THE TEXAS MURDERS

Books by James Patterson
Featuring Texas Ranger Rory Yates

Texas Ranger
Texas Outlaw

For a preview of upcoming books and information
about the author, visit JamesPatterson.com or find
him on Facebook, X, or Instagram.

RAVES FOR
JAMES PATTERSON

"Patterson knows where our deepest fears are buried... there's no stopping his imagination."

—New York Times Book Review

"James Patterson writes his thrillers as if he were building roller coasters."   —Associated Press

"No one gets this big without natural storytelling talent— which is what James Patterson has, in spades."

—Lee Child, #1 *New York Times* bestselling
author of the Jack Reacher series

"James Patterson knows how to sell thrills and suspense in clear, unwavering prose."   *—People*

"Patterson boils a scene down to a single, telling detail, the element that defines a character or moves a plot along. It's what fires off the movie projector in the reader's mind."

—Michael Connelly

"James Patterson is the boss. End of."

—Ian Rankin, *New York Times* bestselling
author of the Inspector Rebus series

THE TEXAS MURDERS

JAMES PATTERSON
AND ANDREW BOURELLE

Little, Brown and Company
New York Boston London

Little, Brown and Company
Hachette Book Group
1290 Avenue of the Americas, New York, NY 10104
littlebrown.com

First Edition: January 2025

Little, Brown and Company is a division of Hachette Book Group, Inc. The Little, Brown name and logo are trademarks of Hachette Book Group, Inc.

The publisher is not responsible for websites (or their content) that are not owned by the publisher.

The Hachette Speakers Bureau provides a wide range of authors for speaking events. To find out more, go to hachettespeakersbureau.com or email hachettespeakers@hbgusa.com.

Little, Brown and Company books may be purchased in bulk for business, educational, or promotional use. For information, please contact your local bookseller or the Hachette Book Group Special Markets Department at special.markets@hbgusa.com.

ISBN 9781538711002 (trade paperback), 9781538711019 (hardcover library), 9781538768761 (large print), 9781538711033 (ebook)
LCCN 2023946043

10 9 8 7 6 5 4 3 2

CCR

Printed in the United States of America

For Ron and Roberta Bourelle

PROLOGUE

ONE

ISABELLA HEARS THE unmistakable vibration of a rattle-snake tail, freezing her in a cold chill.

The seventeen-year-old girl raises her eyes from the stream—she was drinking from water hardly deeper than a puddle—and sees the snake on the other side of the bank. Its head is raised above its slithering body, thicker than a Coke can and stretching to longer than six feet. The scales are olive and gray in the distinctive diamond pattern.

The girl blinks her eyes to determine if she's hallucinating. She's lost track of the number of days she's been crawling through the desert, dragging her useless leg behind her while following the trickle of the creek bed meandering through rocky canyons of sagebrush and prickly pear cactus. She's been surviving on water and the tiny fruit buds blooming on cacti. She knows she can't go on much longer like this.

She should crawl backward, but she can hardly move. She

hasn't eaten in days. Her hands are scraped raw and bloody, with several fingers missing the nails. And her right leg—the worst of her injuries—is broken in multiple places. Her shin bone is bent at an unnatural angle and bruised deep burgundy, her knee is almost as big as a volleyball, and her ankle is so swollen that she's long since removed her shoe and left it behind.

The last thing she needs is a snakebite.

If treated quickly, snakebites aren't fatal. She knows that. But she is already knocking on death's door. A dose of venom squirted from the fangs would finish the job within a day.

That is if the snake is even real—not just her starving brain playing tricks on her.

As if in answer, the tip of the tail stands vertically, and the snake shakes the segmented point again, producing a rattling sound that sends a fresh chill down Isabella's spine.

She's not hallucinating.

She's face-to-face with a real rattlesnake.

And if she doesn't back away, the snake is going to strike. If there wasn't a trickle of water separating them, it might have already attacked.

Once, when she was younger, she watched an uncle on the reservation kill a rattlesnake, but he had the benefit of wielding a long-handled shovel in one hand and a machete in the other.

She doesn't have so much as a pocketknife.

Isabella attempts to ease backward, but when she tries to lift her stiffened leg, the limb screams in pain. Isabella's eyes drop from the snake to the water, and she catches a glimpse of her own reflection. Her skin is coated in dirt and sweat and blistered by the merciless sun. The left side of her face is swollen and marred with a deep laceration that feels hot with infection. Her hair dangles down around her face, the strands tangled and dirty, knotted with twigs and cactus needles. Her face is coated with dust, her lips dried and cracked, her eyes wild.

She looks like some kind of cavewoman out of a movie, more animal than human.

Seeing herself like this, what's become of her, ignites a rage inside her. Adrenaline floods her bloodstream. She looks around for some kind of weapon. She spots a rock within her reach. Roughly the size and shape of a football, the rock is half submerged in the water. Balancing on her one good knee, she attempts to pry the rock loose with both hands.

The snake lifts its rattle and shakes it again—the last warning she's going to get.

She frees the rock and holds it over her head.

"Come on!" she growls at the snake, her teeth clenched.

The snake lunges forward, mouth open in a wide V, just as Isabella slams the rock down in an explosion of water.

Everything happens so fast she's unsure if she hit it.

Then she sees a reddish color clouding the water. The snake's long body flops around but the head remains under the rock. The death throes last for almost a whole minute before the snake's body finally goes limp.

When Isabella shoves the rock aside and pulls the snake up, she sees the creature's neck is smashed at the base of its skull, its mouth still hanging open, the forked tongue limp between its fangs.

She drags the body onto the bank and digs her finger-nails into the scaly skin of the belly. It's hard work without a knife, but she starts to peel the outer skin from the snake with a fevered determination. Her uncle breaded and fried the snake he killed, but she recalls the flavor being bland, like sinewy fish. The meat was full of tiny bones. She never wanted to eat snake again. But now she finds herself salivating, ready to devour the meat raw.

As she works, she remembers her uncle skinning the snake he killed. He cut the head off, then nailed the body to a board, where it dangled lifelessly while he peeled the scaly outer layer. Isabella's mind is a fog of hunger and exhaustion, but she tries to remember something her uncle said to her as she watched. Some lesson she's forgotten. The memory is right there at the edge of her grasp.

A sharp, stinging pain shakes her awake from her thoughts.

The snake's mouth is clamped onto her forearm, the fangs embedded in her muscle, two syringes emptying themselves of poison. As she tried to tear off its skin, she must have triggered a muscle reflex.

Now she remembers the lesson.

Make sure to cut the head off, her uncle had said. *A rattlesnake can still bite after it's dead.*

TWO

ISABELLA YANKS HARD on the snake, tearing its fangs out of her arm. She flings its body against the rocky ground with a *smack*. She grabs the stone she used to kill it and begins bashing the creature's head with all her remaining strength.

She realizes she's screaming.

In anger.

In pain.

In defiance of the fact that she knows she's going to die.

When the snake's skull is no more than a bloody pancake, she hurls the rock out into the canyon and sobs into her hands. She examines the bite marks in her forearm, two red punctures the size of pencil lead, with the flesh swelling around them.

Already she can feel the effects of the poison. Nausea rolls through her body in waves. Her breathing shallows. She blinks her eyes, her vision suddenly blurry.

The sun is setting, filling the western horizon with an orange glow. She wants to simply lie down next to the water and close her eyes.

Let death take her.

No, she thinks. *I will fight to the end.*

She doesn't bother trying to eat the snake. That would waste too much time. Instead, she resumes her days-long crawl downstream. The creek has been flowing through a sandstone canyon, with the land only now beginning to flatten out. In the falling darkness, the desert air cools her feverish skin. A numbness overtakes her pained limbs. The earth underneath her keeps tilting with vertigo, threatening to dump her sideways.

But she pushes on.

Time slips by in a blur.

She wonders if she's already dead. Is this the afterlife? Crawling through a dark desert for all eternity. She collapses onto her back and stares at the stars spinning above her in a whirlpool.

Go ahead, Death. I'm ready.

She blinks her eyes and the sky turns bluish—she's lived to see another sunrise. But she knows it will be her last. Her labored breathing drowns out the only other sound, the faint trickle of water.

She thinks she hears a vehicle on a road but knows her mind must be playing tricks on her. When she hears it again, she rolls onto her stomach and pushes herself up to look around. The sun is rising, filling the landscape with light. A blurry boxy shape glides across the horizon, glinting in the sunlight.

"Help!" she screams. "Help me!"

The car keeps on going. Out of sight.

She hobbles forward. She retches, although nothing comes up.

The road is too far. She focuses on a boulder ten feet away. *Just make it to that rock*, she tells herself. Then when she gets there, she picks out a cluster of cacti as her new goal. Then a yucca plant. Piece by piece, she chips away at the distance.

Until finally she spots the raised berm of a roadway and a corrugated metal cylinder carrying the stream underneath.

Just make it there, she tells herself. And when she does, she crawls onto the warm blacktop and lies on her back on the center yellow line. Overhead, a hawk circles.

She closes her eyes. She has no fight left.

Screeching brakes pull her from unconsciousness.

"Oh, my God," a woman says. "Is that the missing Indian girl from the news?"

A man dribbles water into her mouth. Isabella coughs it up. Then gulps more.

"Not too much," he says. "You don't want to throw up."

Time slips forward and other cars have stopped. Paramedics are there. A police officer.

As strong arms lift her onto a stretcher, a cop asks, "What happened? Where have you been?" The voice urges her that if someone abducted her, the more she could tell them right now, the more likely they would be able to find the person responsible.

"They did this to me," Isabella mutters, barely audible.

"What?"

"I can't believe they did this to me," she says, and begins to sob.

"Who?" the cop asks.

"You don't know?" she says, looking at the cop's confused expression.

The officer's hand is poised over a notebook, ready to write down whatever she tells him.

But Isabella thinks of what she's been through—and those responsible—and she decides in that moment to never speak of what happened.

Not to anyone.

No matter what.

PART I

CHAPTER 1

Four years later

THE ARROW SOARS silently through the air and strikes the target a hundred yards away with a *thunk*.

I lift my binoculars to see where the arrow hit.

Dead center.

Bullseye.

In my Texas Ranger uniform of shirt, tie, boots, and cowboy hat, I lean against the fence and watch as the woman nocks another arrow and draws back her bow. Even through the rustling noise of the small crowd, I can hear the creak of the bowstring. She stands poised, the muscles in her arms taut. The other competitors—all men—have been using modern compound bows with cams on the strings and peep sights to make aiming easier. They have wrist releases to draw back the string. But the woman, a Native American wearing a uniform from the Ysleta del Sur Pueblo Tribal Police, has only an old hickory bow she pulls back with three fingers—and no sight to aim with except the tip of the arrow.

And yet she's been cleaning up against all her competitors. They started shooting at forty yards and worked their way up to one hundred. She's so far ahead in points that she could miss the target entirely and still win the competition.

She releases the arrow, and this one strikes dead center, too.

I applaud along with the small crowd gathered to watch. The woman takes no notice. She draws back her third and final arrow.

Her body is the picture of concentration. Spine arched. Right arm drawn back into a tight V. Left arm holding the bow as straight as the arrow she's about to fire. Her hair is pulled into a single braid that runs down the length of her back. Her eyes squint ever so slightly. She holds the bowstring back by her jawline, touching the corner of her mouth with the tip of her forefinger. Then, in a fluid motion, she releases the tension on her fingers and lets her hand slide back, gently brushing her shoulder.

The arrow launches forward, cutting an arc through the air as it travels the length of a football field.

I hold my breath along with everyone else watching.

The arrow strikes the target, not only in the center area, but so close it seems to be touching the other two arrows. The only way she could have a tighter pattern is if she'd split the arrows like Robin Hood.

The crowd—not nearly as big as the demonstration of

talent deserves—applauds the woman. Her competitors, gracious losers, take turns shaking her hand to congratulate her. She nods her head politely. She doesn't smile.

Over the PA system, a voice announces the winner. *Ava Cruz.*

I'm at the second annual Texas Law Enforcement Charity Shoot, a fundraising event held on a massive shooting range outside of San Antonio. Sheriff's deputies, state troopers, highway patrol deputies, and Texas-based representatives from the FBI, ATF, and DEA are all here showing off their shooting skills to raise money for the Texas Fallen Officer Foundation.

I'm slated for the fast-draw competition.

I skipped the event last year, caught up in an investigation. But this year my captain called me up and told me he entered me in the contest.

"Rory," he said to me, "the Texas Rangers didn't win a single event the first year. I want you to change that."

Wandering around, waiting for my competition, I stopped on a lark to watch the archery contest, mostly because I thought the archers deserved an audience as much as the shooters. As someone who's honed his weapon skills to an art, I can appreciate the female officer's dedication to become that good.

I step forward to go congratulate her, but before I get two feet, a hand clasps my shoulders.

"So you decided to show up this year?"

I turn to find a man dressed in a loose button-down shirt and a ball cap lettered FBI. He stands an inch or two under six feet, and has dark hair and a big, confident smile.

"Hey, Ryan," I say, extending my hand. "Good to see you."

It's Ryan Logan, an FBI special agent in charge based out of Dallas. He and I have crossed paths a few times, but mostly we know each other through our reputations.

Ryan is a quick-draw specialist. Aside from having an impeccable record with the FBI, he spends his free time going to shooting competitions throughout Texas and the Southwest. Though my captain entered me this time, I'm no stranger to fast-draw competitions like this. In my twenties, I used to enter them for fun—and even won a few. But Ryan's familiarity with this scene goes far beyond my experience. Going into today, I knew that as last year's winner he'd be my toughest competition—the clear favorite.

Over the PA system, we hear an announcement that the fast-draw competition will begin in five minutes.

"Ready to have your ass handed to you?" Ryan says affably.

CHAPTER 2

I SLING MY duffel bag over my shoulder and walk with Ryan toward the fast-draw area. The shooting range spans acres set up for various events. We can hear the *pop-pop* of trap-shooting shotguns in the distance, as well as the less frequent report of rifles in a long-range event on the other side of the property. Although most of the competitions use wax bullets, not real rounds, keeping people safe with all this shooting going on requires a lot of organization and strict rules for crowd containment. The folks behind the event have done a good job.

"Congratulations on your medal, by the way," Ryan says, as we wind our way through throngs of uniformed officers and spectators eating cotton candy and corn dogs. "The ceremony's coming up soon, right?"

What we're talking about is the Medal of Valor, the Texas

Rangers' highest honor. Only a handful of Rangers have ever earned the award.

Next week, they'll be giving it to two.

I'm getting one.

Unfortunately, the other award will be given posthumously.

My old lieutenant, Kyle Hendricks, died in the line of duty helping me make a major drug bust in West Texas last summer. I would just as soon have the focus be on Kyle's sacrifice. But everyone in my life is treating the award like a big deal.

"How are things in Dallas?" I ask Ryan to change the subject.

"Oh, I'm not in Dallas anymore," he says. "I've got a new assignment. I'm bouncing around state to state."

Ryan explains that Congress has recently created a task force to investigate an epidemic of Native American women going missing each year. He's been charged with coordinating the Southwest region's arm of the task force, working with tribal, state, and local police, along with the Bureau of Indian Affairs and FBI.

"You must know the woman who just won the archery competition?" I ask, hooking my thumb back toward where we came from. "Have you worked with her?"

"Oh, I know her," he says, rolling his eyes. "I wouldn't exactly say we work together. Some of these reservation police don't quite play nice with the federal government."

Ryan and I arrive at the quick-draw area, where a large crowd has gathered. As we proceed to the shooting area, I can hear people talking about us—about Ryan being a competition ace, and about my reputation of being good with a gun. Unlike Ryan, most of my shooting experience is in real-world situations.

As the competitors line up facing a wooden fence about thirty feet away, the event host briefs us on how the contest is going to work. Between us and the fence, metal targets two feet in diameter are displayed at about waist height.

The metal targets are coated in lithium grease to mark where the wax bullets strike. There's a light, covered in Plexiglas, in the center of the target. And each target has an impact sensor that will clock the speed of the shot.

In fast-draw competitions, if the competitors are any good, no one will be able to tell who wins with only the naked eye.

In the first round, the targets are placed fifteen feet away. Then they'll be moved back another three feet for the next round, and another three for the final. Twenty-one feet might not seem like a lot, but when you're shooting from the hip, you've got to be a hell of a shot just to hit the target, let alone be able to do it with any kind of speed.

We get to shoot three times each round, and the average scores decide who moves on. The top two shooters from each group in the first round move on to the next, but after that it's single elimination.

For safety, the crowd will gather behind us. Ordinarily I wear a SIG Sauer P320 on my hip. But a semiautomatic pistol is strictly forbidden in a contest like this. Today, that gun is holstered at the small of my back. On my hip is a Ruger Vaquero, a six-shot single-action revolver. The single-action makes shooting fast even more difficult because you have to cock the hammer back as you draw. I'm a little rusty with the Ruger, and I'm just hoping I can hold my own against someone like Ryan.

"Shooters on the line," the announcer says, and the first five of us take our place.

I position myself on the far left, and Ryan takes the spot directly to my right.

I dig my cowboy boots into the dirt like a batter getting into position beside home plate. I focus my eyes—shaded by my Stetson—on the target in front of me.

I wrap my hand around the smooth rosewood grip of the revolver.

I slow my breathing, trying to keep my nerves under control.

"Shooters set," the announcer says.

The crowd is silent in anticipation.

The light flashes, and I pull the gun, cock it, and squeeze the trigger—all in one fluid motion that takes less than half a second. The air fills with *pop*s as the other competitors do the same.

I look down the end of the line to see the times displayed.

The guy to the far right, a highway patrol trooper out of Odessa, recorded a time of 0.687 seconds.

The next officer, a female detective from Houston, recorded 0.551.

The middle guy, an embarrassed DEA agent, missed the target completely.

Then comes Ryan's score: 0.315.

All the scores—those who hit the target anyway—would be more than respectable at any event held by the most elite quick-draw organizations.

Ryan's is downright amazing.

I open my mouth to tell him so, but he has a look of unpleasant surprise on his face as he examines the numbers.

I check my own time.

0.314.

Ryan's perturbed expression disappears and is replaced by a friendly smile.

"Hot damn, Yates. That's some fine shooting," he says. "This is going to be fun."

CHAPTER 3

THE ANNOUNCER DECLARES enthusiastically that the matchup of two world-class fast-draw competitors is something special. He's not being hyperbolic.

For pros who practice this stuff every day, anything in the 0.3 range is an excellent day's work. It's possible to go lower, but very rare. There probably aren't twenty people in the last twenty years who have shot faster than 0.3 at any organized competition.

Ryan and I aren't there, but our first shots are pretty damn close.

For our next two shots, Ryan and I both shoot in the mid-0.3 range, easily making it to the next round. Round 2 is single elimination, but Ryan and I aren't in the same group.

Ryan goes first and doesn't disappoint, easily winning by hitting the target all three times in 0.379, 0.344, and 0.319 seconds. His fastest just barely hits the edge of the target, but that doesn't matter in this competition. They say close only matters in horseshoes and hand grenades, but apparently it matters in fast draw, too.

In my round, I score 0.359, 0.347, and 0.330—each one a full tenth of a second faster than any of my competitors, each one in the center of the target.

For the final round, they move the targets back to twenty-one feet, and the five top shooters all line up on the line.

So far, no other competitors have drawn faster than 0.4 seconds, so even though there are five of us on the line, everyone knows the contest is really between Ryan and me.

The crowd has grown large—and raucous—but when the announcer says, "Shooters set," everyone quiets down.

The light flashes, and our hands fly to our guns.

Ryan's bullet splats against the edge of the target for a time of 0.310.

My time—dead center—is 0.322.

The announcer shouts the scores and the crowd erupts, no one able to believe what they're witnessing. I can't believe it myself. I'd told myself not to worry too much about winning, just to have fun. But I'm caught up in the fervor of the crowd.

I want to win.

We have two more shots remaining. Ryan gets set on the line, the picture of concentration. His body is tensed, his eyes focused. I do the same. When the light flashes, I snatch my gun as fast as possible.

I nail the target's center for an unbelievable time of 0.309.

I look over and see Ryan's time: 0.306.

Ryan has a grin on his face as he glances over at me.

"It's still anyone's ball game," the announcer states. "Well, I mean, between Yates and Logan, that is."

I'm behind, but we're talking about fractions of seconds here. All I need is an excellent draw—and for Ryan to have one of his worst.

The other three shooters confer and all decide to bow out, letting the two of us face each other head-to-head.

"It's been fun, Rory," Ryan says to me.

"You're the fastest I've ever seen, Ryan. You've made me faster than I thought I could be."

"Same," he says.

He looks confident that he's got this in the bag. I tell myself to forget he's there. I'm not shooting against him. If I do my best and still lose, then Ryan earned it and I have nothing to be ashamed of. I'm shooting for *my* best time.

"Shooters on the line," the announcer says, but we're already there, digging our feet in, getting our bodies set, our minds focused.

I slow my breathing.

I can feel my heartbeat calming down.

"Shooters set."

I empty my brain and concentrate only on the light bulb. When it flashes, my reflexes take over. The wax bullet explodes in the center of the target.

I relax and holster the gun, knowing I've shot my best.

I look at Ryan's time, an extraordinary 0.299.

My heart sinks for an instant, knowing he beat me. But then it swells with respect. If I'm going to lose, then at least I lost to a member of the 0.3 Club.

Ryan takes off his hat and scratches his head, looking back and forth between his time and mine, as if he's trying to do math in his head. I look at the digital readout above my target and can't believe what I'm seeing.

0.284.

I assume I've still lost—he was too far ahead—but damn it if I'm not proud of that shot.

"You're not going to believe this, folks," the announcer declares. "We've got a tie."

The crowd is abuzz. There's nothing in the rule book about what happens in a draw. We overhear the organizers weighing their choice—letting the tie stand or disappointing an edgy crowd.

"Give it to Yates," someone calls. "His shots were more accurate. That FBI guy barely hit the target half the time."

Ryan and I both turn our heads to see whether he's right about that. On the final shot, at least, Ryan barely hit the bottom edge of the circle. My shot was dead center, which means that not only was it faster, but it was more accurate.

"Hell," Ryan says, irritated. "It's these wax bullets. They're not exactly precision loads."

Hearing this, one of the organizers has an idea and leans in to talk to the others. A moment later, they wave over Ryan and me.

"Fellas," he says, "we're thinking we need to make a change."

"What are you proposing?" I ask.

"Let's switch things up a bit," the organizer says, "and use real bullets."

CHAPTER 4

USING REAL LOADS in a quick-draw contest feels reckless. From the moment he says "real bullets," I have a bad feeling, like the careful plans for audience safety are being abandoned for something a group of drunken frat boys would do around a campfire on a Saturday night.

"I'm sorry to disappoint you," I say, "but I've got to hit the road. I'm happy to concede victory to Ryan."

"Hell, no," Ryan says. "If I'm going to win this thing, I'm going to win it fair and square."

"It won't take long," the organizer says. As if reading my mind about my real concerns, he adds, "We'll make sure to do it safe."

Someone suggests that famous quick-draw artist Bob Munden used to slice playing cards in half with his shots. So our targets would be the flat edge of the cards, hardly bigger than a sewing needle.

"We can set up some kind of contraption to hold the card up in front of the target with the impact sensor," the organizer says. "To win you've got to cut the card *and* have the best time."

"It'll destroy the sensor," someone says, but the others seem to think the damage will be worth it for the spectacle.

I tell them that my concern isn't the target or the impact sensor but whatever's on the other side of the wooden fence. The bullets are going to fly right through.

"There's eight feet of rubber tires over there," the organizer assures me.

"Well, does anyone have any playing cards?" Ryan asks.

The men look around at each other in comical confusion.

Ryan and I can't help but laugh, but behind us, the crowd is restless.

Ryan says, "How about we do what ol' Jelly Bryce used to do?"

Jacob Adolphus Bryce—known as "Jelly"—was a famous FBI agent in the 1930s, '40s, and '50s, who many people believe was the fastest gunman ever to live. In several shoot-outs, he shot men who already had their guns aimed at him—drawing and firing faster than they could squeeze the trigger. But he also did a lot of contests and performances, showing off his shooting skills for audiences.

I've always thought that Ryan fancies himself a sort of modern-day Jelly Bryce. He does plenty of the performance shooting, but—so far—he lacks the real-world reputation Bryce also had.

Ryan explains that Jelly Bryce used to hold a quarter at shoulder height, with his arm extended, while his other hand rested on his gun. When he dropped the quarter, he could draw and shoot it as it passed his waist. Back in the 1940s, *Life* magazine did a photo spread with some kind of state-of-the-art camera showing Bryce's skill in freeze-frame steps.

"Let Rory and me try it," he says, digging into his pocket and pulling out two quarters.

The organizers like the idea, and as much as I don't, I go along with it. I don't want to disappoint the organizers or the crowd. And—to my own surprise—I find that I want badly to win.

I reach into my duffel bag and pull out my hip holster for the SIG Sauer. If we're using real bullets, I'm using my pistol of choice. I see Ryan doing the same, loading live rounds into the Glock he carries on the job. The announcer explains to the restless crowd what the tiebreaker will entail.

There are a good fifty people, half of them law enforcement personnel, crowded around the shooting area in a crescent moon. As the organizer backs them away, I spot Ava Cruz, winner of the archery competition.

The other half of the spectators are civilians. I figure they contributed good money to the fundraising event, and I ought to at least give them a good show. I spot a young woman carrying a toddler in her arms—the boy has straw-colored hair and is wearing noise-canceling headphones—and I tip my hat to her and give her a smile. She beams back at me, doing her best to keep the restless child from squirming out of her grip.

Ryan volunteers to go first and steps into position.

"Shooter on the line," the announcer says, and when Ryan's ready, he adds, "Shooter set."

In a flash, Ryan drops his coin and draws his gun. The *crack* of the shot is so much louder than the wax loads we used before.

He reaches down and picks up his quarter.

"Damn," he mutters. "I missed it completely."

The crowd groans with disappointment, and the announcer explains that it's my turn and if I hit the quarter, I'll win the contest. Ryan hands me the quarter and wishes me good luck, winking to say that he really hopes I miss.

I face the fence in front of the barricade of rubber tires. I hold the quarter out at shoulder height and place my other hand on the grip of my SIG Sauer, which feels much more familiar to me than the handle of the Vaquero.

This is my gun.

I try to tune everything else out, focused only on the task at hand. Like before, with my incredible 0.284 shot, I am in an almost meditative state. Nothing exists but me and the shot I need to make.

I let go of the quarter.

My hand yanks the pistol.

Somewhere in front of me, I spot a slight blur of movement—a fistful of straw.

My brain registers that it's the child who was squirming in his mother's arms. He's wriggled free and darted into my shooting lane.

But my reflexes are on automatic pilot.

The gun is already in my hand, swinging up.

My finger is inside the trigger guard, squeezing.

CHAPTER 5

SOMEHOW THE SYNAPSES in my brain send the message to my hand in time. I let the coin fall and thrust my gun high up in the air, stretching my finger outside the trigger guard. The silence—when we were all expecting a *bang*—has a strange, sobering effect on the crowd. I hear gasps of terror and then exhalations of relief.

The mother runs past me and scoops up her little boy, who seems oblivious to the danger he was in. Crying, the woman clutches him in her arms, thanking me profusely and apologizing at the same time.

My heart pounds as fast as I ever remember it pounding, even in the most heated of battles. My legs are wobbly. My whole face feels numb, and I blink back tears.

The organizers are looking at each other with expressions that say, *What should we do?*

"Do you want to try again?" one of them asks. "We'll do a better job of keeping the crowd back."

I holster my gun.

"Gentlemen," I say, "I'm calling it a day."

The crowd gives me the biggest round of applause of the afternoon.

"Rory," Ryan says, putting a hand on my back. His voice is full of genuine respect. "That was the finest gunmanship I've ever seen. You're the winner in my book."

I tell him that I'm happy with a draw.

"We all had fun and nobody got hurt," I say. "That's all I care about."

Ryan takes my hand and holds it up, and the two of us stand for a moment with our arms raised in joint victory, letting the audience give us another round of applause. I have to spend a few minutes shaking hands and talking to folks, but I'm eager to get out of there. It's late in the afternoon, and I've got a three-hour drive ahead of me to get home to Redbud. More important, I feel a little sick to my stomach and just want to sit in my truck and decompress.

As I'm heading toward the exit, however, I spot Ava Cruz. She's buying a lemonade from a stand, with her bow and arrow slung over her shoulder across her body. I break my stride and approach her.

"That was some nice shooting I saw you do earlier," I say to her.

"That was some nice *not* shooting I saw you do," she says.

"I'm Rory Yates," I say, extending my hand, "from the Texas Rangers."

"I know," she says, shifting her lemonade to her left hand so she can shake. "I'm Ava Cruz from the Tigua Tribal Police."

"*I* know," I say, and grin.

She has a cool disposition, and I can't tell whether it's just her ordinary demeanor or she doesn't like me.

Or both.

"Where'd you learn to shoot a bow like that?" I ask.

She explains that she grew up going to Native American festivals throughout the West. There are various competitions—dancing, drumming, jewelry making. Her specialty was archery. She practiced whenever she could.

"This was easy," she says, tilting her head back toward where the contest had occurred. "Stationary targets. When I was a girl, I used to have a ratty old foam ball. I'd have my friends kick it, and I'd shoot it while it rolled. Or shoot it in midair."

I nod, impressed.

"The practice paid off today," I tell her. "Those other competitors didn't stand a chance."

She shrugs. "My police chief made me come. I wish I'd stayed on the Pueblo. I've got a case I'm working on. It feels wrong to be out playing games when a woman's missing."

I nod, understanding where she's coming from. In law enforcement, it's easy to let the desire to help others consume your thoughts, even when you're not on the clock.

"Your case," I say. "Anything the Rangers can help you with?"

She smirks. "No thanks."

I squint, trying to figure out what she's implying.

"No offense," she says, taking a sip of lemonade, "but the Texas Rangers used to round up the Indigenous people of this land and drive them out of the area or lock them up on reservations. Your organization has a long history of wrong-doings against Indians."

I'm taken aback. The Texas Rangers have been around in one form or another for nearly two hundred years—before Texas was even a state—and I'm aware that not everything in the Rangers' history is something to be proud of. But history is also complicated—not always black and white—and I know there were Native Americans among the earliest Texas Rangers. Regardless of the history and all its shades of gray, I am very proud of the modern Rangers, an elite investigation unit that helps solve crimes throughout Texas. It's an honor and a privilege to wear the tin star on my chest. I thought pretty much everyone in law enforcement—inside and outside of Texas—felt that way.

Apparently not Ava Cruz.

"You seem like a decent guy, Rory, but people wearing *that* badge," she says, pointing to the star on my chest, "treated people who looked like me pretty badly in the past. I think I'll pass on asking the Texas Rangers for any help."

I open my mouth to defend the Rangers, but Ava Cruz moves to walk away.

"You did a good thing today," she says. "I'll give you that."

As I watch her walk away, I remember Ryan's reaction when I brought her up. He clearly doesn't have much of an opinion of her.

I don't feel the same way.

One minute with her, and I have a high opinion of her already.

CHAPTER 6

"THANKS FOR COMING, Rory."

I walk into the office of Captain David Kane, the boss I've been answering to while my lieutenant's position has been vacant. The Texas Ranger division headquarters in Austin is about ninety minutes from the Waco office, where I work, and another twenty from Redbud, where I live. But I woke up early and made the drive comfortably, listening to the radio and hoping to hear a song from my ex-girlfriend Willow Dawes. We're still friends, and I get a kick every time I hear her songs on the radio.

This morning I heard two.

"Congratulations," David says, pumping my fist in a vigorous handshake. "It's nice to see the Rangers on the leaderboard from the charity event."

He gestures for me to sit across from him, and he eases behind his desk into his cushioned leather chair. His office is spotless, the oak desk adorned with only a computer monitor, keyboard, and telephone. Shelves on the wall hold pictures of the captain with various Texas dignitaries: Governor George W. Bush, Matthew McConaughey. Behind his chair is a large window, and on each side of it is an upright flagpole—the American flag hanging on one side, Texas on the other.

David is in his late fifties with the big frame of a once muscular man. Even though Father Time has caught up with him, you still wouldn't want to mess with him. He used to intimidate me when I first joined the Rangers, but I've come to see him as a mentor. He asked me to make the drive to Austin today so he could go over what would happen at the Medal of Valor ceremony, but after a few minutes it becomes clear that's not the real reason.

"Have you ever thought about moving up within the Rangers?" David asks, his gray eyes boring into me. "Why haven't you taken the lieutenant's exam?"

"I've thought about it," I say, "but the timing never feels right."

He nods. "I think the timing is right now."

There are only 166 Rangers in the whole Texas Ranger Division, spread out over the 268,000 square miles within the state boundaries—an area slightly bigger than France. Most of us are simply Rangers: top-notch investigators who help Texas's small municipalities and big cities solve crimes. Three lieutenants lead each of the state's six companies. At headquarters in Austin, we also have a few majors and captains, as well as the chief.

David tells me that he thinks the sky is the limit for my

career. They've recently filled Kyle Hendricks's lieutenant position, but he wants me to be ready for the next opening so I can start my ascension as soon as possible.

"You'll be sitting in this office one day," he says, tapping the polished surface of his desk. "Hell, maybe you'll be chief."

I'm filled with both apprehension and pride. A promotion would be an honor, of course, but I don't know if it's right for me. I'm a detective, not a supervisor of detectives. Would becoming lieutenant—and maybe captain someday—really be the best way for me to serve Texas?

I tell him I'll give what he's saying some thought, and before I leave, he asks if there's anything I want to talk to him about.

"Actually, sir, there is," I say, clearing my throat. "At the competition over the weekend, I met a detective from the Tigua Indian reservation. Apparently they've got an active missing person case at the Ysleta del Sur Pueblo. Is there anything we can do to help?"

David sits back in his chair, filling his cheeks and exhaling loudly.

"Did she go missing from the reservation?" he asks.

"I think so."

He seems relieved. "There ain't much we can do if it's on Indian land. And frankly I wouldn't want to get involved even if there was. Cases on reservations get bogged down in a quagmire of agencies: tribal police, FBI, BIA, maybe the sheriff's department in adjoining counties. If it's drugs or guns, you've got the DEA and ATF to deal with. Lots of red tape. Lots of fighting over who's got jurisdiction. When a case gets solved, everybody wants to take credit. When a crime goes unsolved, everybody's to blame. It's a goddamn mess— I don't think throwing the Rangers into the mix would help much."

He goes on to explain what I already know—that Congress has recently created a task force to focus on cases involving missing Native American women.

"My advice is don't get involved."

As I leave his office, I feel disappointed. I don't know the details of this missing person case. And there is no shortage of cases throughout Texas where the Rangers can be a big help—where I'm wanted *and* can be of some use. But the truth is part of me wants to prove Ava Cruz wrong. I'd like to show her that the Rangers can be her ally.

I walk out into the parking lot. The sun is already hot, the air thick with humidity. I stop at my truck, reluctant to climb aboard.

My captain told me to leave this alone, but I haven't always been the best at following orders. And right now I'm the golden boy of the Texas Rangers—he said so himself that the sky is the limit for my career—so if there's a time when I can get away with disregarding my mentor's advice, now is probably it.

But do I really want to jeopardize all the goodwill my supervisors are throwing my way? This is just like me—get a step ahead only to sabotage myself and take two steps back.

But I can't help myself.

I turn around and walk back into the building.

I stalk around the offices, looking for one person in

particular. Finally, I find the office with CARLOS CASTILLO on the nameplate. I knock and crack the door open.

"Hey, Carlos, you got a minute?"

The man behind the desk is thin with a rangy build, skinny but scrappy-looking. He is in his early forties, but his unlined face could pass for a decade younger, and his ink-black hair is trimmed close to his scalp, without a single gray hair in sight.

He looks up from a file and says, "Sure, Yates. What can I do for you?"

"Can I buy you lunch?"

He checks his watch. "It's nine thirty in the morning."

"Cup of coffee?"

He gives me a discerning look, no doubt wondering what I've got on my mind. He had already been a Ranger for a few years when I was hired, and our paths have only crossed a handful of times since then.

He nods and picks up his Stetson. He wears a Colt 1911 on his hip. Rangers are issued SIG Sauers, like the one I wear, but we're given the latitude to choose another pistol to carry if we want.

"How about a beer?" he says. "It's five o'clock somewhere."

I'm so shocked I can't speak. Then his stone face cracks, and a big smile appears.

"Just kidding," he says, and lets out a laugh. "I'll drive."

CHAPTER 7

WE PICK UP two coffees and drive down by the Colorado River. Carlos parks in a gravel area underneath the highway, and the two of us walk along a multiuse path that stretches over the river. The underside of the bridge above us is packed with the nests of cliff swallows, and the birds flit in and out of their gourd-shaped homes.

Overhead, traffic rumbles along.

"So what brings you to Austin today?" Carlos asks, leaning against the railing and looking over the wide river.

Even this early, the sun-shimmering water is full of people floating in rafts or paddling kayaks.

I tell him that Captain Kane wanted to chat with me about the Medal of Valor ceremony. I don't mention the additional reason the captain called me in. I'd heard that Carlos unsuccessfully applied for the recent lieutenant position. He might not like hearing that we could end up being in the running for the same job.

He congratulates me on the Medal of Valor. I don't expect him to attend the ceremony any more than he expected me to knock on his office door this morning. Carlos Castillo has a reputation for working alone. He does good work—no one ever complains about his results—but I'm not sure he has a lot of close friends in the Rangers.

It feels awkward to explain why I've asked to talk to him, especially since I don't really know what I'm looking for myself. I decide there's no better way to explain something than to try, so I start with my encounter with Ava Cruz over the weekend.

"Do you know her?" I ask.

"Twenty-nine million people live in Texas," he says. "What makes you think I know her?"

"Well," I say, stumbling over my words. "I…uh…"

"You thought that since we're both Indians we must be pals?"

I flush with embarrassment. Carlos is the only Texas Ranger in the whole division with Native American ancestry. He knows it. I know it.

"Sixty thousand people in Texas identify as Native Americans," he says. "You think we're all Facebook friends?"

He stares at me with a forbidding expression. Then his facade breaks and a big smile fills his face.

"I'm just messing with you, Rory."

Relief washes over me.

"I actually have met her before," Carlos says, "but I don't know her well."

He explains that he's often assigned cases that involve Native American crimes but that offenses that occur on tribal land are outside of the Rangers' jurisdiction.

The assumption that the missing woman was moved off reservation property onto Texas lands might be a safe one in this case, considering the Ysleta del Sur Pueblo — the residential area of the Tigua reservation — isn't particularly big, only about thirty acres.

He starts to tell me about the federal task force, but I stop him and explain that Ryan Logan didn't seem interested in working with her.

Still, Carlos gives me the same basic advice as Captain Kane.

"There are already too many cooks in this kitchen," he says. "I know it's hard to accept, but sometimes you're better off trusting that the people involved are doing okay without you. The Rangers can't get involved in every case in Texas."

Somehow the recommendation seems more palatable coming from him than my captain. But the idea that the best way to help is to stay out of the way is still a bitter pill to swallow.

Seeing that I'm not quite satisfied, Carlos adds, "I'll tell you what. I'll make a call over to the Tigua Pueblo. I'll offer our help, try to get a little more information on the case. Maybe they'll be a little more open to the offer coming from me."

As we walk back along the path toward the truck, bicyclists and runners zip by us, some of them doing double takes, no doubt wondering what two Texas Rangers are doing out here in a popular recreation area.

It's a beautiful day, and everyone around us is busy

releasing endorphins, but I'm in a somber mood. I think it's the fact that I'm about to be given the Texas Rangers' highest honor, yet I feel unworthy of it. No matter how many cases you break, no matter how many arrests you make, there's always more to be done.

Always more crime.

And the truth is I'm also stinging from Ava Cruz's criticism of the Rangers' legacy. I tell Carlos what she said and then add, "Why did you become a Ranger, Carlos?"

"To pick up girls," he says, opening his truck door. "No one gets more badge bunnies than a Texas Ranger."

I stare at him, shocked, and he smiles that big mischievous grin of his.

"One of these days you'll be able to tell when I'm joking," he says.

CHAPTER 8

THE TEXAS RANGER Hall of Fame and Museum is located right off I-35 in Waco, next to the Company F headquarters, where I spend a lot of my time.

The spots designated for Rangers are already full, with so many out-of-towners coming in for the ceremony. Cars and trucks fill every space, with overflow lining each side of the entranceway. I finally manage to squeeze my F-150 into a gap between a Prius and a minivan near the frontage road.

I walk a hundred yards to the museum entrance, passing a bronze statue of a Texas Ranger astride a horse and carrying the flag of Texas. Inside, I am immediately swarmed by people—dozens of uniformed Rangers, Texas law enforcement officials, friends from my hometown of Redbud— shaking my hand, congratulating me.

Even though the museum is right next door to the Waco office, I don't make it in here often enough. There's a fascinating display of Texas Ranger memorabilia dating back to the 1800s: saddles, spurs, badges, and guns. Lots and lots of guns. Every manner of weapon Texas Rangers have carried is on display, from Henry rifles and Colt Dragoon revolvers used a hundred and fifty years ago to a LaRue .308 rifle identical to the one I keep in the toolbox of my truck and a SIG Sauer just like the one I carry on my hip.

I make my way through the rows of artifacts, past paintings and sculptures of cowboys on the range, to the pop culture gallery with Lone Ranger lunch boxes and posters from movies and TV shows like *Tales of the Texas Rangers* and *Lonesome Dove*. Seeing all this stuff, the reality and the mythology of the Rangers all mixed together, I recall Ava Cruz's criticism of the early Rangers and the grudge she holds against us. But I don't have time to dwell on these thoughts, not with all these people around shaking my hand and congratulating me.

I spot my parents in the crowd, with my two brothers and their wives and children, standing with a pretty young woman whom I don't recognize.

As I hug everyone, Mom gestures to the young woman and says, "You remember Megan, don't you?"

"Megan?" I say, staring at her.

Long dark hair, thick and glossy, falls over her shoulders and frames her face. She has arresting blue eyes, as deep as the Gulf of Mexico, and I feel like I'm struck dumb staring at them.

"You know," Mom says, annoyed that I clearly don't remember who the woman is, "Megan Casewick from down the road."

My eyes go wide with recognition.

"Sorry," I say, embarrassed. "It's been a long time."

The Casewicks have a ranch near my parents' place. Megan is four or five years younger than me, so we didn't quite run in the same circles growing up. I remember driving by their property when I was in high school, and little Megan—probably just twelve or thirteen years old then—would be out riding her horse in the pasture and wave to me. I'd wave back to her, looking so small on a big bay, but that was about the extent of our relationship. I try to do the math in my head and figure that the little girl who used to wave to me must be a year or two into her thirties now.

I give her an awkward hug, and I can see she's a little self-conscious about the situation. Obviously, my mom is trying to play matchmaker.

"Megan is getting her PhD at UTEP," Mom explains, "but she's home for the weekend 'cause she's got a job interview at Baylor. I invited her to come with us tonight." As if her matchmaking intentions aren't clear enough, Mom leans in close and says, as if in confidence, even though it's loud enough for Megan to hear, "She might be moving back to this area."

I talk to Megan as we move through the jostling crowd, trying to be polite. I ask if she's going to come by my parents' get-together after the ceremony, and she says yes.

When we get a moment out of earshot, my kid brother Jake leans in and says, "Megan sure grew up, didn't she?"

His wife drives a sharp elbow into his shoulder. He feigns injury and kisses her cheek.

In the back of the museum is the Hall of Fame, a small circular amphitheater that screens a documentary movie daily. Tonight, the hall has been converted with a small stage up front, where Captain David Kane sits with a handful of state dignitaries, from the lieutenant governor to Waco's mayor.

Attendees are crowded onto rows of benches, others standing along walls adorned with pictures of famous Texas Rangers. A front-row spot has been reserved for my family and me, as well as the family of Kyle Hendricks. He didn't have a wife and children, so his mother will be accepting the medal. I take a moment to approach her.

"I'm sorry for your loss," I say, my voice choked, tears coming to my eyes. "Kyle saved my life and the lives of God only knows how many others. He's a true hero. If it were up to me, this night would be all about him."

"Thank you, Rory," she says, but those are the only words she can get out before she starts crying.

The two of us hug. She feels fragile and small in my arms, and I can't imagine the pain she has to bear for the rest of her life. Over her shoulder, I see my own parents weeping, knowing that one day they could very well be in her position, accepting a posthumous medal for their slain son, as if a piece of tin on a ribbon could be any consolation.

CHAPTER 9

THE CEREMONY ITSELF is mercifully short, with Captain Kane giving a succinct summary of the events Kyle and I were embroiled in—leaving out the gory details—followed by a touching memorial slide show. When it's over, I'm emotionally drained and want nothing more than to go home and flop down on my bed. But I don't want to disappoint all the people my parents have invited to their house.

As my family and I are waiting for the crowd to clear, a familiar face appears out of the mass of people.

"Willow!" my mom exclaims, and gives my ex-girlfriend a big hug. "Rory didn't tell me you were coming."

"I wanted to surprise him," Willow says, breaking from Mom to hug me. "I stood in the back so I wouldn't draw attention."

She might have been discreet earlier, but now she's turning the heads of the people around us. Wearing a modest blue dress, she doesn't quite look as glamorous as she does in her music videos, but her famous face still stands out in a crowd.

We embrace, and over her shoulder I can see the confused expression on Megan's face. I'm sure Mom wouldn't have invited her if she'd known Willow was going to be here. My parents thought the world of Willow and weren't too happy when she and I decided to go our separate ways. Willow and I dated back before she was a star. I was going through a hard time after my ex-wife, whom I still loved, was murdered. I fell hard for Willow and still think of our brief romance as some of the best days of my life. But her career took her to Nashville, and we couldn't make our relationship work long distance. We broke up amicably, but it still hurt.

I introduce her to Megan.

"You didn't tell me you had a new girlfriend," Willow says, her voice chipper and enthusiastic.

"Um," I say, stumbling over my words, "she's not my... um...We're not..."

"Not yet," Jake mutters loud enough for us all to hear.

Megan, flushed with embarrassment, says to Willow, "I'm a family friend." She extends her hand. "I love your album," she adds. "My favorite song is 'Outlaw in a Miniskirt.'" She looks at me with a wry smile. "That and 'Don't Date a Texas Ranger,' of course."

Willow laughs. "That's advice you definitely should *not* take."

We make our way to the parking lot as rain is starting to sprinkle down. Willow says she's got a rental car and doesn't need a ride. But as Megan moves to ride with my parents,

Willow gives her a gentle shove my way and says, "Why don't you ride with the man of the hour?"

Willow winks at me, and Megan and I hurry to my truck to avoid the rain. As soon as I'm on the highway, the sky opens up and unleashes a deluge onto Central Texas. My wipers are going as fast as they can, and still they can't keep up with the downpour. Thunder explodes like a rifle shot, and lightning ignites the sky in yellow light before plunging it back into darkness.

"I hope that wasn't too uncomfortable," I say to Megan. "I mean, with Willow being there."

"I knew Willow was gorgeous and talented," she says, "but I didn't realize how cool she would be."

I try to take the conversation away from Willow and ask Megan what she's studying at UTEP. She explains that she's finishing her PhD in American literature. Over the past few days, she was doing what they call a "campus visit" at Baylor, interviewing for a job there as an assistant professor.

"I've had two interviews now," she says. "The other one is in Mississippi. Fingers crossed the Baylor job works out."

She's been putting herself through school by working as a bartender four nights a week at a little pub on the outskirts of El Paso called the Outpost.

"I don't mind pouring drinks," she says. "But it's not easy teaching classes during the day, working in the bar till 2:00 a.m., then trying to find time to write my dissertation."

I'm impressed—and a little intimidated.

She's smart.

Hardworking.

And—I can't deny—damn good-looking.

She's wearing a red blouse with an ivory skirt, with a slit showing off just a glimpse of her thigh. In the closed quarters of the truck cab, I can smell a dab of perfume, a citrus aroma that suits her perfectly.

I mention that Baylor is my alma mater, and this gives me something to talk about for a few minutes, how much I loved going to Dr Pepper Hour on Tuesdays and cheering for the Bears at Floyd Casey Stadium before they demolished it and built the new one.

After I pull off the highway and head toward the ranch, a car appears ahead of us, stuck on an embankment. It must have hydroplaned and slid off the road. I pull over and pop on my police lights.

"Hang on a sec," I tell Megan, reaching behind my seat for my rain jacket.

Water pelts the brim of my hat as I step into the downpour. The driver rolls down the window a crack and I ask her to try the gas. The wheels spin, spitting mud.

"Hold on," I say. "I've got a tow cable."

I turn around and Megan is there, getting drenched.

"I'll help," she says.

"You'll get soaked," I say, but it's too late—her wet hair is matted to her scalp, her saturated blouse clings to her skin.

"I was raised on a farm," she says, smiling. "A little rain never hurt anybody." I open my mouth to object, but she says,

"I'm not the kind of girl who's going to sit in the car and let a man do all the work. You should know that right off the bat."

"Here," I say, stripping off my jacket and draping it around her shoulders.

I place my hat atop her head — the Stetson never looked so good before.

I haul my tow cable out, and while I attach it to my truck, Megan kneels down in her skirt and hooks it underneath the stuck car. Her high heels are getting muddy, but she doesn't seem to mind. A minute later, the car is free, and we're back on the road, smiling at each other even though our clothes are soaked through.

When we get to my parents' house, Dad says, "What the hell did you two get into?"

The house is full of friends and family, and it's clear the party has already started.

So much for a small get-together.

"We thought maybe you ran off and eloped," Jake says.

I ignore him while I strip off my button-down shirt so I'm only in a wet T-shirt. Mom hands us a couple of towels. As Megan attempts to dry her long hair, Mom fetches a faded Baylor sweatshirt that I bought her for Christmas years ago when I was a student.

"Here," she says to Megan. "Let's see how you look in green and gold."

"If you're done messing around," my other brother, Chris, tells me, "you're wanted in the living room."

"I am?"

As I step around the corner, I see a dozen or so people are gathered around two stools set up in the corner. Willow sits on one of them. The other stool is empty. Two guitars—mine and hers—lean against the wall behind her.

"Sorry," Willow says with a bright smile. "Your family insisted we treat them to a duet."

CHAPTER 10

I TAKE MY seat next to Willow, unsure how I'm going to muster the energy to perform. Two hours ago, I was crying with Kyle's mother in my arms. Now I'm expected to play music.

But all eyes stare at us eagerly. My good friend Freddy Hernandez, who I went to high school with and who has since helped me break more than a few cases as a top-notch medical examiner, stands in the corner with Darren Hagar, another high school buddy, who owns the bar where Willow used to sing. Jake perches on the arm of the couch, next to my parents. Chris sits on the carpet with my three-year-old nephew, Beau, in his lap, who is sucking his thumb and looking like he's about to fall asleep. Megan sits down next to them and looks up at me with a bright smile. She looks good in an old sweatshirt with half-wet hair, and I can picture her like this with the two of us settled in for a chill night of watching Netflix on the couch.

I realize I'm getting ahead of myself, but in this moment, I am at least hoping that she gets the job at Baylor so I can see more of her.

Without even discussing it, Willow and I start with "Mammas Don't Let Your Babies Grow Up to Be Cowboys." It's the first song we ever sang together, and it's also the last song we played the night we broke up. Singing it now feels like we've turned another page in our relationship. We started with the spark of attraction, which turned into love, which led to heartbreak.

Now we've become friends.

After concluding the song, we play a mix, ranging from Miranda Lambert and the Zac Brown Band to Garth Brooks and the Chicks. My nephew—half asleep a minute ago—is up and dancing.

Willow suggests we try Kenny Rogers and Dolly Parton's duet "Islands in the Stream." The song is going well, but I catch a glimpse of Megan in the audience and can see that she feels uncomfortable watching me share a love song with my ex. Up until then, she seemed to be enjoying the show.

I say I've got time for one more, and a couple of people from the crowd jokingly call out that we should play "Don't Date a Texas Ranger." Laughing, Willow says she's been working on a new song and wants to know if she can try it out.

"You just try to keep up, Rory," she says with a smile.

She strums the strings with an upbeat tempo and starts singing lyrics about Texas, belting the words out in quick succession.

Bluebonnet flowers and pickup trucks
Boca Chica and barbecue at Chuck's
Hook 'em Horns, Enchanted Rock
Strolling the San Antonio River Walk
Dr Pepper, pecan pie
The Rio Grande and the big blue sky

From here, she jumps into the chorus:

I hang my hat in Nashville these days
But my heart belongs in the Lone Star State
I love it—the place, the people, everything together
What can I say, y'all? Texas forever!

The small audience is into the song, laughing and grooving along. But Willow kills the momentum by strumming the guitar a final time and saying, "Sorry, that's all I have so far."

Everyone seems to want more, so I start playing the same tune and I add my own lyrics.

Working in the fields, plowing the hay
Floating the Colorado River on a sunny day

Willow beams at me and joins back in. She sings,

The Dallas Cheerleaders' kick line

Unsure for a moment what to say, I add,

Drinking Shiner Bock and feelin' fine

As the audience erupts with laughter, I sing,

Armadillos and rattlesnakes, coyotes and hawks

Grinning, Willow sings,

Sixth Street in Austin really rocks

At this point, the whole room is laughing, waiting to see what we can come up with on the fly. After a pause, Willow sings,

Country music on the radio

Leaving me to conclude,

Let's not forget the Alamo!

Everyone is in stitches, Willow and I included. We do another roll through the chorus to finish the song, and this time everyone in the room shouts *"Texas forever!"* along with us. Willow and I rise and take a quick bow, hugging each other and laughing.

Megan is giggling along with everyone else, but I can't help but sense some reservations from her expression — she didn't entirely like what she saw.

I want to go talk to her, but I'm approached by my friends Freddy and Darren.

"Willow broke up with her boyfriend in Nashville, you know?" Darren says conspiratorially.

"I heard," I say.

"She won't be single long," Freddy adds.

Out of the corner of my eye, I catch a glimpse of Megan by the door, saying goodbye to my parents.

"Excuse me," I say, and squeeze my way through the crowded house.

I catch up with her outside as she's about to climb into her pickup.

"Leaving without saying goodbye?"

"Sorry," she says. "I didn't want to interrupt you."

She looks luminous in the moonlight.

She says she needs to get up early tomorrow and head back to El Paso. She has a long drive, followed by a shift at the bar. She tells me she had a great time and loved seeing me perform with Willow.

"You two really are good together," Megan says.

"Willow's the good one," I say. "She makes me look better than I am."

"I'm not talking about the music," Megan says.

"Oh," I say, shrugging. "Well, it wasn't meant to be."

"You sure?" she says, giving me a serious stare. "You're really over her?"

"Cross my heart."

Neither of us is really sure what to say next. We've both

felt the same spark, I'm certain, but we also don't know if anything will come of meeting tonight.

We might have a future.

We might never see each other again.

"Goodbye, Rory," she says, giving me a hug.

We hold our embrace longer than we need to, and then I watch her drive away.

CHAPTER 11

I'M AT THE sink doing the dishes. Mom is picking up cups and plates as the last stragglers don't seem to be getting the message that the party is over. Behind me, at the kitchen table, my old high school football coach is talking to Jake and Dad—all of them a little drunk—reminiscing about the Hail Mary touchdown pass I threw in the final seconds of the homecoming game my senior year. It seems like every time I hear Coach tell the story, he adds another five yards to the length of my throw.

"Want some help?" Willow says, sidling up next to me and beginning to dry the dishes in the rack.

"Thanks for coming," I say, handing her a dripping plate. "It means a lot."

"You'd do the same for me," she says, wiping the towel over the wet surface. "When I win my first CMA, I expect you to be there."

I chuckle.

"I'll do my best."

As we work in tandem, I ask Willow where she's staying. She says that she didn't book a hotel yet but my mom offered for her to stay in their spare room.

The atmospheric pressure around us seems to change as we both recognize that my house—the house she and I used to share—is just up the hill on my parents' property, a little two-bedroom where the old ranch hand sleeping quarters used to be. It would be easy for the two of us to walk up there together and pretend for one night like things are like they used to be.

Neither of us says it aloud, but we're both thinking it.

I told Megan that I was over Willow, but I wonder if I am. If I'll ever be.

My phone buzzes in my back pocket, saving me from the awkward silence. Willow hands me the towel she's using, and I dry my hands. I check the phone and see the call is from Carlos Castillo. I've been expecting an update, but not this late. It's almost midnight.

"Are you serious about wanting to help with these cases of missing Indian women?" Carlos says.

"Yes."

"Come pick me up," he says. "We're heading west."

He explains that a Native woman from El Paso has gone missing. She doesn't—or didn't—live on a reservation, which means the Rangers can get involved with less red tape.

"It's still going to be a jurisdictional pissing match with the local cops and the feds," he says, "but if you want to get involved, this is probably the way to do it."

I tell him I'll be there as soon as I can.

"You sure you want to?" Carlos says. "I know tonight was your ceremony. I can go alone. I don't mind."

I am exhausted, and if I told him to go without me, I could be in bed within fifteen minutes, sound asleep. Or "sleeping" with Willow. I do the math in my head about how much driving Carlos and I would have ahead of us: almost two hours to Austin to pick him up and another eight or nine hours to El Paso from there. We won't get to the crime scene until at least 10:00 a.m. tomorrow. I consider telling Carlos that I'm going to pass on this case. I'll let him—or the feds—handle it. But I remember Ava Cruz's reproachful words about the Texas Rangers.

"I'm in," I say.

When I hang up, Willow has an expression on her face that she's been in this situation before—watching me run off at all hours of the night. I usually like to think our relationship didn't survive because her career took off in Nashville, but my career got in the way just as much as hers did.

"Where are you going?" she says, sounding disappointed.

"El Paso."

Her eyes go wide.

"I'll start a pot of coffee," she says. "You go to your place, pack whatever you need, and stop back by before you head out. The coffee will be ready by then."

I drive up to the house, only a couple hundred yards away, and change out of my damp pants and shirt and into clean ones. I throw together a duffel bag with a few changes of clothes, a paperback book, and my toothbrush. I'm not sure how long I'll be gone.

When I drive back down to my parents' house, my family is there with Willow. The rain has stopped and insects chirp from the darkness. I take the thermos of coffee and give everyone hugs. As I hold Willow in my arms, I tell her she might as well stay in my house for the night.

"It's a little messier than when you lived there," I say. "But you know where everything is."

She thanks me but says it might feel too weird—too lonely—to be there without me.

I climb into my truck, put it in gear, and wave out the window to say goodbye to everyone. I drive about ten feet before putting on the brakes. I hop out of the truck and jog back into the house, past the confused faces of my family.

"Forget something?" Dad calls after me.

A few seconds later, I come out with my guitar case.

"You never know," I say, sliding it behind the seat. "I might need this."

CHAPTER 12

I MEET CARLOS at headquarters in Austin, where he's sitting on the tailgate of his pickup in the dark parking lot. He takes his shotgun and LaRue rifle out of his toolbox and slides them into mine, alongside my guns and other equipment. He places his bulletproof vest in there with mine as well. Carlos also packed a duffel bag of clothes and moves to put it behind the seat inside the cab. There isn't much room because of my bag and my guitar.

"You really need the guitar?" he asks, raising an eyebrow.

I shrug. "I don't leave home without it."

He offers to take the first shift driving, but I tell him I've just had half a thermos of coffee. He leans back in the seat and tilts his hat over his eyes.

"Wake me when you need a break."

Driving across Texas can be a long, lonely endeavor, especially in West Texas, as towns get fewer and farther between.

It's beautiful country, but at nighttime, there's nothing to see but the occasional jackrabbit darting across the road.

As I drive, Carlos begins to snore. I look over at him and wonder what kind of team Carlos and I might make since both of us have a reputation for doing things our own way.

With nothing to do but watch the mile markers tick by, I let my mind drift to my evening: the ceremony and the party afterward. My thoughts are torn between two subjects and can't seem to decide which to focus on.

Willow.

Or Megan.

I think of how much I enjoyed playing music with Willow again—and what almost happened after. But I'm also thinking about Megan and the way she looked in the rain, her hair soaked and her face aglow in the brake lights.

I'm aware that these thoughts are a defense mechanism keeping me from dwelling on what's really on my mind—the death of Kyle Hendricks. I wish I could go back in time and find some way to save him. But all I can do is try to make sure that it doesn't happen to anyone I work with in the future, including the Ranger sleeping in the seat next to me.

When Carlos finally stirs, there's a hint of blue visible in the sky, signaling the approach of dawn. The summer solstice was yesterday, which means today is the second-longest day of the year. It's going to be an especially long day for me if I don't get some sleep.

When I ask Carlos if he wants to take a turn behind the wheel, he says, "Nah. You might as well push on through. You're good for it, right?"

It takes me a minute to realize he's joking. There's something about his delivery that gets me every time.

I pull over at a rest area so we can empty our bladders and switch seats. It feels strange to sit in the passenger seat of my own truck. I try to relax, but the sun is rising and my body clock keeps telling me it's time to wake up, not go to bed. I feel a strange exhausted tunnel vision and find my eyes focusing on the insects splattered against the windshield instead of the road in front of us.

Outside the window, the transition from the barren hills of West Texas to the crowded city of El Paso is abrupt. One minute, we're in the middle of nowhere; the next, we're in a bustling city, which appears even bigger than its six hundred thousand people because you can easily see across the border to Juárez, a city of more than a million. From the highway, with the muddy dividing line of the Rio Grande hardly visible, El Paso and Juárez seem to bleed together into one sprawling metropolis stretching to the south as far as the eye can see.

It's too late to sleep now, so I ask Carlos, "You think someone from this federal task force is going to be on scene?"

He nods. "Probably."

I ask him what he knows about the task force, why it was created. He echoes the explanation Ryan gave me at the shooting competition, that there's an underinvestigated epidemic of missing and murdered Native American women.

"There isn't even a clear estimate of how many women we're talking about," Carlos says, pulling off the highway and heading toward the missing woman's home address.

"Sometimes Indian women are misclassified as Hispanic or Asian or don't get logged into federal databases for whatever reason. Some estimates say as many as five thousand Native women go missing or are murdered every year."

"Five thousand?" I say, shocked that the number is so high.

At the federal level, Carlos says, agencies like the Department of Justice and Department of Health and Human Services recently formed a coalition, trying to provide education and streamline communication among tribes and organizations. The FBI was brought in to lead the law enforcement effort, but the jury is still out about whether they're much help.

"What happens to the women?" I ask. "Why are there so many?"

"Some run off," Carlos says. "They live on the streets, maybe strung out on drugs. Maybe they come back. Some of them are probably beaten and killed by men in their lives. I suspect a disproportionate number are taken for human trafficking. Who knows? Maybe there's a serial killer out there collecting Indigenous women."

He says the part about a serial killer flippantly. But there are a lot of sickos out there. You never know.

"The bottom line," he adds, "is that Native women are a segment of the population that no one gives a damn about—at least not until recently—so no one really knows why so many disappear."

Carlos pulls off the highway near the university, and as we get close, it's easy to spot where we're headed. The parking lot of an apartment complex is crowded with a half dozen law enforcement vehicles: patrol cruisers, unmarked sedans, a crime scene van, and a big operations van that, if I were to guess, belongs to the FBI.

It turns out I'm right.

As we step out of our truck, Ryan Logan and a handful of other men in suits exit the van and spot us.

"Well, look who it is," Ryan says. "The second-fastest gun in the West."

He's smiling, and his expression appears friendly enough, but there's something underneath—something he can't quite hide—that suggests he's not happy to see Texas Rangers on his turf.

CHAPTER 13

I STRETCH AND try to wake myself up. The day is already hot, but the air is bone dry, nothing like the humidity of Central Texas. The lush green of the landscape back home has been replaced by the barren brown hills of the Chihuahuan Desert. Palm trees ring the parking lot but provide little shade. An irrigation system is spraying the lawn at the apartment complex with water, but it's apparent by the brown patches in the grass that the sprinkler is fighting a losing battle.

A sheriff's deputy lifts the crime scene tape for us to duck under as Ryan walks up the sidewalk to meet us, his pants getting misted from the sprinkler.

I introduce Carlos.

"We thought we'd stop by and see what we could do to help," I say, trying to tread carefully around the questions of jurisdiction and hierarchy.

Ryan hesitates, deciding whether to let us in on what's happening—or try to keep us out of it. I'm hoping our recent history at the gun competition will make him agreeable. But the opposite could be true. He hadn't expected to walk out of the contest tied for first place, and he might hold a grudge about it.

"All right," Ryan says, apparently deciding to be cooperative rather than competitive.

"What can you tell us about the case?" Carlos asks.

"This case?" he says, gesturing in the direction of the apartment, "or *the* case?" He grins as if he's got a secret.

Carlos and I trade glances, not sure what Ryan's getting at.

"This case," he says, nodding toward the apartment complex. "Not much to say. Woman's name is Fiona Martinez. College student. Works part-time at Whole Foods. Last seen two days ago, and she posted on social media just before midnight that night. Her mom expected a call from her yesterday. When the daughter didn't call, Mom called the EPPD. They called me."

"Any connection to the woman who went missing on the Tigua reservation recently?" I ask.

"Just that they're both Indians." He glances at Carlos and amends his statement. "Both Native Americans."

"Tigua?" Carlos asks.

"This girl's Navajo."

"Any sign of a struggle in the apartment?" I ask. "Or evidence that she might have run away?"

"No," he says. "Everything looks normal. Her car is here. No clothes missing as far as we can tell. Car keys and driver's license are on the kitchen counter next to her cell phone."

He tells us there's nothing to see in the girl's apartment but says we're welcome to have a look.

"When you're done looking around," he says, patting the side of his operations van, "come see me in my office on wheels."

We pass a tech dusting for prints at the front door.

It's not a big apartment by any stretch of the imagination. But the woman who rented it — Fiona Martinez, Ryan said — took good care of it. Aside from a few dirty dishes soaking in the sink, the apartment is clean and picked up. Nothing seems particularly out of place.

The furniture is mismatched, probably purchased at thrift stores, which makes sense given that Fiona is a twenty-year-old college student. A small desk in the corner of the living room holds a stack of textbooks. An El Paso Community College student ID hangs from a lanyard draped over a pushpin sticking out of a corkboard.

Also pinned to the board are a handful of photographs. The images depict the same woman from the student ID posing with various people. Several of the pictures show Fiona in traditional Navajo clothes, with feathers and leather hides, at what must be powwows or other festivals.

"What do you make of this?" Carlos asks, gesturing to the kitchen table.

The surface of the wooden table is completely bare except for a single feather — brown with curved markings, and at least a foot long — lying directly in the center.

"Is that a hawk feather?" I ask.

"Too big."

"Bald eagle?"

"Golden eagle," Carlos says. "You can tell by the marbling."

I should have guessed from the size of the feather that it came from a golden eagle. Their wingspans can be six or seven feet, and they are more likely to be found in this area. Bald eagles tend to live around lakes, eating fish, but golden eagles prey on rabbits and reptiles and scavenge in the desert.

None of the techs bagging evidence around us seem interested in the feather, which is surprising to me. I'm not certain off the top of my head, but I'm pretty sure it's illegal for a non–Native American to even own a feather like this. But it's not as if Fiona Martinez's apartment is full of Navajo artwork and decorations.

There are no baskets. No dreamcatchers. No pottery.

Just a single eagle feather sitting in the center of the table as if someone left it there for us to find.

I take a photograph of the feather and ask one of the techs if he can bag it into evidence. He gives me a look that says *I know how to do my job*. Still, I'm not so sure they would have given it much notice if we hadn't said something.

Sometimes when you're in law enforcement, you get hunches, and I can tell by the look on Carlos's face that we both have a hunch about this—the eagle feather means something.

CHAPTER 14

INSIDE RYAN'S OFFICE on wheels, the air conditioner is running, but the air is still stuffy and hot. The interior consists of a bank of computer monitors, radio equipment, and a small desk area messy with file folders. Ryan sits in a sliding desk chair and gestures for us to find seats in front of the monitors.

"I know y'all came over here for this case," he says, grinning like a kid eager to tell his peers about a secret he can't wait to share. "But since you're here, do you want to hear about *the* case?"

He presses a few keys, and one of the monitors displays a mug shot of a man with a rough, leathery complexion and an ugly scar running down his forehead, bisecting his left eyebrow, and culminating just above his jawline. The left eye, which the scar cuts through, is gray and clouded. His good eye is alert and angry. The mug shot is one of those that you take one look at and know you wouldn't want to mess with the guy in it. If looks could kill, whoever took that mug shot would have died on the spot.

"This is Llewellyn Carpenter," Ryan says. "Originally from Dayton, Ohio. Now lives in Roswell. Thirty-eight years old. Former Army. Did tours in Iraq and Afghanistan. Dishonorably discharged. He's been in and out of prison ever since. Narcotics. Possession of stolen property. Assault."

Ryan presses more keys and the other monitors light up with surveillance images of the man standing next to a blue panel van. There are several grainy images of him at a gas station, where he is smoking a cigarette next to the pumps, and a few clearer pictures of him unlocking a chain-link fence at a warehouse and then driving the van through the gate.

Ryan explains that once his team started comparing notes on various missing persons cases throughout the region, they noticed that there were more than a dozen instances where a blue panel van was seen in areas where women went missing. As far east as Houston, as far west as Palm Springs, and as far north as Denver, police reports mentioned a blue panel van, usually listed as a seemingly unimportant detail buried within the notes. It wasn't until Ryan's team started scrutinizing all the cases that they discovered the connection.

The day before a teenager went missing in Sedona last month, a security camera at a gas station got an image of the guy and the van. There was no clear picture of his full face, but the camera did catch his profile, showing the scar, and a clear picture of his left forearm, revealing a distinctive tattoo of a snake coiling around the arm.

"We ran the tattoo through the federal database and came up with a list of matches," Ryan says, entering a few keystrokes until one of the monitors fills with images of half a dozen tattoos similar to Llewellyn Carpenter's. "Once we had the names, we looked for someone with a matching scar. It was easy to narrow down the suspect list."

The van license plate recorded in the security footage came from a stolen vehicle, Ryan says, but the FBI put a stakeout on his last known address in Roswell. He showed up a few days later, and they've been surveilling him ever since. Ryan points to a larger image of the warehouse that Carpenter had driven the van into, a run-down facility with boards over the windows and tumbleweeds lodged against the fence.

"We think this is a major distribution center for a large human-trafficking operation," Ryan says. "Women are brought here, hooked on drugs, and then shipped off to various illegal brothels in the Southwest. We've located two already. One in Tucson and one in Colorado Springs. We're hoping to get a fix on more."

"And this guy's in charge of the operation?" I say, gesturing to the image of Llewellyn Carpenter.

Ryan shakes his head. "He's a kidnapper and driver. He takes women from point A to B. He might be a major player, but someone else calls the shots."

"Who?"

"Don't know yet."

"So where is this warehouse?" Carlos asks.

"And when are you going to bust it?" I add.

"It's right here in El Paso," he says. "And we're going to hit it within the week. We're trying to locate as many brothels as we can so we can take them all down at once. But we believe there are women inside, suffering, so we're not going to wait much longer."

Carlos and I glance at each other, knowing what the other is thinking.

"You need any help?" I ask.

Ryan sits back in his chair. "If y'all want to get in on this," he says with a smug smile, "I guess I could make room on my team for a couple of Texas Rangers."

For a moment, I wonder why Ryan's so agreeable, and then he answers my question for me.

"I don't see how you can do any harm," he says. "Besides, it won't hurt to have the Texas Rangers owing me a favor."

Carlos and I seem to agree that this is a price worth paying because, without consulting each other, we both know that we want in.

"All right then," Ryan says. "Welcome to the southeastern branch of the Federal Task Force on Missing and Murdered American Indians and Alaska Natives."

CHAPTER 15

WE SPEND ANOTHER hour signing paperwork and sitting down at a computer with one of Ryan's agents, who walks us through how to use a few federal databases we didn't have access to before. When Carlos and I finally step outside into the bright sunlight, I'm just about asleep on my feet. I need either a cup of coffee or a nap. Maybe both.

We stop at a place called Mesa Street Grill and eat lunch while we talk.

"What do you think?" I ask, remembering what he said on the drive about how the federal task force might add another layer of red tape to investigations, cluttering things up rather than streamlining them. "Seems like their coordination of cases is paying off."

He agrees but adds that it also appeared as if Ryan only cared about the big trafficking operation.

"He was so excited to show off his plans about raiding

the warehouse that he hardly seemed to care about Fiona Martinez."

Ryan had offered us space to work in the FBI office, but I'm barely awake and need to take a quick nap, so we decide to check into a hotel. As Carlos sits at the desk, leaning over his laptop, attempting to navigate the FBI databases, I dial Ava Cruz of the Tigua Tribal Police.

When I reintroduce myself, she says, "I remember who you are," her tone suggesting that she has better things to do than to talk to me. "Another Ranger called the other day. Carlos Castillo. I haven't had a chance to return his call yet."

I explain that Carlos and I are in the El Paso area—close to the Tigua Pueblo—and that we're investigating another missing Native American woman.

"We found a golden eagle feather at the woman's apartment," I explain. "I was wondering if in your case, the one you told me about, something similar might have been found."

"A Native American with an eagle feather? That doesn't sound unusual."

"It seemed out of place here, though," I say. "There weren't any decorations with feathers or anything like that. And it was on the kitchen table, laid out with nothing else around it. Like a calling card."

She says she didn't find anything like that in the home of the woman she's searching for. I also ask her about any sightings of a blue panel van, and she says that she'll have to ask the neighbors of the missing woman. That's a specific detail that she wouldn't have known to ask about before.

"Would have been nice if the feds had mentioned that," she says.

Even though my phone call hasn't amounted to any leads, at least Ava Cruz's tone has changed. She doesn't sound put out by my call anymore. She sounds intrigued.

When I end the call, Carlos says without looking up from his computer, "It was worth a try."

I tell him I'm going to take a quick nap, and I pull my boots off and stretch out on my bed, still wearing my shirt and tie. I drift off to the sound of Carlos's fingers clicking away on the keyboard.

I expect to be down only for a quick power nap—thirty minutes, tops—but when my phone buzzes, waking me up, the light coming in through the window has changed. Evening is approaching.

"Hell," I say, groggy. "I slept too long."

Now I won't sleep worth a damn tonight. I wish Carlos would have woken me up earlier, but of course that's what he probably thought while I was driving to El Paso. Now we're even, I guess.

"I got some dinner," he says, gesturing to a pizza box sitting on the table. He's eating a slice while still typing away at the computer.

I check my phone and see that I missed a call from Ava Cruz. "Find anything out?" I ask Carlos as I call Ava back and wait as the phone rings.

He says that he's just now getting the hang of navigating these federal databases.

"I feel like a mouse in a maze," he says. "Or a tribal elder trying to use a smartphone."

When Ava picks up, she says, "What you said got me to thinking, so I looked back through some of our old cases to see if there was any mention of eagle feathers."

"And?"

"Another woman went missing off the Pueblo last year," she says. "Rebecca Trujillo. Twenty-one years old. The notes mentioned a feather lying across the woman's pillow."

I motion to get Carlos's attention. He stops what he is doing on the computer, and I put the phone on speaker so he can hear better.

"Any mention in the report of what kind of feather?" I ask Ava.

"No," she says, "but I went through the evidence room and found it. It's here in a plastic baggie on my desk."

"And?"

"I'd say it's about a foot long. Kind of a chocolate-brown color."

"Marbling?" Carlos asks.

"Yeah, I guess that's what you'd call it. There are tan patches."

We text images of the feathers back and forth, and while we're not ornithology experts, all three of us agree the feathers seem to have come from the same type of bird. Maybe even the same bird.

I tell her that we should make sure both feathers are taken to the crime lab in El Paso and see what they can tell us.

"There's something else you should know," Ava says, her guarded tone gone, replaced by a collaborative attitude. "About this missing woman, Rebecca Trujillo."

"Yeah?"

"I said she went missing about a year ago. In fact, she went missing one year ago yesterday. Same day as the girl you're looking for."

Carlos and I stare at each other.

"Both went missing on the summer solstice," Carlos adds.

I feel a chill crawl up my spine.

If Fiona Martinez went missing on the anniversary of Rebecca Trujillo's disappearance, both on the summer solstice, and in both cases a golden eagle feather was left behind, suddenly Carlos's flippant comment about a serial killer collecting Native American women doesn't seem quite so far-fetched.

CHAPTER 16

WE MAKE ARRANGEMENTS for Carlos and me to visit the Pueblo tomorrow and talk with Ava about the cases. Then Carlos and I work until after sunset, searching the computer databases, making phone calls, checking in on other cases we're involved in back in our home offices, and updating our respective superiors about what we're up to here in West Texas. When we finally call it a night, I can tell there's no chance I'll be able to sleep anytime soon. Staying up all night and then taking the nap today have thrown off my circadian rhythms—not to mention what we've discovered about the eagle feathers left behind has me too anxious to relax.

I change into a pair of jeans and a T-shirt, and I tell Carlos I'm going to go grab a beer.

"Want to come?"

"Nah," he says. "Not unless you're planning on crossing over into Juárez to hire a couple of Mexican prostitutes."

"Very funny," I say. "Looks like I've finally figured out when you're joking."

"You think I'm joking?" he says, looking up with a surprised expression. "It's perfectly legal in Mexico. We wouldn't be breaking any laws."

I feel a moment's hesitation—*Wait, is he joking?*—and then his face breaks into a grin.

"You got me," I say. "Again."

In the parking lot of the hotel, I plug an address into the GPS. Twenty minutes later, I park my truck in the gravel lot outside a bar called the Outpost. I debate whether to go in. I felt a spark with Megan last night, but that doesn't change the fact that I was also tempted to rekindle the flame with Willow. If not for Carlos's phone call, I might have woken up next to Willow and spent the morning discussing the possibility of the two of us getting back together.

I remind myself I'm not cheating on anyone by taking an interest in Megan. The bottom line is that Willow and I aren't dating anymore.

When I walk into the bar, I don't spot Megan right away, and I wonder if I've misremembered her saying she is working tonight. The bar is spacious, but not very crowded, with only a few people seated at the numerous round tables. The floors are scuffed hardwood, the walls decorated with neon beer signs. There's a pool table, shuffleboard, and a corner with roping dummies where a trio of college-age kids are practicing their lassoing skills. A small stage is positioned prominently in the room, but no band is playing tonight. Instead, a song by Shooter Jennings plays on the jukebox.

I slide onto a barstool next to a guy who looks a little out of place among the younger crowd. Even more out of place than I do. He's probably in his late fifties, wearing—despite the fact that it's summer—a tan jacket with patches on the elbows. The other patrons all look like college students; he could be their professor.

When Megan walks out from the back room, carrying a rack of pint glasses, she doesn't notice me at first. She's wearing cowboy boots, painted-on jeans, and a Tom Petty T-shirt. Her hair is pulled back in a no-nonsense ponytail.

"Meg," the guy next to me calls, clearly not concerned that she's helping another customer. "How about a refill, love?"

As she looks up at him, she spots me, and her face lights up in surprise.

"What on earth are you doing here?" she asks, coming around the bar to hug me.

"I couldn't wait to see you again."

She gives me a skeptical look, knowing that I didn't drive six hundred miles just to see her.

"Working on a case," I say. "I'll probably be here a few days. Maybe even a few weeks."

She goes back around the bar and pours me a beer. She gets one for my impatient neighbor while she's at it, then she introduces us.

"This is Neil Stephenson," she says. "He's my dissertation advisor."

"Dr. Neil Stephenson," he says, correcting her.

"Rory's a Texas Ranger," Megan says.

"Funny," he says, "you don't look like a baseball player."

"The other kind of Texas Ranger," Megan says, rolling her eyes in mock irritation.

Neil takes a drink, unimpressed.

Megan appears to be the only one working at the bar, so she's soon pulled away and I'm stuck with her pretentious professor. His favorite subject is himself, and he drones on about how he tours Southwestern colleges giving lectures on American literature. As he talks, he doesn't take his eyes off Megan, and I wonder if she realizes that he wants their relationship to be more than just teacher and student.

The clock approaches midnight, and the bar thins out. Besides Megan and me, there's only Neil—I mean Dr. Stephenson—and a couple of guys shooting pool. Megan tells me she's going to close the place down so she and I can be alone. Her professor, who is quite drunk, doesn't seem too happy. I get the impression he is used to sticking around until closing so he can have time alone with Megan. Reluctantly, he orders an Uber while Megan heads over to break it to the pool players that this will be their last game.

"Come on—one more draft!" one of them says loudly, his words slurred. "My bitch girlfriend just broke up with me, and I don't plan to leave until I'm good and shit-faced."

"I think you've already achieved your goal," Megan says, reaching for the guy's empty glass on the rail of the pool table.

The guy's arm flashes out and he grabs Megan's wrist, gripping it tight.

"Now hold it there, honey," he says.

"Let go," she says forcefully.

"Either you fetch me a beer," the guy says, "or I'm going to slap you around like I should have done to my ex."

I rise off my barstool and start walking toward them. The jukebox is already off, and the sound of my boots against the floorboards carries across the room. The man turns his attention toward me, and Megan snatches her arm away and backs up.

"If you want to slap somebody around," I say, "why don't you try me?"

CHAPTER 17

AS I APPROACH the pool table, I try to take stock of what I'm walking into. The drunk guy, wearing a faded Houston Astros tank top, turns to face me. He is short and stocky, with muscular arms and a beer gut, giving me the impression he spends time in the gym, but more likely lifting weights rather than putting in any time on the treadmill. He has a slight grin on his face like the idea of getting into a bar fight makes him happy. His girlfriend just broke up with him, and he's ready to either beat someone up or get beaten up—it probably doesn't matter much which.

Fortunately, his friend doesn't seem interested in joining. He's taller but thinner, and looks sober by comparison. A water glass sits on a nearby table, and I deduce that he is the designated driver who came along to watch over his friend during his mission to get wasted.

"Come on, Randy, let's just go find another bar," the friend says, then, looking up at me, adds, "We don't want any trouble."

"The hell we don't," says Randy, who picks up a pool cue and snaps it over his knee. "Trouble is exactly what I fucking want."

He tosses the thin half of the broken stick aside and holds the other end like a baseball bat. This changes things.

I'm not in the habit of wearing a gun when I'm off duty, so I don't have any weapon on me. I figure I can still probably disarm him, but there's a decent chance I'll get hurt. Plus, I was hoping to get out of this without putting the son of a bitch in jail.

Or the hospital.

Waiting around for the cops to arrive will interfere with my alone time with Megan.

"Either that pretty little bartender serves me one more round," he says, "or I'm going to shove this pool stick right up your ass."

Megan says, "Neil, call the police."

I'd forgotten about the professor over by the bar.

"Hang on just one second," I say, holding up a finger to stall Neil.

I stare at Randy, who looks ready to turn my skull into a home run. Slowly, I reach into my back pocket and pull out my wallet, flip it open, and show him my Texas Ranger ID. He squints his eyes to read.

"You a cop?" he asks.

"I'm a Texas Ranger," I say.

His confidence and anger seem to drain from his body. He looks unsure how to continue.

"Jesus Christ," his friend says, putting his hands to his head. "Put the stick down, Randy. Don't be an idiot."

I'm not sure if seeing the badge makes them more scared of me, or if they're just afraid of what might happen if Randy assaults a Texas Ranger. Either way, Randy doesn't have the same looking-for-a-fight attitude he did a minute ago. He hesitates for a moment, and I brace myself for the attack. Then he comes to his senses and puts his arms up as if I'm holding a gun on him. He doesn't let go of the pool cue—he seems to have forgotten it's even in his hand.

"I'm sorry, mister. I wasn't thinking."

I turn to the friend as I pocket my wallet. "Are you sober?"

He nods his head and from over my shoulder Megan confirms that he's been drinking ice water all night.

"Take your friend home," I say. Then I give Randy a hard stare. "I don't know anything about you, Randy, but I didn't like what I saw tonight. Grabbing a woman's wrist. Talking about slapping your ex around. Trying to start a fight with me. You need to make some changes in your life. This isn't how a Texas man behaves."

"Yes, sir," he says, his skin a shade or two paler than it was when I first approached him.

"One other thing," I add, gesturing to Megan. "This woman is a close personal friend of mine. If you ever set foot in this bar again, I'm going to hear about it. I've got your first name, and I've seen your face. That's enough. I'm a Texas Ranger. I'll find you."

The two men hurry out the door, Randy taking the broken pool cue with him. I follow them and watch as they pull out of the parking lot in a Jeep. I make a mental note of the license number.

When I walk back in, Neil says, "Well, that was quite a display of testosterone."

I ask Megan if she's okay, and she says she is. I tell her that her instincts were right to call the police, and I add that she never should have been working alone in a place like this.

"Normally, there's always at least two people on a shift," Megan says, "but the other guy called in sick."

Megan takes a few minutes to turn off the neon beer signs and finish cleaning up behind the bar. Neil milks the last of his beer and then announces that his Uber is arriving.

"See you on campus tomorrow," Megan calls out as he exits.

A minute later, she and I are finally alone with fresh beers in front of us.

"It's nice that we finally get some time alone to talk," I say.

"I'm not sure I'm in the mood to talk anymore," she says.

"Oh," I say.

I'm surprised, but I also understand. I only hope my part in the "display of testosterone" hasn't diminished her attraction to me.

Megan stares at me with her electric-blue eyes and says, "I'm more interested in doing this."

She leans in to me, puts her soft lips against mine, and we begin to kiss.

CHAPTER 18

OVER THE NEXT two hours, we spend our time kissing *and* talking. It feels good to do both. Since Willow and I split, I haven't spent time doing either with any woman, let alone someone as attractive, smart, and enjoyable to be around as Megan Casewick.

We might have grown up just down the street from one another, but now we live in completely different worlds. She's an academic, spending her days either standing in front of a classroom or with her nose in a book—and not the best-sellers I like to read. She reads smart scholarly books with long sentences, citations, footnotes, and lots of academic vocabulary. As for me, I spend my days visiting crime scenes, collecting evidence, interviewing witnesses, testifying in court, and stopping bad guys. It's hard to say at this point if our differences would be good for a relationship.

Or a disaster.

For now, though, it feels good just to begin falling for someone.

Part of me feels like we could continue this way until the sun rises—talking, kissing, getting to know each other—but we both agree we need to get some sleep. She's teaching in the morning, and I'm due at the Pueblo to meet up with Ava Cruz. I'm not going to change Ava's opinion of the Texas Rangers if I show up bleary-eyed and asleep on my feet.

I walk Megan to the parking lot, where the air has grown cool. That's one nice thing about being in the dry climate of far western Texas as opposed to the humid central part of the state—the temperature cools considerably when the sun goes down.

Before parting ways, Megan wraps her arms around my neck and kisses me again, long and sensually. I slide my hands to the small of her back and hold her firmly against my body. I love the way she feels in my arms.

"I better go," she says finally, and climbs into her truck, an old Dodge Dakota. Before driving away, she rolls down the window and throws an elbow out. "Come back tomorrow night," she says, then checks her watch and adds, "Or tonight, I guess it is."

"I will if I can."

"And bring your guitar," she says with a grin. "You can sit on the stage and play a few cover songs for my customers."

After she drives off, I climb into my Ford and start the engine. My headlights illuminate the only other car in the parking lot, and I catch a glimpse of movement behind the window. My truck's elevated position allows me to see inside. The front seat is leaned back all the way, and a human is lying inside.

I step out of my truck and approach the Nissan Sentra.

Megan's mentor, Neil Stephenson—Dr. Neil Stephenson—is passed out in the driver's seat.

He had told us he called an Uber, but apparently he decided to sleep off his drunkenness instead. At least he's not driving, I think. I watch him for a minute to make sure he's breathing, then I climb back into my truck and drive off, having had only two beers myself, the last of them finished off a good ninety minutes ago.

As I drive away, it occurs to me that Megan's mentor might have hidden in his car, jealously waiting to see how long Megan and I stayed behind together. When I first noticed him, I thought I saw movement. Maybe he was spying on us as we kissed in the parking lot. Then pretending to sleep.

I tell myself I'm being paranoid, and I let my thoughts drift back to Megan, the feel of her body pressed against mine.

I'm already looking forward to going back tonight so I can kiss her again.

CHAPTER 19

YSLETA DEL SUR PUEBLO might have once stood off on its own, away from El Paso, but the reservation has been subsumed by the growth of the El Paso suburbs. As Carlos and I drive to meet Ava Cruz in the morning, I can't tell where the federally designated tribal land even begins. The neighborhoods don't look demonstrably different from those in the surrounding areas: brick houses with mortared stone fences and juniper and cypress trees growing in the patchy yards.

We pass a beautiful old Spanish-style mission. Next door is a large building with a sign reading SPEAKING ROCK ENTERTAINMENT CENTER, which Carlos says used to be a full-fledged tribal casino but has since been downgraded to just slots and bingo. There's a billboard advertising an upcoming concert for a heavy metal band I've never heard of.

Down the street, we drive past an old, boarded-up

community center. Workers driving heavy machinery are digging up the lot across the street, with a sign advertising a new community center scheduled to open next year.

A minute later, I pull my truck into the parking lot of the Ysleta del Sur Pueblo Judicial Facility, one of the bigger adobe structures on the Pueblo, containing both the police department and the courthouse. The front lawn is green and well maintained, a sharp contrast to the mostly brown yards in the Pueblo and surrounding city. The words TRIBAL POLICE DEPARTMENT are stenciled in large red letters above the door of the left wing of the building. I park next to a tribal police SUV. The Ysleta del Sur logo is displayed on the vehicle's white door, showing a star, a bald eagle head, and two feathers, which—unlike the feathers found at the crime scene—are white with black tips.

We tell the receptionist who we're here to see, and Ava doesn't leave us waiting for long. She comes out to greet us wearing her blue uniform and her hair pulled back in a braid, exactly how I saw her at the shooting competition.

She gestures for us to follow her, and she leads us to an investigation room, where photos and notes are pinned to the walls, stacks of paperwork and file folders cover a table, and evidence boxes fill one corner. An older-model box TV sits on a rolling metal stand. The garbage can by the door is full of paper coffee cups and discarded take-out boxes—giving me the impression that Ava has been working day and night on this case.

Ava points to an eight-by-eleven photograph taped to the wall of a young Native American woman with a bright, enthusiastic smile. Her long straight hair cascades down her shoulders and out of the frame. The picture looks like a senior high school portrait.

"This is Marta Rivera," she says. "Age nineteen. Lives with her mom here on the Pueblo. Went missing ten days ago. No sign of struggle. No witnesses who noticed anything suspicious. Nothing to suggest she ran away, either. No clothes missing or anything like that. It's like she just vanished," Ava adds, snapping her finger loudly, "into thin air."

"Does she go to college?" I ask.

"She works full-time at the rec center and takes some classes online from Arizona State."

There goes my idea that maybe she and Fiona Martinez, who attends El Paso Community College, are classmates.

Ava tells us that since we called her yesterday, she's asked Marta's mom if she saw any out-of-place eagle feathers after her daughter went missing.

The answer was no.

"But," Ava adds, "I also looked into your blue panel van."

She explains that she didn't find anyone who remembered seeing a vehicle that fit the description. However, she had already obtained security camera footage from the Speaking Rock casino on the day Marta went missing. One outdoor camera has a good view of one of the main roads through the Pueblo.

The footage has been saved onto a DVD, and Ava picks up a remote and turns on the TV. She plays a few seconds showing cars going up and down the roadway.

"That's the way we came in today," I say.

"There," Ava says, pausing the screen.

The image is grainy, but a van is definitely visible, and it seems to have the same color as Llewellyn Carpenter's vehicle.

"Looks like the one," I say.

We're all quiet for a moment as it sinks in what this might mean.

"The good news," Carlos says to Ava, "is that the FBI knows who that guy is and they're taking steps to rescue at least some of the women he's abducted."

"Hopefully we'll be able to find Marta Rivera and bring her home," I say.

Ava looks dubious.

"You said that was the good news," she says to Carlos. "Does that mean there's bad news?"

Carlos nods. I already know what he's going to say.

"The bad news is that I think our eagle feather victims are a different case entirely. I don't think either Fiona Martinez or Rebecca Trujillo will turn up when the feds conduct their raid. And," he adds, "I wonder if there might be more eagle feather victims we don't know about yet."

CHAPTER 20

AVA MAKES ROOM for Carlos and me in the tight investigation room, clearing space on the table. Carlos and I bring in our laptops and the three of us get to work, hunting through the FBI database and making phone calls. Carlos orders food—another pizza—and we eat lunch while we work.

Given our new access to FBI online tools, it doesn't take long to discover that two years ago, on the solstice, a Ute woman from Durango, Colorado, disappeared and was never found. A year before that, a Kickapoo woman from Houston disappeared.

Also on the solstice.

Also never found.

It takes us longer to figure out if golden eagle feathers had been left behind. I call the Durango Police Department and finally convince someone to look through the old files. There are no feathers in evidence, but the officer I speak with flips through some crime scene photos and sees a feather on a desk in the woman's room. He takes a picture of the picture and texts it to me. The image isn't great, but the size and color of the feather show that it, too, probably belonged to a golden eagle.

Meanwhile, Ava calls the Houston Police Department, and after some digging, they find a feather in an old evidence box. By midafternoon, we've established that for four years in a row, Native women went missing on the solstice, with feathers left behind. In all cases the women were young, between eighteen and twenty-one. We can't yet see any other links between them.

They come from four different tribes—Tigua, Navajo, Kickapoo, and Ute—and it's doubtful any of the women knew each other. Even though the last two—Fiona Martinez and Rebecca Trujillo—both disappeared from the El Paso area, Fiona was actually from Flagstaff, Arizona, and had only recently moved to Texas. Rebecca was already gone by then.

While Carlos continues typing away on his laptop, Ava and I begin discussing what it's going to take to fully look into these four missing persons cases. We'll need access to all four police files. We will need to travel to these different communities, spanning four states, and interview the women's friends and family members. We'll need to examine whatever evidence the local authorities have in storage.

The bottom line: We're going to need a bigger team than the three of us.

"I think it's time we let Ryan Logan know what we've found," I say. "We're going to need help."

"Wait one second," Carlos says, still scrutinizing his

computer screen. Finally, he looks up with a satisfied expression and says, "I think I found a fifth victim."

He explains that four years ago on the solstice, a young woman went missing. She was seventeen, which makes her a little younger than the others. Nothing in the record says anything about an eagle feather, but the disappearance on the solstice is significant.

"Where was she from?" Ava asks.

"Right here on the Tigua Pueblo," Carlos says. "She was last seen at a powwow happening in El Paso, so the local cops and the feds took the lead in the investigation."

"I wasn't here that far back," Ava says. "I was working for the highway patrol up in the Panhandle."

"There's more," Carlos adds, grinning because he knows that he's holding us in suspense.

"Spill it," I say. "Don't leave us waiting."

"She's still alive!"

My eyes go wide.

Carlos explains that the woman—whose name is Isabella Luna—was discovered on a highway eighty or so miles east of El Paso. She'd been gone for ten days and was badly malnourished and seriously injured.

Cuts.

Broken bones.

Even a rattlesnake bite.

"The police and FBI questioned her about what happene' Carlos says, "but she had no recollection. Finally, it look' they gave up trying to get her to remember. They just l' Closed the case."

Ava says that she knows who Isabella Luna is.

"She's a good person," Ava says. "She works in the restaurant at the casino. She's got a smile for everyone who comes in. I knew she disappeared for a while, but it never occurred to me it might be related. I didn't realize it happened on the solstice."

"The police report says she has no memory of anything between performing at the powwow and being found on the highway," Carlos says.

Immediately, I'm thinking about how Isabella Luna might hold the key to breaking this case open. However, I can see the sympathetic look in Ava's eyes, and I'm reminded that we're talking about a person who has clearly been through a lot.

"I hate to make her relive her trauma," Ava says, "but if it can save other lives, we've got to find out what she remembers."

CHAPTER 21

WHEN I KNOCK on Ryan Logan's office door—the one in the FBI headquarters in El Paso, not his office on wheels—he doesn't seem pleased that we've brought Ava Cruz with us.

"I don't mean to be an asshole," he says, "but if you want to talk to me about official task force business, we'll need to speak in private. Only members of the team."

Yesterday morning, he didn't have a problem filling Carlos and me in on all the details about Llewellyn Carpenter and the planned raid. That was before we signed on the dotted line and joined his so-called team. I wonder why he won't extend the same courtesy to Ava Cruz. Maybe it's because yesterday he had the opportunity to show off to a couple of visiting Texas Rangers. Today, he doesn't want to hear that someone outside the task force has something to contribute that his team might have overlooked.

I open my mouth to say I want Ava to stay—she's a part

of our investigation—but she heads toward the door, saying, "It's okay." She lowers herself onto a seat just outside the doorway, looking like a child waiting in the hallway while Mommy and Daddy talk to the teacher.

Carlos and I sit across from Ryan's desk. I take a deep breath. Ryan's attitude has started the meeting off on a bad note, and I can already feel my anger simmering to the surface. I hate when politics and egos get in the way of solving crimes.

"What can I do you for?" Ryan asks, throwing his legs up on the desk.

The office has no decorations, no pictures on the wall. Nothing but a spotless desk and the late afternoon sun pouring in through the window. The office is clearly just a temporary home for him—a place with four walls and a telephone—while he happens to be here in El Paso. In another month, he might set up shop in Phoenix or Albuquerque or San Antonio.

Carlos and I take turns speaking, starting with our discovery of the eagle feather at Fiona Martinez's apartment and concluding with the revelation that Isabella Luna might be able to provide some insight about these eagle feather cases.

Ryan looks skeptical.

"Unless the DNA tests on the feathers come back belonging to the same bird, I'm not sure we can jump to these conclusions. Why don't you just hold your horses on this until we get those tests back?"

"We need to move on this fast," I say. "Isabella Luna was gone for ten days. Our latest victim, Fiona Martinez, might still be alive. The clock is ticking."

"Besides," Carlos says, "it doesn't necessarily mean anything if the feathers came from different birds. No one is saying this guy's got a pet eagle in his garage that he plucks the feathers from."

Ryan smirks.

I plow forward, telling him what we need.

"We want to send teams to the different states," I explain, "so we can conduct fresh interviews and rebuild those investigations from the ground up."

"What for?"

"To find out if there's any link between the victims, for one," I say. "And to look for other connections. Other clues. You said so yourself that no one linked the blue panel van until the task force had an idea of what it was looking for."

As I speak, I can hear my voice getting more and more heated, fueled by the unconvinced expression glued to Ryan's face. I can't help myself—I'm getting pissed.

Ryan looks back and forth between Carlos and me.

"I'm swamped planning for this raid," he says. "I've got all my troops focused on that right now. If you two want to look into this with Robin Hood out there, you're welcome to, but I can't spare another person."

As Carlos and I rise to leave, I know I shouldn't say anything, but I can't help myself.

"Ryan," I say, "if you drag your feet on this and it turns out we could have saved Fiona Martinez and didn't, that's going to be on your conscience."

Ryan, suddenly as angry as I am, jerks his feet off the desk and jumps to his feet.

"Listen here, Rory," he snaps. "I'm juggling teams in five different states. You can't even fathom the responsibilities I have. I don't take the lives of the women who are missing lightly. I intend to save as many of them as I can. And the ones we can't save, I intend to get justice for them by arresting those responsible. So don't come in here riding your fucking high horse about how you think I should be doing my job. You're welcome to head on back to Waco any time you'd like. We were getting along just fine without you."

Ryan and I stare each other down. The camaraderie we shared on the gun range seems a million years ago. We were competitors then, and we acted like friends. Now we're supposed to be working together, and it feels like we're adversaries.

"I'll stay," I say. "And if you were getting along so fine, then why'd you miss these eagle feathers?"

"Whatever," he says, and flicks his wrist to dismiss us from his office.

Out in the hall, Ava Cruz is waiting for us. As we walk to the elevator, Carlos says to her, "Did you hear any of that?"

"All of it," she says as we step into the elevator.

She looks up at me and gives me a nod, as if to say thanks for standing up to the FBI.

It seems I've gained the respect of Ava Cruz, even if I've lost it from Ryan Logan.

I decide I'm happy with the trade.

CHAPTER 22

AS THE ELEVATOR descends, Carlos says, "It's five o'clock. Y'all want to go get a drink?"

"I know the perfect place," I say.

We agree to meet at the Outpost in an hour. I drop Ava back at her station, and then Carlos and I head back to our hotel. We change into jeans and collared shirts that aren't quite as dressy as our work shirts. Then we head over to the bar.

"Well, what's this?" Carlos says as we pull into the lot.

The marquee over the door reads:

PERFORMING LIVE

ONE NIGHT ONLY

RORY YATES

"What on earth?" I say.

As we enter the bar, Megan spots us right away and laughs as she approaches.

"Don't be mad," she says. "I meant it as a joke. You don't have to play if you don't want."

"Oh, he's ready," Carlos says, bumping his shoulder against mine. "He's got his guitar in the truck. Rory never leaves home without it."

It's not lost on me that he's repeating the same words I used when I picked him up in Austin. He gives me his roguish grin.

"Maybe a few songs," I say. "I'll need some liquid courage first."

Carlos and I make our way to the bar. When Megan's out of earshot, Carlos says to me, "I like her. She's got a sense of humor."

"I'm surrounded by comedians," I say.

The Outpost doesn't serve food, but there is a cluster of food trucks just down the street. Carlos goes and buys us some tacos while I order a round of Texas Lagers and get a table. The bar is fuller than it was last night, but it's far from packed. It shouldn't be too stressful to play a few tunes.

Two minutes after Carlos returns, Ava walks in with a muscular Native American man in a white T-shirt. His hair is pulled into a braid as long as Ava's.

"This is my fiancé, Marcos," she says. "I hope it's okay that I brought him. I didn't get the impression we were going to talk business tonight."

Carlos and I welcome Marcos, and the four of us sit for a while, eating tacos and drinking. Ava opts for lemonade instead of beer, and I only sip from my pint, knowing I'll be driving later.

It turns out Marcos is a long-haul trucker and he has a few days off. Between Ava's long hours at the police station and his long hours on the road, they haven't seen much of each other lately, and she didn't want to go out after work without bringing him along.

"Where do you drive to?" I ask.

"Anywhere," he says. "Everywhere."

"Marcos is gone a lot," Ava says, wrapping an arm around one of his muscular tree trunks.

It's a new side of her I haven't seen yet — the picture of a girl in love — and it suits her.

Marcos and Carlos hit it off right away, talking about rezball — a fast-paced, high-intensity version of basketball played in tribal high schools in the Four Corners area and elsewhere in the West.

"I tried to watch the NBA playoffs a few weeks ago," Marcos says. "It's so slow compared to rezball."

"Like watching sloths race," Carlos adds.

As they talk and laugh, I find myself in a moment of awkward silence with Ava.

"Thanks for sticking up for our case today," she tells me.

"I'm not sure it did much good," I say.

She shrugs. "Still. Thanks."

"I get the impression Ryan Logan's not your biggest fan," I say. "Did something happen between you?"

She shakes her head. "Not really. It's just that he's a fed — he wants everyone to kiss his ass. Especially tribal police.

Like we should just be groveling at his feet because he's helping us. I won't do that. You have to earn my respect."

I nod, understanding.

"You earned my respect today," she says.

"Thanks," I say, trying not to make a big deal out of it but truthfully feeling grateful for her words.

Out of the corner of my eye, I see Megan's professor, Neil Stephenson, walk into the bar. When he surveys the room and spots me, he heads directly to our table.

"Ah, shit," I say under my breath. I rise and shake his hand and introduce him to everyone.

"You know," he says, seeing his audience, "Native American literature is my specialty."

The last thing I want is for him to join us, but he pulls a chair from an adjacent table and sits down between Ava and her fiancé. He begins to prattle on about how he travels the West, going to community colleges, universities, and tribal colleges to give lectures and workshops on the work of Indigenous writers. Carlos starts asking him about writers he's read, and one after another Neil says he's not familiar with who Carlos is mentioning. I can't tell if Carlos really is that knowledgeable about Native American authors or if he's making up names and messing with the professor.

With Carlos, I can never tell if he's joking.

Ava and Marcos clearly don't care for our visitor, so I decide now might be a good time to play. Maybe he'll shut up if there's live music. I run out to the truck and get my guitar. The sun has set and the night air is cool on my skin.

I stand for a moment, breathing the fresh air, and prepare

myself for what I'm about to do. I've performed plenty of times, but it always makes me nervous. I tell myself not to worry. I can handle a little gig in front of an apathetic audience. Of course, my real fear is that I'll embarrass myself in front of my new friends—Carlos and Ava and her fiancé—in which case Carlos will tease me endlessly about this.

Knowing his sense of humor, that's a distinct possibility.

CHAPTER 23

MEGAN UNPLUGS THE jukebox, and I spend a few minutes tuning my guitar. No one in the bar seems to be paying any attention to me. There's a rudimentary sound system, which I can plug my guitar into, as well as a microphone for singing.

When I clear my throat and announce that I'm going to play, 90 percent of the patrons don't pay any attention to me. Megan—who has a coworker helping her tonight—takes a break from serving drinks to sit on the bar top, her attention devoted solely to me. Tonight she's wearing a red tank top, but I remember the Tom Petty shirt she wore last night.

I say, "This one's for someone special to me," and I strum the opening of "American Girl," the only song I know by Tom Petty. Megan recognizes it right away, and her face lights up and she applauds.

Slowly, the other people in the bar start to pay attention, and soon everyone is listening to me. Everyone, that is, except for Dr. Neil Stephenson. The professor keeps talking to Ava, who seems to be doing everything she can to ignore him.

After "American Girl," I start in on some of the country tunes I know well: songs by Johnny Cash and Willie Nelson and Tim McGraw. Jimmy Buffett is always a hit, no matter what the crowd is like. I play for about thirty minutes, and by the end there are about a dozen people on the dance floor. I know I should quit while I'm ahead, but I decide to try out Willow's song "Texas Forever" on the crowd. I tell them that this is from Willow Dawes, and the audience lets out a hoot. It seems to dawn on a few of the faces that I might be the Texas Ranger she wrote her hit song about.

I do my best to remember the lyrics Willow sang and the ones she and I came up with on the fly. The whole crowd likes it — it's a Texas crowd, after all — and just like at home, they're shouting *"Texas forever!"* along with me by my second trip through the chorus. I decide to try to make up some new rhymes. I look over at Ava, Marcos, and Carlos, and I sing,

> *The Texas flag and the lone star*
> *Drinking beers at the Outpost bar*
> *The Ysleta Mission on the Tigua Pueblo*
> *Playing bingo at the Speaking Rock casino*

This brings a smile to the face of the usually stoic Ava, and I decide that's a good place to end. I roll through the chorus one last time, and the audience sings practically all of it with me.

After I pack up my guitar, but before I leave the stage, I pull out my phone and send a text to Willow, explaining that I was playing around with her song and came up with some new lines. I feel a little strange, like I shouldn't be texting her, but I tell myself there's nothing wrong with it. We're still friends, aren't we?

Once I hit Send, I look up and see Megan standing at the edge of the stage, beaming at me. I feel guilty, like I've been caught doing something I'm not supposed to.

"That was amazing," she says. Then she gets an ornery twinkle in her eyes, as if she's up to something. "Can you help me lift a keg from the storage room?"

"Sure," I say, unsure why she won't ask her coworker.

I follow her to a storage area behind the bar—out of sight of the patrons—and as soon as we're alone, she grabs me and pulls me into a kiss. We make out, pressing our bodies against each other, for a good minute or two.

"I've been wanting to do that since you walked in the door," she says when we finally stop to take a breath.

I laugh. "I take it you don't really need help with a keg."

Reaching up to wipe some lipstick off my mouth, she asks what I'm doing later tonight, after her shift ends. I know what I probably should do is go to the hotel and get some sleep, but I tell her I'll do whatever she wants.

"Maybe you should come back to my place," she says.

I tell her I'll give Carlos the keys to my truck, and I'll wait with her until closing.

She stands on her tiptoes and gives me a peck on the cheek. I head back out into the bar, where I see Carlos is practicing his lassoing and Neil Stephenson has followed Ava and her fiancé over to the pool table.

I'd been worried that the professor had the hots for Megan, but I'm not sure that's the case now with the way he's following Ava around like a lost puppy. Marcos looks like he's ready to throw Neil through the window, so I figure I better rescue them. I'll go over and start chatting with Neil to give the couple a few minutes to themselves. But first I want to run my guitar out to the truck. I don't want it left behind when I give the keys to Carlos.

As I push through the exit and into the parking lot, I make it about fifteen feet before I spot something that makes me stop short. Parked in the lot, near the door, is a blue Jeep just like the one Randy and his friend drove away in last night. Before my eyes can move to check the license plate number, some kind of blunt object—a broken pool cue perhaps—smashes into my lower back.

I fall forward, wincing in pain, as my guitar case goes flying.

CHAPTER 24

I FALL TO my hands and knees in the gravel as my guitar case makes a dull *twang* sound landing next to me.

The pain in my back is excruciating, like I've just been struck with a bullwhip, and I find myself stunned for a moment, frozen on all fours. Afraid that another blow is going to come—this time against the back of my skull—I roll over and put an arm up in defense.

Three figures—all wielding some kind of weapon—crowd in around me. There's enough ambient street lighting for me to make out their faces in the darkness. Randy, the asshole I almost got in a fight with last night, stands at my feet holding the same broken pool stick he ran off with. His sober and sensible friend isn't with him tonight, but he has two other companions, one holding a tire iron and the other a massive crescent wrench that must be at least two feet long.

"Remember me?" Randy says, smacking the stick against the palm of his hand.

"Randy, my old friend," I say with fake enthusiasm. "I'm beginning to think your girlfriend did the right thing by dumping your ass."

"You little shit," he growls, stepping forward.

I back up, sliding on my butt through the gravel. I keep one arm up in case he takes a swing. Better a broken forearm than a broken skull.

As I scoot backward, I leave my guitar case behind, and one of the men gives it a hard kick, sending it skidding across the gravel.

"Not so tough now, huh?" Randy says, obviously enjoying the sight of me squirming away.

I'm trying to buy time.

I don't have my gun. I'm outnumbered three to one. And they have weapons. The wrench and tire iron are more dangerous than the pool stick, so if Randy's buddies are as willing to commit violence as he is, I could be in serious trouble.

I can think of only one thing to do.

"I'll give you money," I say, reaching into my pockets. "I've got three hundred dollars on me. That's a Benjamin for each of you."

I can see that Randy's friends like the idea of getting paid. Why assault someone for free when you can *not* assault someone and make a hundred bucks?

But Randy isn't interested. "How about we just beat the shit out of you and take the money?"

From the nodding faces of his friends, I can concede that he's made a good counterargument.

I keep scooting backward. We're probably thirty feet from the bar entrance now. Inside my pocket, my hand fumbles for my keys, trying to find the fob for my truck and remember which button does what.

"You know I'm a Texas Ranger?" I say, trying to buy myself a few more seconds.

"You made that clear last night."

"Which means you can't just beat the shit out of me," I say. "You're going to have to kill me. Otherwise, I'll identify you and you'll go to jail for assaulting an officer. Murder is your only option unless you stop right now."

Randy's buddies don't look too happy about this news—apparently they hadn't thought this through—but Randy doesn't seem fazed by it.

"That's the idea," he says. "I'm going to kill you, and then I'm going to go to my ex's house and—"

He stops talking when the alarm on my truck sounds. The headlights and brake lights flash like the Fourth of July.

I only hope it's loud enough for Carlos to hear inside.

"Oops," I say, pulling my keys out of my pocket. "I guess the three hundred dollars are in the other pocket."

"You son of a bitch," Randy barks, raising his stick.

The door of the bar bursts open and Carlos, Ava, and Marcos step out. When he sees what's happening, Carlos shouts back into the bar, "Call 9-1-1!"

Then he runs toward the three men.

Ava and her fiancé follow, both ready to fight.

With Randy and his friends distracted by the three people racing toward them, I hop to my feet.

The trio of men don't seem to know what to do, looking at each other for guidance. They're still armed, but now they're outnumbered. And with the truck alarm wailing into the night, what they probably thought would be a simple assault under the cover of darkness has turned into a chaotic scene for the whole world to see.

Randy hesitates for a second, then he chokes up on the stick like a batter getting ready for the pitch. His two friends look for a moment like they're going to split, but they follow Randy's lead and decide to take their chances.

"Come on!" Randy yells at my rescuers.

This guy must love to fight because he's not going down without one.

I'll give him a fight he won't forget.

CHAPTER 25

I TAP RANDY on the shoulder, and he spins toward me, swinging the broken pool cue like a major-league hitter going after a fastball. I have just enough time to duck, and the stick comes so close to my skull I can feel the wind against my hair. Missing me throws him off balance, and while he's trying to get his feet set, I drive my fist into the lower part of his rib cage.

He lets out a grunt and attempts to swing back, but his feet are tangled up and his arms are holding the stick all wrong—like a right-handed batter who suddenly tries to hit left-handed without switching the position of his hands. I dodge the blow easily this time, and instead of going for the body, I drive my fist into his mouth. He reels backward, dropping the stick and landing clumsily on his butt.

I have time to see how the others are faring. The man with

the crescent wrench is swinging wildly at Carlos, who is quick on his feet, like a lightweight boxer with a long reach. He zips in, hits the guy with a couple of jabs, then slides back out before the guy can put any momentum behind the heavy wrench.

The one with the tire iron swings wildly at Marcos, who barely jumps back in time, but while he's distracted, Ava drops to the ground and sweeps the guy's leg with her own. He staggers, not quite falling, but it causes him to lower his defenses. Marcos swoops in with a killer right cross, and the guy drops like an elevator with a broken cable.

Meanwhile, Randy rises up out of the gravel, wiping his hands. He spits out a tooth and smiles at me, showing the bloody gap in his mouth. He looks more pissed than hurt and charges at me.

I grab him, stepping out of the way as I use his momentum to propel him face-first toward a car, which I recognize as Neil Stephenson's Nissan Sentra. Randy's head collides with the door, making a loud thud and leaving a dent the size of a salad plate.

Randy tries to stand up, but before he can turn around, I grab his left hand and twist his wrist. He groans in pain, and I contort his arm in a way that will either drive him to the ground or—if he resists the pain—do some damage to ligaments and muscles.

It's his choice.

Luckily, he makes the first smart move all night and goes down to the ground in a huff. With his chest in the gravel, I pin his arm behind his back. I look up to see Carlos has his guy in a similar position. The other guy—the one who got run over by the freight train of Marcos's fist—is still out cold.

Randy grunts and looks around with a surprised expression on his face that says, *Is the fight really over?*

Within a minute, everyone from the bar has filed out into the parking lot to get a look. We don't bother to tell them to go back inside. As long as they don't get close, some spectators aren't going to hurt anything.

Ava fetches handcuffs out of her vehicle, and Carlos and I put them on Randy and his friend. Then we let them sit up to lean against the wheels of my truck with their hands locked behind their backs. The third guy starts to wake up around the time the police arrive. They put Randy and his buddies in the back of a cruiser, and take some time interviewing all of us before hauling them off to jail.

I apologize to Neil for putting a dent in his door with Randy's head, and the professor surprises me by shrugging it off and saying, "It gives the car character."

When the hubbub has finally died, the patrons go back inside. Megan waits for me at the doorway. Carlos, Ava, and Marcos all stand with her. As I approach, Carlos gets a phone call and answers it, stepping a few feet away.

"You okay?" Megan asks me.

"My back's a little sore," I say, "but I'll live."

I'm not trying to be macho. I'm sure I'll have a welt—and some aches for a few days—but I know it could have been much worse.

"I'm sorry about all this," Megan says.

"Not your fault," I say, then gesture to the sign advertising a live performance from Rory Yates. "Besides, you wanted a show."

She laughs. "Is life with you always this exciting?"

"Not if I can help it," I say. "I like sitting on the porch and picking my guitar and watching the sun set."

"Sounds nice."

"I just need a good woman to sit on the porch with me," I add. "Maybe she could be reading a book."

"Sounds lovely," she says.

"One thing you should know," I add. "I do get called in at all hours. Crime doesn't stop at closing time. It's usually just getting started. It's hard to make plans."

"You can say that again," Carlos interjects, putting his phone away. "Just got a call from Ryan Logan. The raid's happening at 5:00 a.m."

"You're kidding?" I say. It's already past midnight. "He's just letting us know now?"

I check my phone and see two calls I missed from Ryan during all the fuss.

Still, when I was arguing with him a few hours ago, he probably knew then that the raid would be happening the next morning. Or he would have known that it was at least likely. He could have given us some kind of heads-up. I hate to think he withheld the information just to get back at me for standing up to him.

"If we want to be there," Carlos says, "we need to meet up with the team now."

"You told him we're coming, didn't you?"

"I said I'd be there," he says, "but I told him you just got beaten up and would probably miss it."

I stare at him, shocked. I open my mouth to tell him of course I want to be a part of the raid—and I did *not* get beaten up!

Then I remember who I'm talking to.

"Got you," he says, grinning. "Again."

CHAPTER 26

BEFORE LEAVING, CARLOS and I talk briefly with Ava, who wants to know if she should try to interview Isabella Luna tomorrow without us.

"Might be better if it's just me," she says. "Woman to woman. Tigua to Tigua."

"Just wait," I tell her. "We only have to put it off one day. Carlos and I will be ready then."

"The raid's at 5:00 a.m.," she says. "Can't we do the interview in the afternoon?"

Carlos and I discuss this possibility, but both of us worry that we'll be tied up most of the day.

Ava doesn't seem thrilled about this but defers to us. I know she doesn't like being told what to do, especially by outsiders, but I think she can see the benefit in all three of us addressing this interview with a coordinated plan. I stood up to Ryan today on behalf of our investigation, and tonight the two of them came to my rescue. In a short time, we've become a team.

I tell Marcos it was nice to meet him, and he shakes my hand with his steel vise. After Ava and her fiancé walk to their car, Carlos says he's going to hit the restroom before we leave, which gives me a few minutes alone with Megan in the parking lot.

"I'm sorry," I say. "I'll have to take a rain check tonight."

"I'm not in a hurry," she says. "I just want to spend more time with you. That's all."

"I want that, too," I say. "I'm not leaving El Paso anytime soon."

I stare into her beautiful eyes, sparkling in the streetlights.

"Maybe we're going too fast," she says.

She's right. If we fall for each other while I'm here in El Paso and it turns out she doesn't get the job at Baylor, where will that leave us? Either what we have here in West Texas will amount to nothing more than a summer fling, or I'll be right back where I was with Willow—trying to maintain a long-distance relationship.

"Well, isn't this tender?" a familiar voice says snidely.

Megan rolls her eyes as her professor steps out into the parking lot and eyes us up and down. He doesn't look particularly bent out of shape, and I realize maybe I was wrong about his intentions toward Megan.

When Carlos steps outside, he says to Neil, "Yo, Doc, make sure and find those authors I was telling you about and read up on them. There will be a quiz next time I see you."

After we leave, Carlos and I swing by the hotel to change

back into work clothes, then head toward the FBI rendez-
vous point. The streets are empty. The overcast sky seems to
catch the light of the city, causing a soapy grayness to hang
over the streets.

Both Carlos and I are quiet, focusing on what lies ahead.
The nerves you feel before a raid are like the jitters you feel
suiting up for a football game — only a hundred times more
powerful.

I ask Carlos again why he joined the Rangers, hoping for a
serious answer this time.

"I just wanted to fight for what's right," he says. "I figured
I could do more about injustices in the world by wearing the
badge rather than fighting against it."

Wise words, I think, and then I wonder why he was passed
over for promotion.

Everything I've seen from Carlos has been competent and
professional — aside from his sense of humor, and even that
only makes him more personable, in my opinion. He'd make
a good lieutenant, as far as I can tell. I wonder why Captain
Kane is so keen on grooming me for the next lieutenant position when there's already a qualified candidate interested. I
can hear Ava's criticism of the Rangers in my mind, but I'd
like to think things have changed.

"What about you, Rory?" he asks. "Why did you want to
become a Ranger?"

I shrug. "I didn't have the talent to make it as a country
singer."

He gives me a look that says, *You're not as good at the jokes
as I am.*

"My dad taught me to help people, if I could," I say. "This seemed like a good way to do it. Plus," I add, honestly, "I was good at shooting. I was fast. I was accurate. It came naturally to me. And I liked the discipline of practice, trying to get better and better. It seemed a shame to let the skill go to waste. Of course, I was too naïve to realize..."

When I hesitate, he completes my thought for me: "It's a lot different shooting at a target than a human being."

"Yeah," I say. "Just because you can do one doesn't mean you can do the other." We're quiet for a moment, then I add, "I guess it turned out I could do both."

As we leave the highway and approach the abandoned warehouse where the team is meeting up, I ask Carlos, "Have you ever...?"

"Once," he says, serious, no sign of his comedian side. "Before I was in the Rangers. I was a sheriff's deputy in Maverick County. Went to serve a warrant on a meth dealer accused of statutory rape. He opened the door with a .38. He missed and I didn't." After the truck chews up another half mile of road, he adds, "He was a bad person, just about as bad as they come, but that didn't make it easy."

We pull through a chain-link fence to a lot thrumming with activity. There are several cars and Ryan Logan's recognizable office on wheels. Dozens of law enforcement officials are there, suited up in bulletproof vests and carrying rifles. I spot Ryan talking on his radio and barking orders to the men and women around him.

I don't like the eager, cocky expressions on their faces.

Everyone looks overconfident to me. They all remind me of Randy—excited for the fight to come.

And we all know how that turned out for Randy.

Before stepping out of the truck, I point to the star on my chest and say to Carlos, "Someone has to wear these badges. Better that it's people like us, who take seriously what it means to pull the trigger. It's the people who *want* to shoot that I worry about."

Carlos nods in agreement. "Let's get our vests on. I've got a feeling we might have to use our guns today."

CHAPTER 27

AS SUNRISE APPROACHES, Carlos and I sit inside the command center van with Ryan Logan and a handful of FBI agents and El Paso officers. We're all wearing bulletproof vests and carrying our sidearms. There's a cabinet inside for rifles, and Carlos's LaRue .308 and mine are both in there for easy access. But we're not expected to actually enter the raid.

We're five blocks away.

We're the backup.

Ryan's bank of computer monitors displays images of the warehouse. The FBI managed to discreetly install cameras on the streets in front of and behind the building. Another image comes from a drone high in the sky, giving us a bird's-eye view. The other shots come from the lapel cameras on the SWAT team leaders.

One agent inside the van has headphones on to hear updates on the two raids that will occur simultaneously. That way, he can keep Ryan updated on what's happening at the brothels in Tucson and Colorado Springs.

The air is cool and crisp outside, but inside the van—with all the bodies packed into a small space—the air is stifling. The tension is palpable, as if every person in the vehicle is sweating out their anxiety and adrenaline.

Ryan gives the command for the raid to begin, and soon each monitor displays activity. The lapel cameras provide shaky on-the-ground footage. Meanwhile, we can see the team members coming into view on the roadside cameras. The drone shows the officers from above, small specks crowding in on the building.

The agents in front hold police shields, followed by two men lugging a battering ram, and bringing up the rear is a crowd of officers ready to swarm inside once the front door is knocked down.

They don't make it that far.

Suddenly all of the images are full of gunfire—bright flashes of light out of the second-story windows of the warehouse. The lapel cameras become so shaky it's impossible to tell what's happening. The drone camera shows SWAT agents running for cover behind the few cars in the lot. They return fire but mostly to provide cover for their retreat. As they clear out, like cockroaches running when the lights come on, a few of the agents are left behind, unmoving. They lie prone in the dirt—dead or dying.

At the back of the building, the other SWAT team is pinned down behind a dumpster.

Ryan Logan shouts into the radio for updates, but there's too much chaos for anyone to respond.

One of the lapel cameras is frozen, pointed toward the sunrise, as its wearer lies inert. A red blob slides across the image — blood running over the camera.

"Come on, Rory," Carlos says to me. "Let's get the hell in there."

We grab our rifles and shove through the door into the cool morning air. We sprint to the truck, and I spin the tires. Other agents and officers from the command center come running outside in our wake, including Ryan, who has a deer-in-the-headlights expression on his face.

I flip on the siren and the lights, and we span the five blocks in a matter of seconds.

When we arrive, there's a lull in the gunfire, and I drive right into the middle of the battleground, trying to provide cover for the agents who are pinned down. Carlos jumps out and raises his rifle to the windows where the gunfire came from.

I leave my LaRue behind and heft the battering ram out of the dirt. I run toward the door as fast as I can manage while hauling the fifty-pound hunk of metal. Normally, using this thing is a two-person job, but I'll have to make do.

Someone takes a shot at me, bullets thudding into the dirt by my feet. Carlos squeezes the trigger one time, and the shooting stops. I don't need to turn my head to know he got him. When I'm almost to the door, I swing the ram back and use my momentum to bring it crashing just above the knob. With a thunderous *boom*, the door swings inward.

Inside is complete darkness.

I hear women crying and screaming.

I draw my pistol and grab my flashlight. Then I rush forward into the building with Carlos close behind.

CHAPTER 28

I HEAR GUNFIRE from outside and from through the walls, telling me that the shoot-out between the people on the second floor and the SWAT team has resumed. Suddenly, the building's fire alarm starts to ring out. The sprinklers in the ceiling open up and rain down on the path ahead. I can't be sure if the building is on fire or if this is just a distraction caused by the criminals inside. The more chaos they create, the better off their position will be.

Ordinarily, it's a SWAT team that comes in full force— stunning and confusing and overwhelming adversaries— but in this case, it's our team that's been caught off guard.

I jog down a dark corridor, my Stetson keeping the falling water out of my eyes. The hallway is full of closed doors for what I assume would be offices if this building were used by any ordinary business. Under normal circumstances, Carlos and I would take the time to make sure each room is clear, but right now, my priority is getting to the gunmen on the second floor. I've got to make it easier for the SWAT team to get inside.

My flashlight makes me an easy target but I don't let that stop me. At the end of the hallway, I burst out into a large garage bay, with a ceiling that must be thirty feet high. Carlos is right behind me. I sweep my flashlight through the raining water and see at least three dozen cots with women shackled to the beds. Some are crying and screaming. Some are hiding under their beds with hands over their heads. And some—I'm terrified to see—don't even look awake. If the sprinkler system and all the shooting won't wake them, they're either dead or so high on drugs that they're comatose.

The room seems unoccupied except for the women, but over by two large garage doors, a handful of cars are parked, including Llewellyn Carpenter's blue panel van.

Suddenly, from the other side of the room, muzzle flashes explode out of the darkness. Bullets puncture the wall just to my left. I extinguish my light—no doubt it's what the shooter is aiming for—and drop down onto the wet floor. Carlos hits the deck, too.

The shooter stops firing, and the room is enveloped in blackness. I raise my gun, aiming in the general direction of where he stood. I wait, hoping he'll discharge a round, which will tell me right where he is.

But he doesn't.

He's waiting for me to show myself in the darkness.

Behind me, I hear the slightest sound of movement from Carlos. Then, far off to our left, the sound of something metal clangs against a corrugated panel. I know what it is immediately: Carlos threw something—a coin or maybe a round from his Colt—across the room as a distraction.

It works.

The gunman opens fire toward the opposite wall. The man's face is illuminated by the strobe lighting of the muzzle flashes. I squeeze the trigger of my SIG Sauer, and his head whips back. The shooting stops and the gun clatters to the floor. I jump to my feet and turn the flashlight on to make sure he's dead.

His body is lying in a puddle, the water turning crimson.

We can still hear gunfire outside and from somewhere within the building, but it's muffled by the alarm and the spray of the sprinkler, which creates a white noise that almost drowns everything else out. I sweep the light over the imprisoned women. They are screaming and crying and scared to death—but none of them have been shot.

"How do we get upstairs?" Carlos shouts to the women.

A handful of the prisoners point to the corridor the man I just shot came out of. Carlos and I run across the room, our boots splashing in the water. Behind us, we hear a noise, and we both spin, guns raised. An armed man bursts into the room. I'm on the verge of pulling the trigger before he can get his gun raised.

I lift my gun instead, pointing it toward the ceiling.

It's a member of the SWAT team who made it in behind us.

He raises his gun, aiming, no doubt, at my flashlight.

"Texas Rangers," I yell, spinning the beam so it illuminates my face and—more importantly—my cowboy hat.

In the darkness, no shot comes.

Relieved that we didn't just get killed by a member of our own team, I shout to the man, "Secure this room! We're going after the shooters on the second floor."

Carlos and I race past the body of the man I shot and into the next room, expecting a staircase. Instead, we find an even larger room, this one with a mezzanine running the perimeter of the second floor. We don't need my flashlight to see because the windows on the upper level have been shot out, and for some reason the sprinkler system isn't spraying in here. Several men — four on the left mezzanine and three on the right — fire automatic rifles from the windows down onto the SWAT officers outside. There had been a fourth gunman on the right, but a body lies at the other men's feet — the person Carlos shot from the parking lot, I assume.

Carlos's LaRue thunders next to me, and one of the shooters stumbles backward, tumbling over the railing and dropping to the floor with a thud.

Shooters on both sides of us cease firing outside the windows and swing their guns toward us.

CHAPTER 29

WITHOUT SO MUCH as a word, Carlos and I both stand our ground, him shooting to the left side, me shooting to the right.

Before the first gunman gets his rifle into shooting position, I put a bullet low in his rib cage at an angle that will send it through his heart. While he starts to fall, I move my gun a few inches to the left and squeeze off another shot just as the next shooter is about to pull his trigger. He groans and falls back, pointing the gun toward the ceiling as fire explodes from the barrel. The first gunman has finally landed with a metallic clang against the mezzanine walkway.

I move my gun a few more inches to the last guy. He is a fraction of a second behind his buddies in swinging his gun from the window—he probably assumed the others would take care of me—but instead of waiting until he has me in his sights to fire, he lets the gun rip while he's turning. A wave of bullets strafes the ground, coming my way.

I squeeze off another round, and the wave stops just feet from me.

The man slumps over the railing and hangs with his head upside down, his arms dangling.

I turn my attention to Carlos's side of the gunfight. Only one shooter remains, but before either he or I can take him down, a volley of gunfire blasts through the window from outside, filling him with holes. Then the back door of the warehouse bursts open and SWAT members rush in, guns drawn.

All firing ceases for a moment. There are plenty of sounds—cops running into the building, voices shouting outdoors, sirens wailing, the sprinkler system in the other bay—but compared to the noise of the gunfire, the room feels eerily quiet. Gun smoke clouds the ceiling, drifting in the beams of light spilling in through the broken windows. Glass tinkles down from the shattered windows.

Then we hear a single blast—recognizably a shotgun—coming from the room with the women, and suddenly a commotion of terrified voices overtakes the sound of the sprinklers. Carlos and I rush back to the room, and I try to take in what's happened.

One of the garage doors is rising, filling the room with bright sunlight. The SWAT officer who was the first one to make it in lies on the floor, unmoving. Another figure, covered completely in a heavy gray blanket, inches through the maze of beds like a ghost. I raise my gun but notice there are two sets of feet sticking out of the bottom of the blanket—a pair of men's boots and a woman's bare feet.

I understand what's happening in an instant.

There's a man under the blanket, holding one of the women hostage.

I move closer, keeping my gun on the shapes under the blanket. I think about shooting the man in the foot, but I assume he's got the shotgun we heard a few seconds ago. If I do no more than injure him, he could unload a round of double-aught buck into the poor woman, opening her up like a soda can that's been shaken up and thrown on the ground.

I need a kill shot.

But I don't have one.

SWAT members pour in through the two corridors, aiming their guns at this and that, trying to assess the situation and secure the scene. But in the chaos, no one really seems to grasp what's happening. There are women crying, bodies on the floor, water pouring from the ceiling.

As the garage door rises, Ryan Logan walks casually inside, as if thinking one of his men raised the door and all is under control.

"Hostage!" I shout, pointing to the shapes under the blanket, which have almost made it to the blue van.

Ryan sees what I'm pointing to and draws his gun.

"Don't shoot!" I shout.

Ryan hesitates and seems to understand the situation better now. I run up next to him, as the blanketed shape arrives at the van's side door. A glimpse of arm reaches out from under the blanket to slide the door open. I see it only for an instant, but it's long enough for me to recognize the tattoo of a snake coiled around the forearm.

"Give up, Carpenter!" I yell. "There's no way out."

He ignores me as he wrestles the girl inside the van. I still have no good shot.

"Miss," I shout, "tell us your name!"

"Marta," shouts a scared voice from under the blanket. "Marta Rivera."

My blood runs cold as I realize this is the woman who recently went missing from the Ysleta del Sur Pueblo—the one Ava has been consumed with finding.

Carpenter slams the van door shut behind them. Ryan and I position ourselves in front of the van, along with a handful of other law enforcement personnel. Carlos is leading the effort to get the chained women back and out of the way, in case the situation erupts in gunfire. Their cots screech against the concrete floor as they pull them away by their chains.

Behind the windshield of the van, the blanketed shape moves into the driver's seat. Carpenter is clearly holding Marta on his lap, using her as a shield, but I can't tell where one of them ends and the other begins.

"Shoot the tires," someone yells.

"No!" I shout. "He's got a shotgun. He'll kill her."

The truck engine starts, but Ryan and I stand our ground.

"Rory, we're the best shots in Texas," Ryan says under his breath. "Let's get this son of a bitch."

I'm good with a gun—I once shot a knife out of a man's hand, once shot a bumblebee out of the air—but I can't hit something I can't see.

Ryan doesn't seem so hesitant. His finger moves against the trigger of his Glock.

In a flash, I reach out and slap his wrist down. The gun goes off and the bullet ricochets off the bumper, sending up a puff of dust when it punches a hole in the concrete floor.

Ryan looks at me with surprise and anger.

"What the hell are you doing?" he snaps.

The van engine roars to life, and Carpenter—still hidden under the blanket—stomps on the gas. I tackle Ryan as the van comes within inches of running us down. I fall on top of him and watch as the van speeds through the gravel lot.

"Get the hell off me!" Ryan shouts, pushing me away.

Strong hands grab mine and pull me to my feet.

"Come on, Rory," Carlos says. "Let's catch him."

We sprint to my truck and jump in. As I spin the tires and give pursuit, I hear Ryan yelling, "You better get him, Yates, or it's going to be your ass."

CHAPTER 30

THE VAN IS a few hundred yards ahead of us when I make it to the street. I flip on the siren and turn on my lights, which flash from the grill of my truck and from behind the passenger seat visor.

Water is still dripping off the brim of my hat.

The van takes a hard right and speeds toward downtown. Carlos shouts into the radio, alerting the local police to who we're pursuing and which way we're headed. With Marta Rivera in the van, we don't want to shoot it up or make it crash. We need some backup to cut off the van's route of escape so we can surround it. FBI vehicles join the pursuit from the warehouse, but they have a lot of ground to make up.

We need to get into a position where Llewellyn Carpenter gives up. Or at least gives us a clear shot. I'm assuming he's shed the blanket—otherwise how could he drive?—so if we can somehow get ahead of him, I might be able to get the shot I need.

The van drives recklessly, with no regard for other cars on the streets. It zips into oncoming traffic, passes a car, whips back into its own lane. It's causing such chaos that my truck is getting caught in the congestion of its wake. Everyone is slowing down, stopping in the middle of the street, not realizing until I'm on top of them that my siren and lights are on.

"We're losing him," Carlos says.

I whip the truck to the left so I'm straddling the center line. The cars to my right squeeze over, and the cars coming at me hit their brakes. Up ahead, the van turns onto another street.

"Keep an eye on him," I yell, jerking the wheel left and right to avoid a collision.

"Turn here," Carlos yells.

A few blocks ahead, we spot him taking a hard left.

"He went into a parking garage," Carlos says.

The lights have just changed, and the roadway in front of me is filled with pedestrians crossing the street. I ease forward, honking my horn, as people realize what's happening and hurry out of my way. One man, crossing with his nose in his cell phone, doesn't notice, even when I lay on the horn, and I have to ease around behind him.

Then my foot is back on the gas, and I close the gap to the garage. Carlos tells the dispatcher that we need backup units to block all the exits to the garage. I pull in and start winding my way upward. It's a big parking garage, with multiple options of where to go on each level, several ways up and down.

I don't want Carpenter to slip down behind us, so I take my time, trying to explore every corner of each level before moving up. Other cars crowd the lanes, and I honk my horn so I can get around them.

"There," Carlos says, pointing across the garage to the recognizable blue van just barely visible on the next level up.

I speed to where the van sits in a parking spot. I slam on the brakes and put the truck in park to block Carpenter's escape. Carlos and I jump out and run around the vehicle. My gun is leveled on the driver's side. Carlos, who's ditched the LaRue for his Colt, circles to the passenger door. When I get to the window, I aim my gun inside.

The front seats are empty. Carlos runs back over to my side, where the sliding door is located. With my gun ready, I try the handle and pull the door open, revealing an interior that's empty except for a gray blanket lying in a heap.

There's no sign of Llewellyn Carpenter.

No sign of Marta Rivera.

Carlos runs to the radio. "The van is empty," he reports. "He must have switched vehicles."

I run to the concrete barrier at the edge of the garage and look down at the street. A half dozen cars pour out of the garage—vans, trucks, sedans, sports cars—and there's no telling how many in the street might also have come from the garage.

I hear sirens in the distances, but they're not close enough to block off the area in time.

"Shit," I say, holstering my gun and catching my breath for the first time since all this started. The outside of my clothes is soaked with water, the inside is soaked with sweat, and my mouth is bone dry.

To the east, the sun hovers over the horizon, blasting the landscape in golden light. It's only about thirty minutes after sunrise, yet I feel like I've had one of the longest days of my life. I'm emotionally and physically spent.

Carlos walks up to me and puts a comforting hand on my shoulder.

"We'll get him," he says. "And at least we know Marta Rivera is alive."

But for how much longer? I wonder.

CHAPTER 31

THE SCENE AT the warehouse is abuzz with activity when we get back.

Two fire trucks arrived, although there isn't actually a fire. Crime scene investigators are going through the building with a fine-tooth comb. It looks like a few of the kidnappers were taken alive—agents are leading them in handcuffs to the back of a paddy wagon.

Several ambulances are there, with paramedics treating some of the rescued women while FBI agents and El Paso police take names and information. From what I can tell, the women come from a variety of racial and ethnic backgrounds—white, Black, Latina, Asian—but there's no doubt that a disproportionate number are Native American. The one similarity they share is that they're all young.

Agents have set up crime scene tape around a wide perimeter

to keep the news vans at a distance, but when we drive up, an agent opens a gap for us to pull in.

"You did good today, Rangers," he says through the open window of my truck.

"Thank you."

"Agent Logan wants to see you," he adds.

When we get out of the truck, a handful of agents in SWAT gear approach us and thank us for charging onto the scene the way we did.

"There's no telling how many more of us would have been cut to pieces without you guys coming in to help," one says.

We say we appreciate the sentiment, but I've got a feeling that Ryan Logan isn't going to be quite so grateful.

Ryan's office on wheels has been moved to the parking lot of the warehouse. I knock on the door and peek my head inside. He's on the phone but waves me in. Carlos and I sit and wait, still wearing our bulletproof vests. Still sopping wet.

When he hangs up, Ryan says, "Well, at least the other two raids went off without a hitch. Looks like we've rescued forty-nine women in total. Eight from Tucson. Nine from Colorado Springs. And the other thirty-two from right here."

"That's good news," I say.

He narrows his eyes at me.

"It could have been an even fifty if you hadn't smacked my arm when I was trying to shoot."

"It was too dangerous," I say.

"I knew what I was doing," Ryan says, clearly angry. "Just because you couldn't make the shot doesn't mean I couldn't."

"No one could have made that shot," I say. "Not with any degree of certainty."

He slumps in his chair. "I guess we'll never know."

I can't tell if he's mad because I stopped him from taking the shot or because he didn't get a chance to prove himself in today's gunfight.

"I've got five agents that are seriously injured," Ryan says. "What the hell happened in there, Rory?"

I tell him my perspective. When Carlos and I ran by those office doors upon entering the building, in such a hurry to take out the riflemen so our SWAT team could flood the building, Llewellyn Carpenter must have been hiding in one of the rooms and snuck up on the man he shot in the garage.

"How is he?" I ask.

"Critical."

I lower my head.

Ryan tells us that the fire alarm was pulled in one of those rooms. Carpenter must have triggered the alarm to create chaos, then hid as we ran past. There were other kidnappers there, so it's possible someone else could have pulled the alarm, but my gut tells me Ryan is right.

"You fucked up, Rory," Ryan says. "You should have cleared those rooms. You shouldn't have stopped me from taking the shot. One agent is probably going to die because of you. One of the women is still in captivity. And our prime suspect is in the wind."

I could argue with him, but I don't have it in me. The last time I was in a big firefight like this, Kyle Hendricks was killed. Now a man I never met might die.

I feel as low as I've ever felt as a Texas Ranger.

Carlos is the one to speak up.

"Ryan," he says, "with all due respect, you don't know what the hell you're talking about."

Ryan furrows his brow and glares at Carlos.

"I'm not saying it's your fault that this raid went to shit," Carlos says. "Sometimes these things happen no matter how well you plan. But the bottom line is this thing went to hell in a handbasket from the start. If not for Rory's quick thinking and quick action, you might have more dead law enforcement personnel on your hands."

Ryan opens his mouth to argue, but Carlos won't let him interrupt.

"We passed those front offices, but if we'd taken the time to clear them, that would have cost us minutes. There's no telling how many more of your SWAT agents might have been gunned down while that happened. You have five injured agents, but you ought to be counting your blessings that you don't have twice that many dead.

"It seems to me," he adds, "that you're just pissed because the only reason your operation wasn't a complete disaster is because the Texas Rangers saved your ass." He hooks his thumb to gesture to the world outside the operations vans. "Your men out there are shaking our hands and thanking us. And then we come in here and you decide to throw us under the bus."

Carlos shakes his head in disapproval. Ryan's cheeks are flushed with anger.

"And as for pushing your gun down before you could

shoot," Carlos concludes, "it seems to me you ought to be thanking Rory rather than scolding him. Marta Rivera is still alive, wherever she is. If you'd taken the shot, you were just as likely to put a round through her skull as you were through Llewellyn Carpenter's."

Ryan is clearly pissed, but I'm uplifted by Carlos's words. He's right—the raid was a shit show, but it would have been worse if we hadn't been there. Not better.

"Listen here," Ryan says, his teeth practically clenched while he speaks. "You two are dismissed for the day. Go find Ava Cruz and follow your little eagle feather leads wherever they take you. Don't come to me until you've got something." Gesturing toward the wall and—by suggestion—all the activity at the crime scene on the other side, he adds, "The FBI will handle this part of the investigation. I'll call you if I need you. But don't expect that call anytime soon."

With that, he looks away from us and picks up a report from his desk, acting as if we're already gone.

CHAPTER 32

THAT NIGHT, CARLOS and I sit on our respective beds in our hotel room, watching a rerun of an NBA Championship game between the Miami Heat and the San Antonio Spurs. We bought a twelve-pack of Cerveza Sol, a pint of tequila, and some limes, and brought them back to the room to drink with our dinner. Another pizza.

"Is pizza the only food you eat?" I ask.

"I go to Burger King sometimes," he says. "Did you know they have a special burger just for Rangers?"

I squint at him, showing my confusion.

He turns to me with a grin. "It's called the Whopper Texas Ranger."

I smirk and shake my head. "I thought you were better than a *Walker, Texas Ranger* pun."

We're about halfway into the bottle and twelve-pack, neither of us talking much, aside from Carlos's occasional jokes, which get worse the more he drinks. The day's events have left us a bit shell shocked. Carlos's jokes are probably just a way for him to cope, a defense mechanism for emotional pain.

"You okay?" I ask, remembering our discussion on the drive over to the raid about the emotional toll of killing people, regardless of the fact that these were all bad, bad men.

"I'll be okay," he says earnestly. It's a relief that he doesn't dismiss my question with a joke, but I note he doesn't actually say he *is* okay, just that he *will be*. "You?" he asks.

"Same," I say, taking another swig.

Despite being dismissed by Ryan, we didn't leave the scene right away. We stayed to help out whatever way we could: comforting victims, answering questions from crime scene investigators, advising agents and officers. When we finally felt comfortable leaving, we headed to the hospital to see the agent who'd been shot by Llewellyn Carpenter, but we were told he was in surgery. Back at the hotel around three o'clock, we still had a busy day of phone calls and paperwork. We had to update Captain Kane about what happened and wait for a decision about whether we should be removed from duty pending an investigation—which is customary after a shooting—or keep working. In the end, he opted to let the FBI make the decision since we're currently working on their team.

We also called Ava Cruz and updated her about Marta Rivera. She seemed heartened by the news that the Tigua woman is still alive, but also frustrated that she wasn't rescued. She kept busy while we were involved with the raid.

She arranged for Isabella Luna to come in to the station tomorrow morning for us to interview her. She said Isabella was reluctant, not sure why the tribal police wanted to look into what happened to her four years ago. Ava told her that she might be able to shed some light on other ongoing investigations, and although Isabella said she still can't remember anything, she did agree to come in.

With our work finally finished for the day, Carlos ordered the pizza while I ran out and bought the beer and tequila. Megan saw the raid on the news and called to check on me. She invited me to the bar, and I politely declined. She said she'd try to call later if there was a lull in the crowd, but the bar is offering two-for-one shots tonight and she expected to be busy. I'm glad I didn't go—I'm just not in the mood to socialize in a public place right now. And, besides, if I visited her, I'd have to limit my beers to one or two.

After the day I had, I wanted a few more.

Carlos and I had started the evening by watching the local news. Ryan Logan was interviewed giving an update about the raid, which has been all over the media all day. Ryan spun the event like a total success, which I guess it *nearly* was. Despite Carpenter's escape with a hostage and the injuries, forty-nine abducted women were found and are being reunited with their families.

That's why we get into law enforcement work—to help people.

In lauding the FBI and the El Paso Police Department, Ryan made no mention of the involvement of the Texas Rangers. Carlos had seen enough and flipped through the channels, ultimately selecting the basketball game.

"Man, that LeBron James is something else, isn't he?" Carlos says, taking a drink and turning up the volume on the TV. "He can play defense just as well on Tim Duncan as Tony Parker. Maybe he could hack it in rezball."

I'm not watching. I'm lost in thought, reliving the intensity of today's gunfight. Also, I can't get the images out of my head of the traumatized women, some of them barely clothed, looking around in confusion, many of them stoned on heroin or meth.

I wonder what kind of person goes to a brothel and pays money to rape a drugged woman there against her will. What kind of world do we live in where such a thing happens?

On the bedside table, my phone buzzes. I expect it to be Megan, taking a quick break between serving shots. But when I check to see who's calling, it's Willow. I hesitate, feeling guilty if I take it, but then I remind myself that Willow and I are just friends. I reach for the phone.

I could use a friend right now.

CHAPTER 33

I ANSWER THE phone and step outside, leaving Carlos to watch the old basketball game without me.

"I saw the news out of El Paso and just wanted to make sure you weren't anywhere near there," Willow says.

I chuckle uncomfortably as I walk down the hall toward the exit. "Actually, I was there," I say. "Right in the thick of it."

"Oh, Rory. Are you okay?"

"It's been a hard day," I say, stepping outside into the cool night air.

Light glows over the city, and I can see the Franklin Mountains illuminated in the distance. There's a wooden bench in front of the hotel in a small garden with various kinds of cacti on display. I sit down and stretch my feet out in a small patch of grass.

Willow expresses concern for me, and I talk about what happened without going into too many details.

No need to tell her I shot anyone.

No need to tell her how close I came to getting killed.

Back when we were dating, we used to talk this way after every altercation I got in wearing a badge. This afternoon, when I finally had a free minute, I texted my parents to let them know I was okay. I didn't think to tell Willow. It shouldn't have surprised me that she'd call to check on me. I'm touched by the sentiment.

I shift our conversation away from the raid—it's not helping me to talk about it—and ask her how the new album is coming.

"Not bad," she says. "We've got room for a few more tracks. Oh, thanks for sending those lyrics, by the way. They were wonderful."

I'd forgotten all about texting her the lyrics. The fight with Randy had happened right after, and then the raid.

We share a laugh together about the "Texas Forever" song.

"Any chance you'll use it on the album?" I ask.

"I don't know," she says. "My producer isn't convinced. He says it's too regional and won't appeal to fans outside of Texas."

"Hmmm," I say. "Imagine if Lynyrd Skynyrd's producer said the same thing about 'Sweet Home Alabama.'"

"No kidding," Willow says. "I'll tell him that tomorrow. The band and I are going to play around with the song then. I'll try out the new lyrics."

"If there's anything I sang that you want to use, you're more than welcome to."

"You looking to get some songwriting royalties to supplement your income?" she says in a playful tone.

"Never crossed my mind," I say. "No need to credit me with anything. It's your song. I was just trying to help."

"I appreciate it," she says. "We'll see what happens."

As I talk, I hear a beeping. I pull the phone away from my ear and see I have an incoming call from Megan. Not wanting to interrupt Willow as she talks about the album, I let it go to voicemail.

Willow and I talk for another few minutes, and then I let her go. It's almost midnight in El Paso and even later in Nashville. We used to end our conversations by telling each other "I love you," and it feels weird not to say it.

After I hang up, I call Megan back, but the call goes straight to voicemail. I don't bother to leave a message. Apparently her break is over.

When I go back in the room, Carlos has dozed off on his bed. I turn off the TV and shut off the lights. Lying in the darkness, I try to think about Megan or Willow—anything but what happened today. But it doesn't work. My mind keeps veering to the men I shot, the agent in the hospital tonight fighting for his life, and—most of all—Marta Rivera and what might be happening to her right now because I couldn't stop Llewellyn Carpenter.

It's a long time before I'm able to drift off to sleep.

CHAPTER 34

THE NEXT MORNING, I'm up bright and early, drinking a tall glass of water and taking an Aleve for my headache. Carlos got up even earlier and went for a quick run, back in plenty of time for us to get ready and head over to Ysleta del Sur.

Ava is in the office when we get there, and we come bearing drinks: two cups of coffee for Carlos and me, and a lemonade for Ava.

"Just took a guess you might like this over coffee," I say.

She takes a sip.

"Good guess," she says with a smile.

The three of us sit down to discuss how to approach Isabella Luna's interview. We don't want to scare her, don't want her to feel like we're prying open old wounds. But if there's anything she can remember, anything at all, it might help break this case open for us.

We decide to stand in the lobby so we don't keep her waiting once she arrives.

"I think this is her vehicle," Ava says, as an old Ford Bronco pulls into the lot.

Out steps a young woman with beautiful dark hair, brushed straight down and parted in the middle. She wears a short-sleeved blouse and jeans, along with sandals. As she walks through the parking lot, I notice the slightest hint of a limp—as if all the injuries listed in the police report never fully healed.

Ava greets her with a hug. She introduces Carlos and me, and the young woman looks up at both of us with anxiety she can't quite hide.

"Texas Rangers?" she says, trying to force a smile. "This must be serious."

"We think you might be able to help us with some cases we're working on," I explain.

"So this doesn't have to do with what happened to me?" she asks.

"It does," I say, and then promise to explain more inside.

We lead her to a small conference room, where we sit around a table. We don't sit across from her, like it's a three-against-one interrogation, but spread out so it's more like four people just having a conversation.

Carlos starts by noting that her old police file suggests she couldn't remember anything from the time of her disappearance until she was found.

"It's been four years," he says. "Has anything come back to you?"

Isabella's nervousness seems to amplify. Her breathing has become more shallow.

"No," she says. "I really don't think about it very often. I try not to, honestly. I remember the ambulance. The hospital. But the week or ten days or whatever it was that I was gone are just blank. Like someone reached into my brain with a big eraser and scrubbed them out."

"So you can't remember how your leg was broken?" Ava asks.

She shakes her head.

"You were bitten by a snake, according to the file," I say. "Do you remember that?"

"No," she says. "Nothing."

Carlos asks if anyone had been following her in the days leading up to her disappearance. If anything unusual had happened. Anyone who might have been upset with her.

"I only know what you already know," she says, gesturing to the file folder sitting on the table next to Carlos. "The last time anyone could remember seeing me was at the powwow. This was at Franklin Mountains State Park. The Tigua hosted the powwow, planning to make it an annual thing if it went well. But I think because of what happened to me they just didn't bother to put it on the next year."

Ava explains that while she grew up on the Pueblo, she had been working for the highway patrol elsewhere in Texas at the time. She asks Isabella to tell us about the powwow.

"It was like any other," she says, looking at Carlos and Ava. "You've been to them. There's dancing and drumming. Lots of crafts and leatherwork and jewelry. Food stands with Indian tacos and fry bread." She shrugs her shoulders. "It was just a powwow."

I try to picture this young woman at the event. There would have been plenty of people there who knew her—it was practically in her backyard—and it no doubt would have been a happy occasion.

"You know," she says, "my life is divided in two. Whenever I remember something in my life, I immediately categorize the memory as happening before it happened, or after—whatever *it* is, I'm not even sure. But I don't actually remember anything between the powwow and being picked up on the highway. And I've made my peace with not remembering. To be honest, I don't really want to remember."

I can't fault her for not wanting to remember. But maybe there's something before her disappearance that could help us.

"Do you remember seeing any kind of eagle feathers at the powwow?"

She laughs, a strange sound considering how upset she is.

"There are feathers everywhere," she says, looking to Carlos and Ava for confirmation. They nod knowingly. "Everyone's decked out in their regalia. Lots of feathers on their clothes, their spears, their drums."

She looks back and forth between us.

"What's this all about?"

We glance at each other and—without speaking verbally—agree to give her some information.

"You disappeared on the solstice," Carlos says. "In the years since, four other Native women have gone missing on the solstice from different areas of the Southwest. We believe those disappearances are related, and we think you might have been the first."

Isabella is visibly shaken by the idea that there might be other women.

"You mean other women might have gone through what I did?" she asks.

"None of the others have ever been found," Ava says.

This news seems to shock Isabella, who looks queasy.

"The most recent one has only been gone a few days," I say. "Not as long as you were missing. If whatever happened to you is also happening to her, then she might still be alive. We might still be able to save her. Are you sure there's nothing you can tell us?"

CHAPTER 35

ISABELLA LOOKS LIKE she's on the verge of a panic attack. Her limbs are trembling, her breathing is rapid and erratic. Her eyes have become moist with tears that threaten to overflow and spill down her cheeks. She closes her eyes and puts her head in her hands—as if blocking everything out and trying to focus on her memories.

Carlos, Ava, and I exchange looks. I can tell from Ava's expression that she doesn't want to push Isabella any further. She wants to end the interview, but Carlos raises a hand with his index finger extended. The meaning is clear—let's wait a moment longer and see what happens.

As uncomfortable as this might be for Isabella to face, the life of at least one woman—and maybe more—depends on her memory. Any clue could give us the lead we need in order to break open the case.

Isabella balls her fists up in her hair and squeezes her eyes tightly shut, as if focusing hard might open memories that have been inaccessible. She's clearly gone from feeling scared to feeling angry.

Finally, she opens her eyes and slaps her hands down on the table. "I can't," she says, exasperated. "I just can't. There's nothing in my memory. It's all blank."

Ava, Carlos, and I all indicate that it's okay, that she doesn't need to strain herself anymore.

"We're sorry we had to put you through this," I say.

Ava asks that if Isabella does remember anything—no matter how irrelevant it might seem—would she please let us know?

"Of course," she says, offering us a sad smile. "I wish I could help. I really do."

Ava walks her to the car while Carlos and I wait in the lobby. After a minute, Isabella is smiling again, and I wonder if we made a mistake with all three of us trying to interview her. Maybe Ava had been right and she should have talked to her, woman to woman, Tigua to Tigua.

When Ava returns to the station, we spend a few minutes talking about the interview and how disappointed we are that it didn't give us any new leads. But we don't dwell on our setback. We push ahead.

Ava has developed a plan for the three of us to take care of the out-of-state interviews and investigations we'll need to conduct. She figures we can split into two groups, one to head east to Houston and the Kickapoo reservation to interview as many people as possible associated with the missing woman from that area, Tina White Wolf. The other group will head to southern Colorado to learn about the disappearance of a woman named Chipeta Tavaci, and then swing west over to Flagstaff, where we can talk to family members of the recently vanished Fiona Martinez. Because the Colorado-Arizona team will be conducting interviews about two women, and whoever goes east to the Upper Gulf Coast area will only be researching one, Ava recommends that she and I head north while Carlos stays in Texas.

"If we split up into two groups," she says, "it will only take three or four days, and we'll have a much better understanding about the circumstances surrounding all of these missing women."

"Why don't we split into three groups?" I ask. "Then it will go even faster."

But Carlos agrees with Ava. As Texas Rangers, he and I can travel out of state without much trouble. We just have to notify the police agencies wherever we travel, and because of the badge we wear, we won't get much pushback. But when it comes to county or city police, Ava might not get the same kind of cooperation. On the flip side, Ava might be able to get further than I can when it comes to working with tribal police in other states.

As it turns out, Ava and I need each other.

With a Texas Ranger and a tribal policewoman, we should be able to get reasonable cooperation regardless of whether we're dealing with state, county, or tribal police. Meanwhile, Carlos will go to Houston and the Kickapoo reservation. His mom was a full-blooded Kickapoo—his father Comanche and Mexican—and he knows that part of Texas well.

"When should we leave?" I ask.

"How about bright and early tomorrow?" Ava asks.

"Why wait?" Carlos says. He checks his watch. "We could be on the road by noon."

CHAPTER 36

CARLOS TAKES MY truck, and Ava and I drive one of her tribal police SUVs. We take I-10 to I-25 and head north through New Mexico, talking very little. There isn't any uncomfortableness between us—at least as far as I can tell—but Ava isn't a particularly talkative person. We discuss the cases some, both the eagle feather case and Marta Rivera's situation, but otherwise we ride in silence.

I call Ryan Logan to update him on our whereabouts. I also inquire to make sure that Fiona Martinez wasn't among the women at the warehouse or the brothels. I already know the answer, since in my heart I'm confident the eagle feather victims are part of a different case, but I need to make sure. He listens professionally, but when I ask him if there's any news about Marta Rivera, he says, "Why don't you and your pals keep looking into those eagle feathers and let us worry about the trafficking victims." He says this with an air of superiority that raises my blood pressure, as if he and his men are doing the important work and the three of us are off on some wild goose chase.

I try to convince myself that a whole battalion of law enforcement officials are looking for Marta and that I should feel confident that they'll find her. I feel myself torn between two cases. I *know* this case is important, but I also wish I could be searching for Marta.

Outside the window, the New Mexico countryside rolls by: brown hills dappled with sagebrush, rocky buttes rising from the earth, vast swaths of land without a human structure in sight besides telephone poles and electrical towers. The sky is blue from horizon to horizon without an ounce of humidity to dull the brilliant hue.

We stop for the night in Santa Fe, getting separate rooms at a hotel near the plaza. After a short break, we meet up and find a restaurant with a balcony overlooking the town square. The adobe buildings are full of art galleries and restaurants, and the area is bustling with tourists. A shaded walkway is full of Native American artisans sitting on rugs, selling jewelry and crafts.

New Mexico has its own style of food—different from traditional Mexican or the Tex-Mex I'm used to—and I enjoy my bowl of green chile stew, a side of enchiladas, and especially the sopapillas and honey served after the meal.

Bored with our lack of conversation—I might be the strong silent type by some standards, but Ava takes it to another level—I ask my companion how she met Marcos. She explains that she's known him since she was in high school, but they only started dating when she returned to the Pueblo to start working for the tribal police.

"How long has he been driving a truck?" I ask.

"Five years or so," she says. "He's always been a bit of a loner, so it suits him."

Trying not to come across like I'm prying into her personal business, I gently ask how she likes him being on the road so much.

"It works for us," she says. "I work long hours. He works long hours. When we do manage to get free time together, we make the most of it. We're thankful for what we get."

"That's a healthy way of looking at it," I say. "My relationships always seem to fail because we can only focus on the time we don't spend together instead of the time we do."

"What about that bartender?" she asks. "How's that going?"

I shrug. "It's all a bit up in the air."

"What's with her professor?" she asks, and can't hide her smile.

We both laugh out loud, thinking of Neil Stephenson and his pretentious demeanor.

"I think he's got the hots for Megan," I say.

Ava makes a face telling me that she disagrees.

"What?" I ask.

"I think she might have the wrong skin color," Ava says.

Thinking of his love of Native American literature and the way he followed Ava around like a puppy the other night, I realize she might be onto something.

"Either way," Ava says, "I'm pretty sure you don't have anything to worry about. That girl only has eyes for you."

"Thanks," I say. "That reminds me, I probably should call her and tell her I can't stop by the bar tonight."

I excuse myself and find a secluded spot on the balcony, looking down on the plaza. The sun is sinking, and a band is setting up on a gazebo in the middle of the lawn.

"Hey," Megan says when she answers. "Sorry we missed each other last night."

I remember that I didn't take her call because I was talking to Willow.

Megan tells me she's got the night off and was going to spend it working on her dissertation, but if I want to hang out, she'd set her computer and books aside.

"Bad news," I say. "I'm in Santa Fe."

"Over by Galveston?"

"No, no. Up by Albuquerque."

"Oh, lucky you. I love Santa Fe."

"I wish you were here with me," I say, as the band starts to play an interesting folk-rock mix, with a woman with a beautiful vocal range singing in Spanish.

I picture Megan and me down on the lawn, dancing to the music. Then I think about what Ava said about focusing on the time you get to spend with the person you care about, not the time you spend away.

"I'll be back in El Paso in a few days," I say. "How about we go out then?"

"Rory Yates," she says in a playfully coquettish tone, "are you asking me out on a date?"

"Yes, I am."

"I'm glad you can't see my face right now, because I'm blushing."

This makes me smile.

As we chat, my phone beeps. I have an incoming call from Willow.

"Do you need to get that?" Megan says. "Is it anything important?"

"No," I say.

This time I ignore the call from Willow.

CHAPTER 37

THE NEXT DAY, we head north. On the drive, we spot pronghorns grazing in the high plains. The land is desolate and beautiful, with occasional signs telling us we're passing through one reservation or another. When scanning through the radio stations, we hear a DJ speaking to the audience in Navajo.

When we cross over the border to Colorado, the landscape becomes greener, tall mountains spring up around us, and the hills fill with pine and spruce trees. We pull into Durango around noon, crossing a bridge over the rushing waters of the Animas River and making our way toward the center of town. We wait at a railroad crossing while an old narrow gauge locomotive whistles and chugs smoke into the air before pulling out of town to carry tourists into the mountains. Down Main Avenue, the adobe architecture of Santa Fe has been replaced by big brick buildings that preserve the look of what the mountain town might have been like a hundred years ago.

We stop by the police station first, where the officer I talked to on the phone has already photocopied the whole case file for us. We spend some time talking with him, learning very little, and I take only a moment to flip through the folder, glancing at the photos. I'll have time to scrutinize the file later, but for now I want to interview the woman's father, who owns a jewelry store down the street.

When we enter the store, a fiftyish white woman is working behind the counter. Ava asks to see Frank Tavaci, the owner, and as she heads into the back room to find him, I take a moment to look around.

The store specializes in Ute and Navajo jewelry, with display cases full of silver bracelets, necklaces, and rings adorned with turquoise and other colorful stones. Other items decorate the walls: an alabaster pipe, a beaded horse bag, and ornamental dreamcatchers with stars and moons as their centerpieces—but no feathers, eagle or otherwise.

Frank Tavaci walks into the showroom and introduces himself. He has short black hair and is a walking advertisement for the store, stylishly wearing several items of jewelry. We explain what we want to talk to him about, and he says that he'd rather speak at his house, which is only a few blocks away.

"You could see my daughter's bedroom," he says. His voice shakes a little with the words, and I can tell that even though it's been two years, the wounds caused by his daughter's disappearance are fresh.

We say we'd like that, and the three of us set out on foot.

Only a couple of blocks off Main Street is a strip of historic-looking houses, and Frank leads us to one. The interior is decorated with the same artist's sensibilities as the jewelry store. A bull skull with everything except the horns covered in colorful stones hangs on one wall. A display of vibrant beaded lanyards hangs from another. Beautiful pottery adorns the mantel of a large stone fireplace.

I notice that one of the items is a beautifully decorated urn. When Frank notices where my gaze is, he says, "My wife's remains. Breast cancer." He nods toward an empty space next to it. "I pray that my daughter is still alive, but if she isn't..." His voice cracks before he finishes. "I wish they could find her so that I might put her next to her mother."

We sit on a leather couch, and Frank sits opposite us on a matching love seat.

"What can I tell you about my little Chipeta?" he asks, his voice quavering.

He pulls himself together as he describes a young, energetic girl. She'd been a regular at powwows and festivals through her teenage years—competing in various art competitions—but she'd recently outgrown those events and had become focused on her studies. She'd been living at home, taking classes at nearby Fort Lewis College while working a few hours at the store. She was nineteen at the time of her disappearance.

He opens a drawer in the end table next to the couch and pulls out a framed picture.

"I used to keep this out," he says, handing the frame to me, "but it hurt too much to see her all the time."

The image shows a pretty girl standing in a mountain meadow, with a simple white sundress exposing her shoulders. She wears a silver necklace. Her features resemble her father's, and her hair, probably as naturally black as his, is augmented with russet and gold highlights.

"She is beautiful," Ava tells him, and I'm glad she's careful to use the present tense—she *is* beautiful—rather than the past.

We ask for him to tell us about the circumstances of her disappearance, which sound eerily similar to those of Fiona Martinez's.

Nothing missing.

No signs of struggle.

No packed bags.

Even her phone and her wallet were found in the house.

"She was living here at the time," Frank explains. "The cops came and took a bunch of pictures, but nothing ever came of it."

We go through various questions about whether she'd noticed anyone following her, whether a person watching her at a powwow might have left an impression, any customers at the jewelry store who showed special interest in her.

The answers are always no.

Frank shows us Chipeta's bedroom, which he says he hasn't touched since her disappearance. There are posters of bands, shelves full of books, a closet of dresses and shoes. There are plenty of examples of artwork—paintings, pottery, beaded blankets—that are good but don't seem quite as professionally polished as what we saw in the living room. Frank confirms my suspicion that these were created by Chipeta.

I look around, then stop to pay particular attention to a display of photographs of the girl with friends. Some show Chipeta dressed in Native regalia, clearly taken at powwows or festivals. Others show her hiking or skiing or dressed for a high school dance, some of these with Native friends but others with white and Latina girls.

"In one of the police photographs," Ava says to Frank, "there was a picture of an eagle feather. Does this ring a bell?"

Frank has a puzzled look on his face, then he seems to remember.

"When I say I haven't touched anything, that's not entirely true," he says, opening the closet door and pulling out a box. "I did clean up. My daughter didn't always keep her room tidy."

I recall the crime scene photos and remember that the room did look a bit messier than it does now. Frank opens the box and rummages around inside. He stands up holding an eagle feather by the quill.

"Is this what you're looking for?" he asks.

CHAPTER 38

LATER THAT AFTERNOON, Ava and I get on a Zoom call with Carlos to discuss what we've found out so far. We're sitting on a balcony where we rented rooms at Purgatory Resort, which is a ski resort in the winter and is open in the summer for activities like mountain biking and ropes courses for kids. My laptop is open on a chair, facing Ava and me. Behind the computer, the view is spectacular, with mountains all around, the tallest in the distance still capped with snow.

Through a pixelated image on my laptop, Carlos explains that the woman he's researching, Tina White Wolf, was by all accounts a troublemaker. Both her mother and father, who are divorced, agreed on this. She had been suspended from school more than once growing up, had been arrested a few times for shoplifting and underage drinking, and had failed out of community college shortly before her disappearance.

"Everyone says she was charismatic and fun to be around. A natural leader. But," Carlos adds, "she seemed to be drawn to trouble, like a moth to flame."

The parents said that sometimes she would take off for a few days without telling anyone where she was going, which is why they initially weren't concerned by her disappearance. The father, Carlos explains, had always feared he would lose his daughter to serious drugs or serious crimes, and when she disappeared, he worried that his fears had finally come true. But as the days passed and there was still no word from her, the mother felt certain something else was wrong.

"Her mom says Tina had never gone a week without at least checking in," Carlos explains. "As much trouble as she was, she never wanted her mom to worry—at least not for long."

Ava points out that it's interesting how different the girls were. They came from different tribes and different areas of the Southwest. Some grew up on reservations, some didn't. They also came from different socioeconomic backgrounds: some well off; some quite poor.

"The only thing these girls had in common," Ava says, "was they were young, pretty, and Indian."

"I don't know," Carlos says. "There's something else about them, too. They all excelled at something. You said Chipeta was an artist. Well, Tina was apparently an excellent drummer. Despite her troubles growing up, she always competed at festivals. Didn't one of the girls have a bunch of ribbons from dancing competitions?"

After some discussion, we determine that each of the four

victims had a special interest when it came to exploring her Native American heritage. But Ava points out that we could find that in any young woman. Her interests might be soccer or piano or playing video games, instead of dancing or drumming, but still any missing woman would have passions that she was good at.

"You're probably right," Carlos concedes, "but I feel like there's something here we're just not quite getting."

Carlos also obtained the golden eagle feather found at the scene, which the Houston police had in an evidence locker. He holds it up encased in a plastic bag.

"Looks just like the others," he says.

"Ours, too," I say, holding up the one Frank Tavaci gave us, also in an evidence bag.

When he gave it to us, the girl's father explained that he couldn't remember seeing it in the house prior to her disappearance, but hadn't thought much of it when he found it while cleaning her room. Chipeta was artistic—she was good at beadwork, pottery, any type of arts and crafts. He assumed she'd picked it up somewhere with plans to make something with it.

"Any word about the DNA tests on the other feathers?" Carlos asks me.

"No. I asked the lab to give them priority, but I haven't heard anything. I'll check right now."

Carlos and Ava keep talking, and I step inside my hotel room and dial the crime lab. I give the tech who answers the phone the file number and wait.

"It's supposed to be fast-tracked," I explain.

That's one of the benefits of being a Texas Ranger. When you send something to the crime lab, you can ask for it to be prioritized. Otherwise, getting results could take months. It's a privilege I don't like to use unless it's important.

"This is part of the whole FBI Native American task force, isn't it?" the technician asks. After a few more moments, in which I can hear keys typing on a computer, the tech says, "Looks here like Agent Logan took it off the priority list."

"What?"

I guess the FBI's priority supersedes the Texas Rangers'.

Now I know how local cops feel when one of our requests bumps theirs.

The tech explains that the task force has recently bombarded the lab with various items—guns for ballistics matching, evidence bags filled with hair or clothes for DNA testing, dozens of blood samples for examination—and Ryan apparently wanted those at the top of the queue.

"He must have thought these feathers weren't as important."

I can't help but think Ryan's deliberately trying to delay our investigation. Is he punishing me because of what happened at the raid? Is he bitter because of our tie at the shooting competition? Or just holding a grudge because I stood up to him?

Either way, I'm fuming when I hang up the phone.

"Listen to what Ryan Logan did," I say to Carlos and Ava.

After I explain, I can tell Ava is livid, but she doesn't express her opinion verbally. I'm not so stoic about it.

Scrolling through my contacts to find Ryan's number, I say, "I'm going to give that son of a bitch a piece of my mind."

Unfortunately, I get Ryan's voicemail.

"It's Rory," I say. "Call me."

That's all I say, but there's no mistaking my tone—Ryan will know I'm pissed and ready for a fight.

CHAPTER 39

AFTER DOING SOME interviews the next morning, we strike out for Flagstaff, passing by a herd of elk on our way out of Durango. The scenery on the drive is beautiful, the forested hills of Colorado becoming red desert plains adorned with amazing rocky buttes, then transforming again into sparse prairies foregrounding distant mountains. As we get closer to Flagstaff, the famous San Francisco Peaks — a volcanic range of ten- and twelve-thousand-foot mountains blanketed with thick pine forests — rise out of the prairie.

Over the course of the five-hour drive, I await a call from Ryan, but never get it. I was mad yesterday, but I've calmed down a bit since then. Carlos had cautioned me that ripping Ryan a new one isn't going to make things any better.

"You know part of this job is diplomacy," he'd said before ending our Zoom call. "Getting tough with Ryan isn't getting us very far. We need to figure out a new approach."

Besides, Carlos said, the results of the tests can wait. And Ryan might even be justified in bumping our feathers for some of the other materials. The human trafficking case is important—the people behind it are still out there, and several more women are likely being held against their will.

"It's easy for us to think our case is the most important, but that's the thing about law enforcement—there are too many cases competing for our attention at any given moment."

It took a restless night for me to think about it, but now I'm inclined to agree with Carlos. I've got to figure out a new way to deal with Ryan.

We head into the city of Flagstaff, which is a lot like Durango only bigger and more crowded, and drive to a gift shop where Fiona Martinez's mother works. The store is full of everything from sweatshirts and Southwest tourist trinkets to Native American arts and crafts: rugs, pottery, jewelry, and kachinas—little carved statues of spirit deities. Dreamcatchers hang from the ceiling, but none with eagle feathers, as far as I can tell.

We don't immediately see an employee, but after a moment, a fortysomething woman walks in wearing shorts and a T-shirt with a picture of the iconic Route 66 road sign on it. I introduce Ava and myself, and Ruth Martinez takes us into a back room where we can talk in private. The room is packed with cardboard boxes and assorted items: stacks of folded T-shirts, piles of rugs, an open box of coffee mugs, a spinner rack of postcards, a basket of chunks of petrified wood and volcanic rock, and a clear plastic bag full of jackalope stuffed animals.

Ruth clears some folding chairs so that we can sit.

"How can I help you?" she asks.

I can see Ruth's resemblance to her daughter, based on the photographs I've seen of Fiona. She's very pretty, just like Fiona, but she wears her grief on her face, with puffy hammocks of skin hanging under her eyes, the whites themselves red with swollen blood vessels. Her hair is streaked with gray.

We ask her the usual questions: Does she know of anyone who would want to harm Fiona? Does the eagle feather we found at Fiona's residence look at all familiar? The answers, as with the other victims, don't help much. But I get a better sense of who Fiona is. Her mother describes her as a thoughtful, introspective girl. She loved to read and to weave—she could spend hours doing either.

"She'd weave the most beautiful rugs," she says, then gestures to the pile in the corner. "Much better than this massproduced garbage we sell to tourists."

"Why did Fiona move to El Paso?" I ask. "She was going to El Paso Community College, but she could have just as easily gone to college here."

She explains that Fiona wanted to get out of the Flagstaff area and try living someplace new. She was working at Whole Foods here when an opening became available in El Paso, and she applied for the transfer. She was a dreamer, looking for an adventure.

"It could have been anywhere," she says. "She would have gone to Phoenix or Denver just as willingly. It just happened to be Texas. I didn't want her to go, but I never thought anything like this would happen."

We've been operating on the assumption that the previous eagle feather victims are probably dead, but I can't forget that there's a chance that Fiona is still alive. Isabella Luna, if she was the first victim, was gone for ten days before she was discovered. Fiona hasn't been gone that long yet.

Ruth Martinez is obviously thinking along the same lines, holding out hope that she'll see her daughter again. Unlike Frank Tavaci, who seems resigned that the best he can probably hope for is to recover his daughter's remains so she can take her place in an urn on his mantelpiece, Ruth isn't ready to give up. She makes it clear she thinks Fiona is alive.

"We're moving forward with the assumption that she's alive as well," Ava says.

"It's not just an assumption," Ruth says. "I can feel it." When we say nothing, she adds, "I don't know how to explain it, but I'm her mother. I know that if she was dead, I would sense it somehow."

I've heard this kind of thing from family members before — grieving parents or siblings who believe in their hearts that their loved one is still out there, sometimes even after years. It's heartbreaking to finally deliver the news that the person they believed was alive was actually long dead. But something about Ruth Martinez's certainty makes me believe she might be right. It also fills me with fear because even though Fiona could be alive right now, she might not be when we eventually find her.

"I promise we're going to do everything we can to bring your daughter back," I say, and even though I shouldn't, I add, "Alive."

CHAPTER 40

AT MIDAFTERNOON OF our second day in Flagstaff, Ava and I go out to a late lunch to discuss what more we need to do in Arizona. Our work feels pretty much done here, and so our discussion focuses on whether we should leave for Texas tomorrow morning or get a few hours of driving in today.

We're at a pizza place called Oregano's, and I text Carlos with a photo of the thick deep-dish pie we're about to eat.

Jealous? I ask.

A minute later, I get a text back. It says, Are you? and includes a photo of my guitar.

I laugh. I can't help myself.

I left my guitar in my truck when I loaned it to Carlos. I guess I was wrong when I said I never leave home without it.

I'm short on gas money, Carlos texts. I'm going to hit up a pawnshop before I drive back. You think I can get $20 for this?

Ha ha, I text back. Very funny.

As we devour the pizza, I take a moment to reflect on the relationships I've formed with Carlos and Ava. A lot of times Rangers work alone, so it's been nice to have not one but two great partners on this case.

Carlos and I work well together. We didn't say a word during the whole gunfight, but we worked successfully and in tandem the entire time.

It's been a little harder to get to know Ava, as a police officer and a person. But beneath her steely exterior, I've seen her conduct interviews, review case files, and carry herself with the professionalism and poise of a sensitive woman who genuinely wants to help people. I'm glad my positive first impression when I met her at the shooting competition proved accurate—and that I've shaken her questionable first impression of me, so she and I could develop this working relationship.

And friendship.

The relationships with Carlos and Ava have made this assignment with the FBI's task force a gratifying experience. Which wouldn't have been the case otherwise, especially considering the strained relationship I now have with Ryan, who was my rival at the shooting competition but, as far as I'm concerned, never needed to be my rival on the job.

As I finish off my last piece of pizza, my phone buzzes, and I see that—speak of the devil—it's a call from Ryan.

"Hey, Yates," he says in the kind of friendly tone he used at the competition. "Where are you right now?"

"Flagstaff," I say. For a moment, I'm expecting him to scold me for being here, and I open my mouth to explain what we're doing and what we've discovered.

But he isn't calling to fight.

"How fast can you get to Phoenix?" he says.

"About two hours, I think."

"Excellent," he says. "I need a favor."

He explains that the police have found a Honda Civic abandoned in Phoenix that matches the description of the vehicle they believe Llewellyn Carpenter used after abandoning his van in the garage. Security footage from the garage showed Carpenter throw Marta Rivera in the trunk and take off, only about thirty seconds before Carlos and I got there.

"I'd send someone else from the task force," he says, "but it's a six-hour drive from El Paso. I could put someone on a plane, or go myself, but that's a lot of expense if it's the wrong vehicle. Since you're in the neighborhood, could you help me out?"

"Glad to," I say, then, knowing there's bad blood between them, I add, "Ava Cruz from the Tigua Tribal Police is with me."

Across from me, Ava takes a sip from her lemonade while watching me closely, trying to figure out what we're talking about.

"No problem," he says, surprising me. "Take her with you. I just need you to make an initial assessment. If it looks like our guy's vehicle, I'll probably come up myself."

I ask him if there's any word on Marta Rivera.

"No," he says. "But if that's the car we're looking for, she might be in Phoenix."

He surprises me again by asking if we've discovered any-thing of interest on our trip.

"Well, we've got four feathers now. All from victims who went missing on the solstice. One year apart."

"About that," he says, "there's something I need to tell you."

He starts to explain that he asked the lab to bump the feathers in favor of evidence from the raid. I tell him that I already know and—now it's my turn to surprise myself—I tell him that I understand. I'm thankful for Carlos advising me to proceed with caution. If I'd let Ryan have it two days ago, I doubt he'd be asking us to go to Phoenix right now.

"Now that you've got all four," Ryan says, "maybe we'll see if we can squeeze them back to the top of the list."

I thank him and hang up the phone, thoroughly flab-bergasted.

"Wonders never cease, I guess," I say.

"What happened?" Ava asks, taking another sip from her lemonade.

"Got a lead on Marta Rivera's kidnapper," I say. "We're going to Phoenix."

CHAPTER 41

DRIVING FROM THE mountains to the desert, we drop almost six thousand feet in elevation. As we get closer to the Phoenix metropolitan area, the landscape sprouts ten- and twenty-foot saguaro cacti, which stand in the sunlight on practically every hillside in sight. There are hundreds of them, beautiful and statuesque, with their arms reaching up like strange humanoid aliens.

Then the roadway flattens out, and we begin the long journey through a metro area that seems even more sprawling than El Paso and Juárez put together. The address Ryan gave me is actually in Tempe, but the cities here—Scottsdale, Mesa, Chandler, Glendale—all bleed together into one endless collection of neighborhoods and strip malls, with the occasional brown hill rising from the flat landscape to break up the monotony. The roads are lined with palm trees, and every person we see is wearing as little clothes as possible:

flip-flops, short shorts, tank tops. I check the weather app on my phone and see that it's 111 degrees outside.

We drive past Sun Devil Stadium and the big brown hill with Arizona State's signature yellow A on the side, then pull into an apartment complex, which looks like mostly student housing judging by the age of the people walking around. A Tempe Police Department car is parked in the lot, blocking in an old Honda Civic.

When we step out of the air-conditioned car, the heat is suffocating.

The officers introduce themselves and say that they were told to keep an eye on the vehicle until we got there. After we've had our look, they'll call to have it impounded. If it's the car we're looking for, the FBI will want it taken to a crime lab in Phoenix, where they can tear it apart, looking for evidence.

"A tenant reported the car," one of the officers explains. "All the parking spots are assigned to apartments. The tenant ignored it for a couple of days before leaving a note under the windshield wiper explaining that this was her parking spot, but the car never moved."

"The keys were in it," the other officer adds. "I bet he was hoping someone would steal it."

The officers say that they've already done a preliminary dusting for fingerprints on the driver's side door, steering wheel, and gearshift. They're waiting on the results, and lab technicians will be more thorough later. But if I can ID the car now, that will tell them how important it might be.

Ryan texted me a few images of the car Carpenter was

driving. The pictures—screenshots taken from the security footage—aren't very clear, but I do my best to look back and forth between the images and the vehicle. The color is right. The year and make and model all look right, as far as I can tell. The car in the pictures had a sticker in the upper corner of the windshield, like the kind you get after an oil change, and sure enough this car has a small Jiffy Lube decal in the same location. The car in the photo also had a bumper sticker, although it's impossible to tell what it said. This car has a sticker in the same spot that says, DO YOU FOLLOW JESUS THIS CLOSE?

I ask to see inside, and, without touching anything, I lean in to look around. I can't see much that would help me determine if this is the correct car. It's practically empty inside, the exception being a brochure folded and wedged into the cup holder advertising a massage parlor in Scottsdale.

Sweat is rolling down my body inside my shirt, but I'm determined to be thorough about this, regardless of the heat.

I ask if the officers have looked in the trunk. They haven't. As one reaches to unlock it, I have a fear that we're going to find Marta Rivera in there, her body stinking and bloated from the heat.

As the lid pops open, I'm relieved to see that the trunk is empty.

Ava and I lean down to scrutinize the interior, and Ava is the first to spot a hair caught in the trunk carpeting, barely visible in the harsh sunlight. We leave it where it is, but look at it carefully, trying to discern its length and color. The color is dark—not just brown, but black. Just like the hair of the girl in the picture Ava showed us when we first arrived at the Tigua Tribal Police Station. The strand is at least two feet, which is very long, even for a woman.

"Do you know how long Marta Rivera's hair is?" I ask Ava.

"Almost down to her butt," she tells me. "That's the way her parents described it."

I reach for my phone to call Ryan, but Ava stops me, bringing my attention to something else. The underside of the trunk lid, sticking up almost vertically into the air, is smeared in a way that's barely visible. I don't see them at first, but when I step to the side, to look at a different angle, it's clear that there are dozens of fingerprints inside, stretching from one side of the trunk lid to the other. Someone inside put fingerprints all over the interior.

In fact, the smudges form a pattern.

"Are those words?" I wonder aloud.

Ava and I and the other cops are squinting, trying to figure out what we're looking at. It's hard to make out all the smudges—we'll need to dust for prints to do that—but it doesn't appear that they are random.

"It's upside down," Ava says, tilting her head sideways.

I do the same, and then I see it. Once we've dusted for prints, the message will be more visible, but I can see enough to make out the muddled, uneven words:

MARTA RIVERA

HELP

CHAPTER 42

I CALL RYAN LOGAN and tell him what we found.

"Hot damn," he says, excited. "Good work, Yates."

"It was Ava, actually, who spotted the prints."

"Well, good work, Ava!" he says.

Those are words I never thought I'd hear him utter.

All animosity between us seemingly forgotten, Ryan says he's going to take an FBI plane to Phoenix and lead the team of technicians who will scrutinize it for more evidence.

"You and Ava can head back to El Paso, if you want," he says.

Despite the heat, the sun is lowering in the sky. Sunset is probably only an hour or two away.

"We might as well stay the night," I tell Ryan. "Anything you want us to do while we wait on you?"

"No," he says. "You've done good work. Go find a hotel with a pool and take it easy."

When I hang up, I relay our conversation to Ava.

"I guess whatever stick was stuck up his ass finally fell out," she says, and we both burst out laughing.

I'm glad the Tempe officers have gone back into their air-conditioned vehicles and didn't hear that. But it feels good to laugh. We're giddy, I guess. Finding this car has us both feeling like there's hope to find Marta Rivera alive.

"Well," Ava says, "for once, I think Ryan Logan has a good suggestion. Let's go find a hotel with a pool and get the hell out of this heat."

I give her a look that says, *I've got another idea.*

"We could do that," I say, then point inside the car to the brochure in the cup holder, "or we could go check out this massage parlor."

She gives me her own look: *Are you sure we should?*

"It can't hurt to drive by," I say. "We don't have to go in and order Swedish massages."

Ava asks if we should call Ryan Logan and let him know what we're doing. I already know what he would say. He wouldn't want us interfering. But the hope that Marta Rivera is alive is spreading inside me like a wildfire. I can't sit idly by a swimming pool when I might be able to do something to help.

"Nah," I say. "No need to involve him until we know something."

We say goodbye to the Tempe police officers, and we drive over an invisible city line to Scottsdale, where the shopping centers become more upscale and the houses get bigger and more expensive-looking.

I expect the parlor to be in a strip mall, but the SUV's navigation system takes us off the main thoroughfare. At the threshold to a residential area stands a small brick building with a sign that says MASSAGE UTOPIA. The nondescript structure itself looks more like a dentist's or optometrist's office, with nothing except the no-frills sign to suggest otherwise. The blinds are all drawn and there are no cars in the small parking lot.

A CLOSED sign hangs in the window.

"Drive on by," I say. "We're not exactly inconspicuous in this tribal police vehicle."

As she turns the corner, I crane my neck to look down the alley at the backside of the building. While the front of the building showed no signs of life, the back of the building is bustling with activity. One man carries clear garbage bags full of something—maybe bedsheets—and tosses them into the back of a parked pickup truck. Another comes out with an armload of paperwork and shoves it into a fifty-gallon drum, which is already piled high with discarded papers.

A bottle of lighter fluid sits on the ground next to the barrel.

"They're clearing out," I say. "They're about to burn their evidence."

"You think this is one of the brothels?" Ava asks, looking in her rearview mirror but not altering the way she drives so as not to call attention to us.

"Must be," I say. "Pull over up here."

"What should we do?" Ava asks, easing to the curb.

"Better let Ryan know," I say, grabbing my phone while looking around to see if anyone has noticed us.

When the FBI agent answers, he says, "I'm heading to the airport now. I should be there in about two hours."

"Something's going on," I say. "It might be over in two hours."

As quickly as I can, I relay what I saw at the massage parlor.

"Just sit tight," he says. "Keep an eye on them."

"And if they clear out before you get here?" I say. "What if they burn evidence?"

"Just stay put," he tells me.

"There could be victims in there right now, Ryan," I say, losing my patience. "What if they load up a van full of missing women and drive them away?"

"Follow them and don't get spotted," he says, and I want to argue with him that we can't exactly keep a low profile in Ava's police SUV.

The civility and friendliness Ryan spoke with earlier is gone, and he's taking a tone like a parent talking to a child he knows is about to do something against the rules.

"You're there in an observation role only, Rory. Do not engage with these people in any way. I'll be there with a team as soon as I can."

"Shit," I say after he hangs up.

In the rearview mirror, I spot a van pulling into the alleyway. It's white, not blue, but otherwise it looks similar to Llewellyn Carpenter's van. Perfect for hiding people in the back.

"They're going to load up the women," Ava says in a panic.

I step out of the car and tug off my tie and untuck my dress shirt and undo the buttons, letting it hang open over my T-shirt. I remove my gun belt but stick my SIG Sauer in the back of my pants, wedged in by my belt and covered by the untucked shirt.

I drop my hat onto the car seat. Then I unpin the star on my shirt and toss it next to the hat.

"Do I look like a cop?" I say.

"No," she says, "but you don't exactly blend in. I don't think people wear dress pants with cowboy boots around here." She pops open the glove box and pulls out a trucker hat with the words TOMBSTONE ARIZONA stenciled across the front panel and an illustration of a grave marker next to it.

"Here," she says. "This is Marcos's."

I put the hat on.

"Better," Ava says. "What's the plan? What are you going to do?"

"I don't know," I say. "But I can't let that van leave with any women in it."

I tell her to stay put. There's no need to discuss the prospect of her coming with me. My disguise might not be perfect, but she's wearing her Tigua Tribal Police uniform—she's even more conspicuous than the car we're driving.

"If you hear shooting," I say, "call for backup."

With that, I turn on my heel and head down the sidewalk, like Wyatt Earp heading over to the O.K. Corral.

Only I don't have Doc Holliday or anyone else to back me up.

CHAPTER 43

I WALK INTO the alleyway like I belong there. Two white men standing outside — one throwing papers into the barrel, the other spraying what's inside with lighter fluid — look up from what they're doing with confused expressions on their faces.

I notice one of the guys has a revolver tucked into the waistband of his jeans. If the other is armed, the gun is hidden.

"Can I help you?" the one with the gun asks.

"I'm here to drive the van," I say, smacking my hand against the side of the panel van, which is parked next to the pickup truck I saw earlier.

The two men look at each other. The one with the gun is thin, with a scruffy red beard and a face full of acne scars. He's wearing an Ozzy Osbourne T-shirt and flip-flops, which look oddly casual for a guy with a revolver tucked into his waistband. The other guy, with a bald head and a belly like a watermelon, is wearing a purple Phoenix Suns jersey and matching shorts.

If I was confident that it was only these two guys here—with only one of them armed—I'd go ahead and draw my gun and try to arrest them. But someone—maybe Llewellyn Carpenter, maybe somebody else—pulled up in that van and disappeared inside the building. And there could be others in there, as heavily armed as the men at the warehouse raid.

For now, I decide I better keep up this charade that I'm one of them.

"Boss sent me," I say.

"Who?" the guy in the Phoenix Suns outfit says.

"The boss," I say, emphasizing it like they should know who I'm talking about.

"Mr. Z?" the one with the gun and the Ozzy Osbourne shirt asks.

I nod, not knowing what else to do.

"Llewellyn didn't say nothing about that," the other guy says, turning his head toward the back of the building. It looks like there are two rear exits: one door that hangs open, and another that's firmly shut.

"How many women you got in there?" I ask, then I try the name I heard them use. "Mr. Z didn't say what kind of a shipment to expect."

"We only got four left," the Phoenix Suns fan says.

"Five," Ozzy Osbourne says. "Counting the one Llewellyn brought."

Marta.

She's inside.

My heart rate—already jacked—accelerates even more.

"Well, let's get this show on the road," I say. "Let's get 'em loaded up."

I step forward toward the back door. I'm not entirely sure what I'm doing, but now that I'm in the middle of this situation, I have to commit all the way. I guess I'm hoping I can somehow convince these guys to let me drive off with the five kidnapped women. It might actually be possible if Llewellyn Carpenter, who must be in there somewhere, doesn't spot me. These guys don't recognize me, but I'm certain he would. Marcos's TOMBSTONE ARIZONA trucker hat isn't much of a disguise.

As I pass the truck, I spot a shotgun lying on the bench seat. Ozzy Osbourne follows behind me and, when we get to the threshold, instructs me to go down a hallway lined with doors, some ajar, some closed.

"First girl's in here," he says, gesturing to the closest closed door.

I try the handle, but it's locked. The guy pulls out a key ring and opens the door. The room is dark, and I reach for the switch. Colored lights come on, illuminating the figure lying on a mattress on the floor. It's a young white woman, wearing only a T-shirt and underwear, with tangled hair and a body full of bruises. Lying next to her on the floor is a squirt bottle of lubricant, a box of condoms, and a cardboard box of discarded syringes.

She lifts her head, squinting against the light, and says in a gravelly voice, "You got my stuff? I need it."

Her lips are flaky with dead skin, and her eyes have the distant, disconnected look of a junkie only interested in the next fix.

"You're coming with me, darlin'," I say, trying to play the part. "I got your next fix in the van."

When she doesn't move, the guy I'm with grabs her by the arm and yanks her to her feet.

"Easy there," I say. "No need to hurt the merchandise."

He ignores the comment and shoves her into my arms.

"You take her on outside," he says. "I'll get the next one."

"Come on with me, darlin'," I say, guiding her down the hallway.

"Where's my fix?" she says.

Her body is flaccid, like a wilted flower, and I have to support most of her weight to keep her moving. She smells like she hasn't had a bath in weeks.

"I'll do anything you want," she says to me, her voice pleading. "I'm a real good girl."

"Everything's going to be okay," I say, keeping my voice low.

When we step out into the sunshine, I freeze in my tracks.

Llewellyn Carpenter is there, holding Marta Rivera—her face recognizable from her photograph, her hair down to her butt just like Ava said—firmly by the arm.

Carpenter takes one look at me and, as I feared, recognizes me. He yanks a gun out of his waistband while tugging Marta toward him to use her as a shield.

"Texas Ranger!" he shouts. "Kill the son of a bitch!"

CHAPTER 44

I DRAW MY gun, but—again—I don't have a shot. Carpenter holds Marta in a chokehold, positioning his body behind hers. She tries to fight, but she's clearly debilitated—either high on heroin or weakened by waiting for her next fix.

With his free arm, Carpenter swings his pistol over her shoulder and points it in my direction. I grab the woman I've been propping up and shove her back inside the building. Carpenter's pistol thunders, and bullets crash into the drywall next to me, throwing white dust into the air. I hurl the woman down inside the closest open doorway and dive on top of her. She's screaming—now fully awake from her addiction-focused haze—and thrashing around in a panic.

Carpenter stops shooting, and I hear a scuffle outside.

"Stay here!" I tell the woman and rise to my feet.

She scurries on all fours into the corner of the room and curls into a tight ball, like a schoolkid in a tornado drill.

Just as I step out of the room, Ozzy Osbourne—the red-bearded guy with the revolver—is rushing down the hall, and we practically collide. Only a few feet away, he swings his big gun at me. With my left arm, I reach out and grab his wrist, pushing his arm against the wall. He squeezes the trigger. Flames leap from the barrel, and a loud *boom* fills the narrow corridor. I try to jam my SIG Sauer against his chest, but he grabs my gun arm in the same position and shoves my arm up into the air. I angle my wrist, but I still don't have a shot.

We push and pull against each other. He's not a big guy, but he has a wiry strength, and it's all I can do to hold on to his squirming wrist. It's just a matter of seconds before he'll be able to twist his long-barreled gun into a decent shooting position. I use my weight to pin him against the wall with my shoulder. With my head lowered, I notice again that he's wearing flip-flops. I lift my foot and drive the sole of my cowboy boot down against his bare toes.

He grunts in pain, and this gives me the moment I need to yank my gun hand free from his grip. I aim my gun, intending to tell him to freeze, but my shifting position has caused me to lose my grip on his arm. He swings his gun on me.

We fire at the same time.

His bullet sails through the folds of my open dress shirt, coming within inches of slicing through my rib cage.

My bullet punches him in the cheekbone, and he slides down to the floor, leaving a trail of brains on the wall behind him.

A vehicle engine roars outside, and I rush toward the exit.

As I step into daylight, I notice two things simultaneously. The first is that the van is speeding away, no doubt with Llewellyn Carpenter and Marta Rivera inside. The second is that the Suns fan stands behind the cover of the pickup truck, aiming the pump shotgun at the doorway.

I dive back inside as he lets loose a series of thunderous blasts. I pin myself against the floor, and chunks of wood and drywall rain down on me.

He stops firing, and I rise to a crouching position, my gun ready. I try to figure the odds of running out and getting a good shot before he lets loose with another blast.

Not good.

"You stay right where you are!" I hear the man yell. "I'm going to get into this truck and drive away. Don't try to stop me, and you might live another day."

I don't hear him climbing into the truck. Nor do I hear the engine coming to life. Instead, I hear footsteps—careful, cautious—approaching the doorway.

He's coming after me.

I raise my gun, ready for him to step into my path.

Then I hear the click of a gun being cocked. Not a shotgun. A handgun.

"Stop right there," I hear a familiar voice say.

Ava.

"Put the shotgun down—gently," she says. Then a moment later: "It's okay to come out, Rory."

I step forward, ready to fire, but the Suns fan is standing with his hands up. Ava's sidearm is leveled on the back of his head. The shotgun is lying on the ground.

"Thanks, Ava," I say. "I'm glad as hell to see you."

"Put your hands against the wall," she says to the guy, and when he does it, she holsters her gun and handcuffs him. "I called for backup," she tells me. "There's an APB out for the van. Was it Carpenter?"

"Yes," I say, realizing just how dry my mouth is. I swallow. "And he took Marta. Again."

CHAPTER 45

TWO HOURS LATER, the sun has set and the scene is swarming with police vehicles, their red and blue lights strobing in the darkness. Press vans are parked on the street. Scottsdale police officers, Maricopa County sheriff's deputies, and a whole team of crime scene technicians are working the scene. The four women have been taken to the hospital. The shotgun-wielding basketball fan has been taken to jail.

Ryan Logan and a small team of FBI agents arrived about fifteen minutes ago. When he saw me, he said, "Wait here," and pointed to a spot on the sidewalk. Then he walked into the scene to be briefed.

Ava stands with me as I wait. I feel like a criminal awaiting his day in court.

I've since tucked my shirt back in and strapped on my gun belt. My Stetson is back on my head. My clothes are dirty and there's even a bullet hole through my shirt, but at least

I look a little more like a Texas Ranger. I don't know where Marcos's TOMBSTONE hat is—I lost it somewhere in the chaos of the gunfight.

We wait for what seems like a long time until finally an agent I recognize from the raid comes to fetch me.

"Special Agent Logan would like to see you," she says, and leads me to the back of the building. As we walk, she says conspiratorially, "Ryan's not happy."

"I figured," I say.

"But for the record," the agent says, "I think you did a good thing. Here and at the warehouse in El Paso. You've got nerves of steel, Ranger. You've got my respect."

"Thanks," I say.

Ryan is waiting for me in the lobby area of the building, which is decorated to look like a real massage parlor. He's leaning against the counter, his head lowered in thought.

Before he says anything, I start my defense.

"They were going to move the girls," I say. "I had to act."

He raises his head and glares at me. "I told you to stay put," he says.

"They were going to move the girls," I say again.

"I told you to follow from a distance."

"We were in a police vehicle," I argue. "How discreet could we be?"

He shakes his head. "All you want to do is hog the spotlight, Rory. You rush in to danger so you can be the hero. I think the Rangers giving you that Medal of Valor has gone to your head."

"I don't give a damn about being a hero," I say. "I don't give a damn about any medals. And I damn sure don't care about any spotlight. But what I do care about is saving lives. By my count, we saved four today."

"But not Marta Rivera," he says pointedly, and this statement silences me.

He's right. I can't count what I did today—or at the raid—as a success when she's still out there, still in harm's way.

I don't have it in me to argue with Ryan anymore. I stand quietly and take my punishment.

"Here's the thing, Rory," he says, approaching me and locking eyes with me, only a foot or two away. "You're reckless. You're not a team player. You run in, guns blazing, without thinking there might be another option. This devil-may-care attitude might work in the Rangers, but it's not working when it comes to my task force. You're not the kind of person I want on this team. I gave you a second chance, with a very simple task: 'Go to Phoenix and look at a vehicle.' Somehow, you turn those instructions into a goddamn gunfight in the middle of a residential area."

"What are you saying?" I ask. "Are you kicking me off the task force?"

"You're out," he says. "I don't want to see you on my crime scenes. I don't want you investigating these missing women. I don't want to see your face for a long, long time." He can't seem to help himself from adding, "And if you show up at next year's charity shoot, I'm going to take great pleasure in wiping the floor with your ass."

So that's what this is all about? I think.

Part of me wants to argue with him. His assessment is

completely unfair. The real reason behind his attitude is a simple emotional response. He's mad he couldn't beat me in the competition, and he's jealous that I keep performing well in real gunfights when he spends most of his time on the sidelines. His own agent just complimented me on "nerves of steel." Ryan wants to be a modern-day Jelly Bryce — the kind of agent who can perform in shooting competitions *and* in the field. The truth is Ryan Logan is jealous that I'm the one with a reputation like his hero.

But I'm tired of fighting. I've been butting heads with him since day one. I've been in two gunfights now. I've saved lives. I've done good police work. And still I can't get the cooperation I need to keep going.

He's firing me, but in my heart, I'm also quitting.

No matter what I say to defend myself, my actions, or my record since joining the task force, Ryan can always counter with two words: Marta Rivera. The bottom line is I've failed her.

Twice.

Ryan waits for me, as if expecting an argument. Instead, I tip the brim of my hat to him and exit without saying a word.

When I arrive at Ava's vehicle outside, I say, "Let's go back to El Paso."

"What happened?" she says.

"I'm off the task force."

She shakes her head in disapproval. I'm not sure if she's mad at Ryan for kicking me off the team or angry with me for not fighting to stay on.

"So that's it?" she says.

"That's it," I say. "It's over. At least for me."

"What about Marta Rivera?" she asks. "What about Fiona Martinez? What about the promise you made to Fiona's mother?"

I don't answer. I don't know what to say.

I tried.

I failed.

I give up.

I can't say those words aloud. But she can see what I'm thinking anyway. What I see on her face cuts me to the bone. It's disappointment.

Disappointment that the Texas Ranger she'd come to believe in has proven her right after all.

PART 2

CHAPTER 46

FIONA OPENS HER eyes with the approach of sunrise. The dark sky is bluing, the stars disappearing. The change is gradual, at first, and then the sun explodes from the horizon, washing the landscape in golden light.

Lying on her side on a slab of sandstone, Fiona uncurls from the fetal position she's been huddled in all night. Desert days are scorching, but the nights are cool. There is no comfortable in-between temperature except for a few hours after sunrise.

Her lips are dry and cracked, her breath hot. She slides herself, dragging her useless legs, to the streambed that trickles through the desert canyon. She can't get enough of the cool water, which she slurps hungrily. The creek is only an inch or two deep, but the water is the main reason she's still alive. She's eaten some cactus buds, a few insects, and one lizard she was lucky enough to grab and choke down, scales and skeleton and all. But she knows it's the steady stream of water, which she's able to fill her belly with several times a day, that's keeping her alive.

She remembers learning in school that a person could survive a long time on water alone. How long? Ten days? Twenty? She never guessed she would be in a position to test this out for herself.

She's lost count of how long it's been since she was abandoned here. It hasn't been nearly twenty days, but the prospect of starvation is only one of her problems. Her injuries are another.

She's sure there are broken bones in both of her legs. On her right, the ankle is swollen to an unbelievable size, the flesh a cadaverous purple color. Her left leg is worse, the lower part bent at a noticeable angle, telling her that both bones must have snapped. She's thankful that neither bone is jutting out through her skin, but there must be internal bleeding. Maybe a growing infection.

She is stuck in a canyon created by the stream, which has etched itself into the hard stone over time. On one side of the creek is wide-open desert, full of sagebrush and the occasional prickly pear cactus, ocotillo shrub, and desert spoon stalk. On the other side of the stream is a steep cliff face, at least forty feet tall, towering over her.

She woke up the first day, nauseated with pain, at the base of the cliff. She thought she was in a pile of branches, but as the sun came up, she realized she was among the bones of women who came before her. There were three women, as far as she could tell. Clearly the remains had been pulled apart by coyotes or other scavengers, the skeletons no longer intact and in different states of decay. But she'd counted three skulls, the most recent of which still had patches of hair attached and remnants of skin, flaking off like parchment in an ancient book. One skeleton had a beautiful silver necklace still tangled in the vertebrae of the neck.

Fiona had clambered down into the creek bed to get away from the bodies and to find the water she could hear trickling through the rocks. She discovered a small overhanging shelf of rock that gave her protection from the sun during the hottest part of the days. She's been there ever since, hoping someone will come to rescue her. She spent much of the early days crying—in pain, in fear, in self-pity—but now she has no tears left.

Each time she sleeps, she wonders if she'll be closing her eyes for the last time.

Death must be close now.

She'd thought someone would find her. Surely they must be searching. But the girls who came before her, if they weren't killed on impact, they must have thought the same thing.

And now there is nothing left of them but bones.

Fiona has considered striking out on her own. If she's going to die, why not die trying to live? In her mind, she's made a plan to travel downstream. Going downhill—even at such a minuscule angle—will be easier than uphill. But each day, when faced with the decision of whether to leave, she finds that she doesn't have the strength.

Now, lying next to the trickling water, she asks for a sign.

She catches movement out of the corner of her eye, and when she looks up, spots a scorpion crawling from underneath a rock.

It's not the kind of sign she was looking for.

The creature skitters forward silently, its tail straight back, its pincers upright as if probing the air. The scorpion—about an inch and a half long—approaches her hand, lying flat against the sandstone.

Fiona is as still as a statue.

The scorpion's exoskeleton is a pale yellow color, and Fiona can't help but think how otherworldly it looks—how prehistoric. Scorpions like this were crawling on rocks when dinosaurs walked the earth. The thought of this—the scorpion surviving through millions of years of planetary changes—makes her think that perhaps this *is* the sign she needs. The universe has sent her a survivor—what better sign could she receive?

The scorpion crawls forward and steps onto the back of Fiona's outstretched hand. Goose bumps rise on her skin, but otherwise she stays frozen. She wants to scream and yank her hand away, but she wills herself not to. Still, the scorpion senses something, and its tail raises from a flat line into a C-shaped arc—the barb at the end ready to strike.

Fiona could try to kill it—try to eat it—but she isn't confident she'll be fast enough. And she has another idea.

She'll let the scorpion decide for her.

If it stings her, she'll close her eyes and let the poison finish the job her injuries and her starvation have already begun. But if it crawls off of her arm and leaves her alone, then she'll rise to her hands and knees and begin crawling down the canyon.

That's the bargain she makes with herself.

If it stings her, she'll let herself die.

If it doesn't, she'll fight to live with everything she has left.

She stares at the scorpion, perched on her skin, and waits for its decision.

CHAPTER 47

MARTA WAKES ON the floor of a van, aching and sick. The metal beneath her is cool. The interior of the van will become hot later when the sun beats down on it, the walls blistering to the touch, the floor emanating heat like an oven. But for now, the van's interior feels chilly, like the refrigeration aisle of a grocery store.

Which is nice because she's already feverish.

Already sick.

She can't remember the last time she ate, but it isn't food she craves.

It's the other stuff.

She can't believe how quickly she's become hooked. When one of the men—sometimes the one they call Llewellyn with the snake tattoo, but sometimes others—brings a small baggie of brown powder, her heart races with anticipation. She waits subserviently as they pour the powder into a spoon, heat it with a lighter, suck the substance up into a syringe. She lets them wrap the rubber strap around her arm, tap her skin for the vein to fatten and become distinct.

There is a moment of pain, like a bee sting, then she closes her eyes and floats on a cloud of bliss better than anything she's ever felt before. And when the clouds disappear and she feels the metal floor beneath her again, the sickness returns.

Sweating.

Stomach cramps.

An aching in her muscles, even her bones.

Marta sits upright, leaning her back against the wall, blinking her eyes awake. The van isn't moving, she notices. The only window is a metal mesh rectangle between her metal holding cell and the cab. She scoots forward to get a look. Her limbs are shaky, and it's all she can do to rise to her knees to look through the metal X's.

Llewellyn, the man who kidnapped her and who has been dragging her around in one car or another since the day the police showed up at the warehouse, isn't in the driver's seat. She spots him through the windshield, pacing and with a phone to his ear. He's waiting for someone on the other end to pick up.

Behind him, Marta sees only hills of sagebrush. No buildings or structures. The sun has recently risen, giving the landscape a warm radiance.

"Mr. Z," he says when the person finally answers. "Yeah, it's Llewellyn."

She's heard this name a few times—Mr. Z—but has never

seen the person it belongs to. The men all use the name with an air of respect.

Llewellyn explains to Mr. Z how the cops showed up at the brothel where they'd been keeping Marta. He explains how he'd shot at the Texas Ranger and fled before the Ranger killed one of the men and arrested another.

"Yeah, it was that same Ranger. That piece of shit just won't go away. He's like a turd that won't flush."

Llewellyn listens. He heads toward the van, and Marta ducks her head down. She pins her back to the metal, with her head just below the window, and tries to listen.

"Okay, I've got a pen," Llewellyn says. "Give me the address again."

A minute later, Llewellyn fires up the engine of the van. He puts the phone on speaker as he pulls onto the road.

"You think it will work?" Llewellyn asks.

"I think so," says a confident voice over the speaker. *"It will look like an accident. And even if they figure out it wasn't, it will distract them for a while."*

Mr. Z—whoever he is—has a slow, confident way of speaking. To any outsider, every Texas accent might sound the same, but growing up on the Pueblo, adjacent to El Paso, Marta can tell more from the way Texans talk than just the state they're from. Mr. Z is an upper-class good ol' boy. There's money behind his Texas twang.

"Besides," the voice on the phone says, *"we just need this Texas Ranger out of the way. That will give us time to shut down operations for a while. We need to consolidate the merchandise and hang low. We'll set up some new brothels in a month or two."*

"What about the girl with me?"

"Bring her to my place before you ditch the van and set the trap."

Marta knows she should be afraid. Going to Mr. Z's place can't be a good thing. But the truth is, this fills her with hope. If Mr. Z is the boss, he'll have plenty of stuff to make her feel better. She looks at the needle marks on her arm and is ashamed for feeling this way.

"What about the guys they arrested?" Llewellyn asks as the van rumbles down the highway. "You think they'll talk?"

"No one will talk," Mr. Z says. *"They all have something they care about. Wives. Mothers. Children. Dogs. If anyone talks, they know I'll have you arrange an accident for their loved ones just like there will be an accident for that Texas Ranger."*

"You just say the word, and I'll take care of whoever you need me to," Llewellyn says. "You know I like kidnapping these girls, but I much prefer..."

He doesn't finish, but Marta feels she knows what the rest of the sentence is: *I much prefer killing people.*

The thought sends a chill up her spine.

"Yes," Mr. Z says conversationally, as if they are discussing the weather, *"we all have our own personal appetites."*

Llewellyn ends the call, and Marta sits leaning against the wall, her arms curled around her knees. She steals a glance through the window into the cab. Llewellyn is facing the windshield, where the highway leads off into desert hills. Her captor reaches for the radio and flips through the channels, finally settling for a sports talk show with the DJs discussing the odds of any of the El Paso Chihuahuas getting called up to the big leagues this year.

Marta gets an idea. She doesn't know if it will help, but she can't do nothing.

She crawls toward the back of the van, checks the window to make sure Llewellyn hasn't leaned over to look back at her, and then positions herself by the back door. She takes her index finger and presses it firmly against the metal. Then does it again.

And again.

And again.

Until she's written a message to whoever finds the van—maybe that Texas Ranger they were talking about.

She only hopes he gets the warning in time.

CHAPTER 48

CARLOS DRIVES WEST.

He's halfway between Houston and San Antonio, where he plans to grab a quick bite to eat, then push on to El Paso. It will take a good ten hours to get there. Maybe eleven.

The scenery of Central Texas is in sharp contrast to where he's headed. The blue of the sky is washed out with humidity, and the landscape is flat and covered in unruly chartreuse grasses. Crocodile-green trees line the roadway.

He's anxious to get back. The trip was necessary, although he's not sure how much the interviews will help in the end. It's what he's been doing in the evenings—going through the victims' phone records and social media accounts—that has proven the most fruitful.

He's got news for Rory and Ava.

He'd been saying that something about the case felt out of reach, some connection among the women. He hasn't figured

223

it out, not entirely, but he's closer now, and he needs their input.

Rory's truck is pretty much identical to his own, yet it feels weird to drive someone else's vehicle. He wishes there was some way to swing up to Austin and get his own, but then he'd be abandoning Rory's vehicle in the capital.

As the miles roll underneath him, Carlos thinks about his relationship with Rory. He hadn't known what to expect when they'd first teamed up. Rory had a reputation for being cool in a gunfight but a hothead in other situations. Carlos has found both to be true. Sure, Rory can be impatient, temperamental, argumentative. But his heart is always true to his task. He tries to do the right thing. Period.

Texas Rangers don't ordinarily work with partners, which suits Carlos just fine. He works better alone. Usually. But it's been a nice surprise to have a partner on this case that he's been proud to work with.

Carlos's phone rings, and he expects it to be Rory with an update.

Instead, it's Ava.

He puts the call on Bluetooth and says, "I'm on my way back to El Paso. Did you two make it?"

"Sort of," Ava says, her voice indicating that something is wrong.

"What happened?" Carlos asks, keeping his eyes on the road. In the distance, he can make out the tallest buildings of San Antonio. "Let me guess: Rory was grumpy the whole time because he didn't have his guitar?"

"Rory's out," she says.

"What do you mean 'out'?"

"He quit. Or got fired. I'm not sure which. Maybe both."

Ava explains what happened at the brothel — the shoot-out, rescuing the women, Carpenter escaping, and losing Marta *again*. She says that Ryan Logan booted Rory off the task force. Then Rory and Ava drove through the night to get back to El Paso. Rory texted the woman they'd met at the bar, Megan, and asked to be dropped off at her house.

"We got there just before the sun came up," she says.

"What did Rory say?"

"He said he was sorry. That's all."

"And what did you say?"

"Nothing. I'm disappointed in him."

Carlos takes a deep breath. "Me, too," he says softly.

So much for having a partner he could be proud to work with.

CHAPTER 49

I WAKE UP with harsh sunlight blasting through the blinds. I feel groggy and disoriented, trying to remember where I am and why on earth I've slept so late.

Then I remember: I'm at Megan's.

And I slept this late—whatever time it is—because I didn't go to sleep until after the sun was already up.

I sit up in bed. I'm still wearing my pants and T-shirt, but my tie and belt are draped over a chair in the corner, my boots on the floor underneath. My duffel bag sits on the floor, my gun belt tucked inside of it. My hat is perched atop the back of the chair. The dress shirt that I wore yesterday is nowhere to be seen, and neither is the tin star that was pinned to it.

A glass of water is sitting on the bedside table next to a hardback book. I take a big drink. The bedroom is small, with a compact desk in the corner and a bookshelf on one wall. Some of the titles I recognize from college English classes—*Ceremony*, *Rain of Scorpions*, and *Bless Me, Ultima*—but mostly they're scholarly books I've never heard of, with words in the titles I've never seen before, like *Intertextuality*, *Narratology*, and *Paraliterary*.

I sit for a few seconds and blink the sleep from my eyes, then finish the water.

On the way to El Paso last night, I texted Megan and asked if I could come over instead of finding a hotel. I'd had a rough day and needed a friend. She worked at the bar until two o'clock, then waited up for me. When Ava dropped me off around five, Megan gave me a big hug, but there was no kissing, no making out. Getting lucky was the last thing on my mind.

We were both so tired we lay down on her bed, me in my pants and T-shirt, Megan in a pair of gym shorts and a tank top. With the sunrise leaking in through the blinds, I didn't think I'd sleep—but I passed out like I'd just been given a sedative.

Now I rise to my feet, stretch my stiff muscles, and leave the bedroom. The soreness in my back from getting hit by the pool cue is gone, but I have plenty of fresh aches and pains from yesterday's events. I follow the sound of a TV, turned low, and find Megan in her living room, her fingers clacking away on her laptop. A small TV sits against the wall, a commercial advertising a used-car lot in El Paso. The salesman, a fiftysomething man with hair that's too blond and skin that's too tan, boasts about the lowest prices and most extensive inventory on this side of the border.

"Good morning, sunshine," Megan says when she sees me.

"Morning," I say, my voice hoarse. "What time is it?"

She checks her monitor and says, "Time for a late lunch, if you're hungry."

"In a minute," I say, and I slump down onto the couch. "I feel like I've been hit by a truck."

She closes her computer and sets it on the coffee table, then picks up the remote and silences the used-car salesman just as he's getting into a fervor over his stock of pre-owned vehicles. I notice my dress shirt is dangling from a plastic hanger suspended from a curtain rod. It's been ironed and looks brand-new—except for the bullet hole. My star, which had been pinned to it, is lying on the coffee table.

"I washed your shirt," she explains. "I would have done your pants, but I didn't want you to wake up to find me undressing you and get the wrong idea."

I smile, and we both share a chuckle. It feels good to laugh, but the reprieve is only temporary. I feel sad, guilty, useless. I keep telling myself I tried—it was Ryan who kicked me off the task force—but I can't shake the feeling that I've let everyone down.

By everyone I mean Ava and Carlos, but also Fiona, who might still be alive, and Marta, who definitely is—or at least was last night.

I should call Carlos, but the fact that I haven't heard from him already tells me that Ava's done it for me. I'm sure he's pissed at me, too. He probably thinks I should have been more diplomatic, found a way to stay on the federal team. Word has probably already gotten back to Captain Kane. I wonder what he's going to think. He never wanted me involved in these cases anyway, so he might actually be relieved.

I run my hands through my hair and look around the apartment. A part-time bartender/part-time teacher/full-time student can't make much money, but Megan seems to have done the best she can with limited means. The mismatched furniture and down-home wall decorations all work together to create an eclectic, comfortable living space.

"I'm sorry I crashed here," I tell Megan. "I don't mean to dump my troubles on you."

I'm sure this isn't the reunion she was hoping for, especially after I called her a few days ago and promised to take her out on a proper date. Instead, I've shown up at her place, beaten down and in no shape to be any fun at all.

"Why don't you wait until tomorrow to head back?" she says.

I tell her I can't go anywhere until Carlos returns my truck anyway.

"Good," she says. "Spend one day here. With me."

CHAPTER 50

"CAN I ASK you a question?" Megan says.

It's been about an hour since I woke up. Megan made faji-tas for lunch while I took a shower and threw on a pair of jeans and a T-shirt. We've just finished eating at a little two-seat table nook in the same room as the TV and couch.

"Shoot," I say.

"Interesting choice of words."

"What do you mean?"

She gestures over to my shirt hanging by the window, sun-light streaming in through the hole.

"Is that a bullet hole in your shirt?"

I nod, wondering what she's thinking. The prospect of dat-ing a Texas Ranger always sounds good to women until they realize they could lose you at any time. Willow always had a hard time dealing with it.

Megan places a comforting hand on my shoulder.

"I'm here for you," she says. "If you need to talk, we can talk. If you want to do something else to take your mind off of everything you've been through, we could watch a movie or sit around reading books. Whatever you need."

Megan looks beautiful with the bright sunlight pouring onto her skin, which doesn't have—or need—a stitch of makeup on it. Her blue eyes catch the light and shine like the cobalt surface of a beautiful mountain lake.

I've never really been one to open up about what I'm feeling, but Megan's sincerity prompts me to start talking.

"On the drive last night," I say, "I was thinking about Wyatt Earp. You know who he was, don't you?"

"He was a gunfighter from the Wild West, wasn't he?" Megan says. "Kurt Russell played him in a movie. Or maybe it was Kevin Costner."

"Both," I say. "He was a lawman. He might not have been much better than some of the outlaws he went after, but he has a legend that follows him, a mythology that makes him a hero in everyone's mind."

Wyatt Earp was on my mind because of the TOMBSTONE hat I borrowed from Ava, but on the drive I started thinking about how there was a famous gunfight in which his coat was shot through on both sides with buckshot, yet somehow none of the rounds hit him. It reminded me of my shirt, where the bullet passed through the front and the back on the left side. It looks like the bullet would have gone right through me, but that's only because the shirt was open and hanging at the time my attacker squeezed the trigger.

I rise and examine the hole in my shirt. The shot was so close that there are burn marks around the entrance hole.

"Wyatt Earp never got shot once," I say to Megan. "Not in his whole law enforcement career. People he rode with got shot or killed. His brothers did. Doc Holliday did. But he didn't." I put my little finger through the front hole, the edges crisp from the scorch marks. "Supposedly, shots passed right through his coat without hitting him. Bullets went through his hat. One even hit his boot heel, they say. His saddle horn was shot off, I think. But he was never hit. Never so much as a scratch.

"I don't know for sure," I add, "but I get the feeling that at some point Wyatt Earp figured he'd used up all his luck. He hung up his gun and retired from law enforcement."

Megan listens without interruption. I meet her eyes.

"I've had some close calls," I say, pointing to the shirt as if she needs a reminder. "I feel like I've used up all my Wyatt Earp luck. One of these days, a bullet is going to find its way home. I'll be either hurt or killed. I'll be in a hospital, or I'll be in a casket."

I walk back over and sit next to Megan, who keeps her ocean-deep eyes fixed on me.

"Unless I hang up my gun and call it a career," I say, "that's where I'm headed. My parents will have to go to one of those Medal of Valor ceremonies and accept the award on my behalf. Posthumously. My luck's run out. I can feel it."

"Do you want to hang up your gun?" Megan asks.

"I don't know," I say. "Maybe getting kicked off the task force is the sign I need. I don't seem to fit in with the way things work these days. My help isn't wanted. I'm fighting the good guys as much as I am the bad guys. Maybe it's time for me to call it quits. Maybe it's time for me to ride off into the sunset."

Megan encourages me to give it some thought, not rush into any decisions.

"The thing is," I say, picking up my tin star from the coffee table and looking at my distorted reflection in the metal, "without this badge, I'm not sure who I am."

CHAPTER 51

MEGAN AND I spend the day together. We sit in the shade on her back patio, drinking sweet tea. We each have a book— mine is a John Grisham paperback from my duffel bag, hers is a scholarly book about multimodal pedagogy, whatever that is—but we talk more than we read. We chat about Red- bud and what it was like growing up there. Our conversation turns to Baylor and how much I liked it as a student and how much she hopes she gets the job there.

Megan is easy to talk to. What's happening in my life— getting kicked off the task force, disappointing Carlos and Ava, my inability to save Marta or crack Fiona's case—is never far from my mind. However, I find that I'm able to laugh with Megan and enjoy myself despite the mess my life seems to be in.

As we talk, I'm able to imagine a future with Megan. And maybe that future doesn't need to involve law enforcement.

Maybe I should turn in my badge, hang up my gun. I've done some good with my career. I should be able to quit and be proud of what I've accomplished.

I've had these kinds of thoughts before. This time feels different. Like maybe it really is time to call it quits.

But I'm afraid I would always feel a nagging guilt that I could have done more.

How much do I have to give? I wonder.

As evening approaches, the sky darkens with clouds, and we head back inside and eat dinner. After the sun sets, we move to the couch, trading tea for wine, and our conversation turns to Megan's dissertation, an archival study of diary entries from early Mexican American immigrants. The project sounds fascinating—and difficult—and I'm reminded how smart Megan is and how different our worlds are. I wonder again how compatible we might be.

"What's the deal with your professor?" I ask. "Neil." Then I correct myself. "Dr. Stephenson. Is it weird for a professor to hang out in a bar with one of his students?"

She explains that he's a widower and she's encouraged him to come to the Outpost instead of drinking alone at home.

"I'm a PhD student, not some naïve undergrad," she says. "I know Neil's got an ego the size of Texas and sometimes you can't get him to shut up, but he's a good mentor. I've learned a lot from him."

"Do you think he's got the hots for you?"

"He's old enough to be my father."

"So?"

"No," she says. "With me, once he's had a few drinks, all

he talks about is his wife. He's lonely, but he's not looking to shack up with any of his students."

I nod, seeing Neil in a new light, with a new level of sympathy.

My ex-wife and I were divorced when she died, but still it wrecked me. I can't imagine what it must be like to spend twenty or thirty years with someone and then lose them.

As Megan and I have talked, we've slowly slid closer together on the couch. When I showed up at sunrise, it didn't feel like the time or place to start making out, but we've spent the day together, getting to know one another, and now, with just a little bit of alcohol in our veins, it feels like we're both ready to make things more physical.

"God," I say, staring into her shimmering blue eyes, "I hope you get that job in Waco."

"Let's not think about that right now," she says. "Let's just enjoy the moment."

She leans forward and her warm lips brush against mine. I kiss her softly at first, then with more firmness. My tongue reaches out and finds hers. We shift on the couch cushions and press our bodies together. I hold her close to me with my palm on the small of her back. She untucks my T-shirt and runs her hands up the ridges of my stomach. I lower my mouth to the crook of her neck and kiss her warm skin. She throws her head back and lets out a soft, erotic moan, her thick chestnut hair cascading down the arch of her back. She runs her fingertips up the inside of my thigh, shooting electricity into my bloodstream, and now it's my turn to let out an involuntary moan.

"Take me to bed," she whispers in my ear.

I don't argue.

Megan throws her legs around my waist, and I lift her into the air. I hold her up, her arms around my neck, and we don't stop kissing as I shuffle toward the door to her bedroom. I lay her down on the sheets and we kiss. I raise myself onto my knees and strip off my T-shirt. She reaches to my belt and tugs the strap free from the buckle.

A loud knock comes from the front door. She and I freeze, like high school kids caught by their parents. Her expression tells me she's wondering the same thing I am: who is it and—more importantly—can we ignore them?

"Open up!" a familiar voice shouts. "We got a report that a Texas Ranger is being held hostage here by a beautiful teacher-slash-bartender."

"Shit," I say, giving Megan an I-can't-believe-this-is-happening smile. "It's Carlos."

She lets out a good-humored groan.

"Worst timing ever," she says with a laugh.

CHAPTER 52

"HEY, PARTNER," CARLOS says when I open the door. "Ride with me over to the airport, and I'll rent a car there. You can have your truck back and be on your way."

Carlos looks like a Texas Ranger should, Stetson atop his head, shirt pressed, pants unwrinkled, star on his chest polished to glint in the porch light. Seeing him makes me feel like I've let the whole state of Texas down.

"So you heard from Ava?" I say, feeling ashamed that I didn't call him today.

"Yeah," he says, shrugging. "Seems like Ryan Logan had it in for you from the start."

His demeanor suggests that nothing is wrong, that he isn't bothered by the turn of events, but I know that's just an act. And it's working. The suggestion that me turning tail and heading home isn't a big deal hurts even more than if he'd tried to reprimand me in some way.

I invite him in while I put on my boots and get my stuff. He tips his hat to Megan, who offers to get him a glass of water or sweet tea, which he declines. Carlos's wandering eyes stop on the shirt hanging from the curtain rod. He appraises the bullet hole but doesn't say anything.

I wish I could read his mind.

I turn toward the bedroom, where my duffel bag is, to get my gun and a change of clothes. I know I won't be doing any sort of official Ranger business, but still I feel like I should dress the part. Carlos looks like a Texas Ranger action figure fresh out of the box—I should at least try to look professional.

Before I get to the bedroom door, I turn and ask Carlos if he just got back from Houston.

"I stopped and got the feather from Ava," he says. "Dropped them both off at the lab. Then I came here."

"Have you had dinner?" Megan asks. "You want a bite to eat before you hit the road?"

He declines. A few minutes later, I'm ready.

Megan walks onto the porch with us. The dark sky is filled with gray, frothy clouds, and gusts of wind push the trees of the neighborhood around.

I kiss Megan goodbye, telling her that I'll be back. Her hair dances in the wind. "I'll wait up," she says, and winks.

Carlos and I head toward the truck, both veering to the driver's side.

"Oops," he says, laughing. "Mind if I drive your truck one last time before turning her over to you?"

I concede, and once I'm in the passenger seat, I say, "Look, Carlos, about what happened..."

He waves me off. "You don't have to explain a thing."

Again, this nonchalance bothers me more than any other kind of reaction I might have anticipated. I expected him to argue and try to convince me to fight Ryan for a place on the team. Or perhaps we would commiserate together. We could both bitch about how unfair it is. But this reaction—not caring at all, or at least pretending not to—bothers me more than I would have expected.

"Before we go to the airport," Carlos says, "mind if we make a quick stop?"

"No problem," I say, not knowing what else to say. He is driving, after all.

"Where are we going?" I ask, then make an attempt at a joke. "Is there a sale on pizza somewhere?"

He ignores my attempt at humor and says, "Just going to see somebody."

I start to feel nervous. What does he have up his sleeve?

A few minutes later, we pull into the University Medical Center of El Paso, which I recognize because Carlos and I stopped here after the raid to try to see the man who'd been shot by Llewellyn Carpenter. The agent, whose name is Marvin Mercer, had been in surgery at the time.

"Let's go check on him," Carlos says. "What do you say?"

"Have you heard from Ryan about his status?" I ask.

Carlos shakes his head. "Nope. I figure we owe it to him to at least check."

My stomach is in knots as we walk through the halls of the hospital. Carlos stops at a nurses' station and tells a man in scrubs that we're looking for Marvin Mercer, an FBI agent brought in after the recent raid.

He looks back and forth between us, registering that it's a couple of Texas Rangers making the request.

"I suppose I can let you see him," the man says, "but he won't know you're there. He's in a coma."

CHAPTER 53

WHEN WE PUSH through the door to his room, we spot Marvin Mercer lying unconscious on the bed, various tubes and wires hooked up to him. Sitting next to the bed, keeping an eye on him, is an agent from the task force I recognize from the crime scene. She wears business attire, and I get the impression she came straight from her shift to the hospital.

"Sorry to interrupt," Carlos says, taking off his hat in a polite gesture.

I do the same.

"It's no trouble," the agent says, rising and introducing herself as Kara Prince. She says she's known Marvin since they were in the FBI academy together.

There are only two chairs in the room, and she offers them to us. Carlos and I decline and position ourselves next to the bed, looking down at Marvin. His eyes are closed and his skin is as pale as a corpse, but his chest rises and falls in a regular rhythm. There's an oxygen tube up his nose, and a nearby monitor informs us of the steady *beep beep beep* of his heartbeat.

"How is he doing?" I ask, my voice cracking.

"Don't know yet," she says. "A bulletproof vest doesn't do much to stop a shotgun at point-blank range."

My breathing becomes shallow. Kara notices and says, "Ranger, you don't have anything to feel guilty for. It's not your fault."

I nod, but I don't feel good about what I'm seeing.

Carlos is looking at me more than Marvin, and I meet his gaze.

"Was this your plan?" I say. "You'd bring me in here to see this, then try to tell me I should stick around?"

"I didn't really have a plan," Carlos says, "but, yeah, if you want my opinion, I don't think you should go."

Kara looks up at us in confusion. "Do you two want to be alone?" she asks.

"We'll step out into the hallway," Carlos says, putting his hat on and tipping the brim.

"I'm sorry for what happened to your friend," I say on my way toward the door.

As we're about to walk out, Kara says to me, "You're not leaving the task force, are you?"

Carlos answers for me. "Agent Logan kicked him off."

Her eyes go wide, then turn angry. She tells us that all the other agents have been glad to have us on the team. "What you guys did at the warehouse, the way you raced in there, you've got nothing but respect from everyone on the task force." Then she gestures toward Marvin, lying unconscious on the bed. "He would tell you the same thing if he could."

"Thank you," I say, and tip the brim of my hat as we walk into the hall.

Just outside the door, Carlos and I stop and stare at each other under the LED lights.

"It's your choice whether you go back to Waco or not," he says, "but before you leave, I want to say something."

I nod, and we wait for a nurse to walk by.

"You asked me before why I became a Texas Ranger," he says. "I did it because I believe in the idea of the Texas Rangers. Sure, there are plenty of black marks in the history of the Rangers. Hell, the Rangers used to run people who looked like me out of the state. The modern Rangers—the *idea* of the modern Rangers—is to fight for what's right, no matter what. No matter the obstacles."

"What would you have me do?" I say.

"Be a goddamn Texas Ranger," he says, gesturing to the star on my chest. "Or take that off."

A doctor and a nurse walk by, pretending not to notice two Texas Rangers engaged in a heated conversation in the hallway of the hospital.

"Ryan kicked me off the task force," I say, hating the whining sound in my voice. "I did my best. He still kicked me off."

Carlos grimaces. "I don't give a damn about Ryan Logan and his ego. I don't give a damn about some federal task force. You don't work for the FBI—you work for the State of Texas. You took an oath to protect the people of Texas, and I don't care if the whole Federal Bureau of Investigation stands in your way, I expect you to do it."

I don't say anything. My heart is pounding. Part of me feels like I'm a kid being lectured by my dad. Part of me feels like I'm a teenager being given a pep talk by my football coach. Another part feels, even though Carlos and I are equals, like I'm being told what I need to hear by a superior officer.

Carlos might not be a lieutenant yet.

He might never be.

But in this moment, he's *my* lieutenant.

"If I stick around," I say, "Ryan might kick you off the task force, too."

"We don't need the FBI," he says. "The FBI needs us."

I take a deep breath. I think about what I told Megan, how if I stick around, I'm bound to take a bullet one of these days. Will I end up like Marvin Mercer on the other side of this hospital door, unconscious and one step from death's door?

Will I have to give my life?

"All right," I say. "I'm in."

His only response is a nod of the head.

"I'm sorry for my . . ." I trail off, not sure what to call it. *My moment of weakness?*

"No need to apologize to me," he says, "but you might have to earn back Ava's trust."

"I will," I say.

He suggests the three of us should meet first thing in the morning at the tribal police headquarters.

"I've got some information that I want to share with you," he says.

As we're about to leave, Kara, the FBI agent, pokes her head out from Marvin Mercer's hospital room.

"I didn't mean to listen in, but you guys were pretty loud," she says. "You might want to know that police have recovered a vehicle they think was Llewellyn Carpenter's."

"Where?" Carlos asks.

"Right here in El Paso," she says. "EPPD is on the scene. Last I heard, Ryan Logan was flying back from Phoenix. Wheels on the ground any minute. If you hurry," she adds, looking around as if someone might be listening in, "you might be able to beat him there."

CHAPTER 54

CARLOS AND I jog through the parking lot to my truck.

"I'm driving," I say, and he tosses me the keys without argument.

With the lights and sirens going, we speed through the streets. Within minutes, I pull into the entrance of Ascarate Park and drive past a playground and baseball diamond on my way to a cluster of vehicles with flashing blue lights. The crime scene is in a parking area next to a fishing lake about forty or fifty acres wide. A handful of EPPD vehicles, their blue lights reflecting on the black surface of the lake, surround a van that looks just like the one Llewellyn Carpenter fled in when I saw him at the brothel in Phoenix. A flatbed tow truck has backed up, ready to load the vehicle.

We duck under the police tape without asking permission and approach the van.

"Wait just a goddamn minute!"

Ryan Logan approaches from the side.

My heart sinks. Looks like we didn't beat him here after all.

"What are you doing here, Yates?" he sneers. "I told you I didn't want to see you anywhere near my crime scenes."

"Who says this is your crime scene?" I snap. "Last I heard El Paso was in Texas. And you see this here." I point to the star on my chest. "This means I'm a Texas Ranger."

He glares at me, and I glare back. We're only a few feet apart, and the tension between us fills the air like static electricity ready to explode. The wind gusts around us, and across the lake, blue serpents of lightning snake from the clouds to the horizon.

"You see this?" he says sarcastically, pulling out his badge, "this means I work for the United States government. If you want to get into a jurisdictional pissing match, be my guest. What do you think your commander is going to say if he gets a call from the attorney general of the United States?"

"He'll probably tell him, 'This is Texas—you feds either help my boys or you get the hell out of their way.'"

Ryan harrumphs. Around us, every EPPD officer and FBI agent has frozen, watching the confrontation. It's like an impromptu match between two heavyweights has just broken out, and they have ringside seats. Ryan and I have gone a few rounds before, but those were just warm-up bouts. This time, I intend to fight Ryan Logan with everything I've got.

"Rory, you've only been involved in one little part of this investigation. I'm overseeing the whole damn thing. Did you know that every single person we've arrested has shut their mouth tighter than a clam and we can't get a bit of new intel from them? We've rescued all these women, but we haven't stopped the people at the top. Whoever they are, they're going to either get away scot-free—or rebuild.

"Go ahead and pat yourself on the back for saving a few women and nabbing a couple bad guys," he continues. "It's my job to bring down the whole empire. Don't forget that you're just a tool for me, an instrument, and you've proven more trouble than you're worth. You're easily replaced."

As much as I want to tell him to go fuck himself, I try to keep my comments slightly more professional.

"Even though you don't seem to have any respect for me," I say, "I have a hell of a lot of respect for you, Ryan. You're a good agent. I can tell that. You're juggling who knows how many agents and officers, coordinating efforts in multiple cities and states. You've got a responsibility I've never had to deal with. But I know a thing or two about working with other people. I'm a Texas Ranger, and my job is to range across the state, helping different agencies and sheriff's offices, and the way you're going about it isn't the best way. You push people around, and anyone who doesn't bend to your will, you cast them aside. Let this lowly Texas Ranger give you some advice. You need to learn to work *with* people."

"Rory," he snaps, "I don't need your advice. I'll do my job however I damn well please. You're welcome to go home and do yours the way you want."

"That's the thing, Ryan. This is Texas. I am home. I'm going to investigate crimes in my state, and if you don't want to work with me, you damn sure better not work against me."

He glares at me, visibly angry. But he knows he's not getting rid of me. I hate to embarrass him in front of all his subordinates, but he didn't leave me much choice.

"Fine," he says finally. He sweeps his arm toward the van. "You're free to examine the crime scene. You've got five minutes. We need to get this van out of here before the sky opens up and the rain washes away all our evidence." As I start to move, he adds, "Don't touch anything. And if you see anything worth noting, you tell me. No keeping secrets."

"I wouldn't dream of it," I say, stepping past him. "I know how to work *with* people."

CHAPTER 55

AS CARLOS AND I approach the van, Ryan shouts to all the people who've been watching our melee, "All right, show's over. Go back to work. Or turn in your resignation. I don't give a damn which."

I catch a few glances from the agents and officers on scene, all of them displeased with Ryan. He's losing the respect of his team. I can see it.

Why can't he?

Carlos pats me on the shoulder and says quietly, "If Ava had been here, that would have done the job to regain her trust."

"Thanks," I say, and the two of us circle around the van, looking for anything that might give us a clue to where Llewellyn Carpenter—and Marta Rivera—might be now.

Agents have left the side doors and the rear door open, but no one is dusting for prints. I'm guessing they want to get the vehicle to the crime lab for that, although judging by the clouds overhead, I'm not sure they'll make it.

In Phoenix, with the bright sunlight, we were able to spot the smudges left behind by Marta's fingerprints. But now it's almost midnight, and the glare of industrial work lights—not to mention flashing bulbs from atop the cruisers—makes it impossible to spot any kind of print with the naked eye. If Marta Rivera has left us another hidden message, we'll have to wait to see what it is.

Carlos and I turn our attention to the cab of the van, which is empty except for a large Styrofoam soda cup from a gas station. Otherwise, there's nothing of interest. No massage parlor brochure stuffed into the remaining cup holder. Nothing in the glove box, which is hanging open.

I ask one of the techs if he's willing to lift the cup so we can look underneath. He seems put out by the request, but he doesn't say no. First, though, he takes pictures to preserve its original position, then—with rubber gloves on his hands—raises the cup. Underneath is some kind of paper, scrunched into the bottom of the cup holder.

I lean forward to get a better look, shining a flashlight so I can see clearly.

"Don't touch it," the tech cautions.

I tilt my head left and right, trying to make it out. When I figure out what it is, my breath catches in my throat.

"It's a receipt from the Speaking Rock casino," I say. "On the Tigua Pueblo."

"From when Marta was kidnapped?" Carlos asks.

"No," I say. "It's time stamped. It's from earlier today. He must have stopped there and cashed out some chips before dumping the van here."

"Why would he do that?" Carlos wonders.

What I'm wondering—but not saying aloud—is what did he do with Marta when he was in the casino doing who knows what. It's entirely possible he injected her with heroin and left her in the back of the van, but he might have dropped her off somewhere. Another brothel or another warehouse.

"Let's go check it out," I say to Carlos.

"Should we tell He Who Shall Not Be Named?" Carlos asks.

"Yeah," I say. "I promised him I wouldn't keep any secrets."

We go in search of Ryan Logan, who is leaning against a police vehicle with his phone to his ear. He sees us and we wait at a distance until he's finished.

"What now?" he says, pocketing his phone.

Carlos explains what we found.

"We're going to go check it out," I say, then reluctantly add, "If you want to send someone with us, you're welcome to."

Carlos adds, "Technically, I'm still on your task force. So if you want to consider me as your representative, I can do that. Unless you kicked me off, too."

He glares at us. I know he wishes we would just disappear.

"Fine," he says. "Tell me if you find anything."

As Carlos and I head toward the truck, I say to him, "You know, when Ava and I found that brochure for the massage parlor in Phoenix, that felt like Carpenter made a mistake. He screwed up by leaving that behind. But this," I add, "it's hard to believe he'd make the same mistake twice."

Carlos says that Carpenter probably never thought we'd

find the car in Phoenix. He might not even know that's how we found the massage parlor. And as for the van, it was pretty well emptied out. Maybe he forgot about the receipt under the cup.

"Maybe," I say, starting the truck's engine. Once we're headed toward the Pueblo, I ask, "Do you want to call Ava and tell her we're headed her way?"

"Yeah," Carlos says, pulling out his phone. "It's time to get the band back together."

CHAPTER 56

TWENTY MINUTES LATER, Carlos and I wait for Ava next to a sculpture near the front entrance of Speaking Rock Entertainment Center. With lights shining from below, the bronze statue shows a muscular man with his arms spread, feathers hanging from them like wings. The sculpture is perched above a pool of water, glowing blue from lights below the surface. A stage has been erected next to the statue, but whatever concert they've set up for isn't happening tonight.

The wind has died down to a stiff breeze, and the clouds overhead are breaking up. The sky had been threatening to rain, but it hasn't carried through on the threat.

Ava approaches in her uniform, all business, and gives me a curt nod.

"You're back?" she says.

"I'm sorry," I say, then gesture to Carlos. "I just needed someone to remind me why I wear this badge."

Carlos smacks me on the back.

"Rory was just constipated," he says, and even Ava can't help but crack a smile at his remark. "He's had a healthy bowel movement," Carlos continues, "and now he's ready to get back to work."

We all laugh together, and, at least for now, the tension of the reunion has been alleviated. Without further discussion, we head inside.

Though nothing by Las Vegas standards, the casino is larger than I expected—and bustling with activity. The light is dimmed. The building has multiple wings, all packed with slot machines, where patrons sit drinking from daiquiri glasses and beer bottles. On one side of the casino is a large bar, with flat-screen TVs displaying various late-night recaps of the day's sporting events. On the other side is a room with a BINGO sign above the entrance. The air is filled with the noise of the slot machines electronically mimicking the sound of coins spilling into trays.

We make our way through the maze of machines to the cashier's cage, where we let Ava do the talking. She asks to speak with a manager, and a minute later, a Tigua man approaches. He has short hair graying at the temples and wears a white shirt with a black bolo tie. Ava, who apparently knows him, introduces us.

"We're looking for this man," Carlos says, showing him a photo of Llewellyn Carpenter. "Apparently he cashed some chips in today and got a receipt."

We tell the manager we'd like to look at security footage before and after the time the receipt was stamped. He looks skeptical, like he doesn't want to get involved with two Texas Rangers, but Ava says, "You'd really be doing us a favor, Xavier."

He relents and tells us to follow him. He leads us to an employee door tucked out of sight, and then the three of us walk down a well-lit hallway to a door marked SECURITY. He leads us inside, where a uniformed guard mans a bank of computer screens. Xavier tells the man the time of the stamp, and the guard rewinds one of the computer screens.

A minute later, we're looking at the black-and-white image of Llewellyn Carpenter walking up to the cage to buy chips. It's clearly him, the snake tattoo visible on his forearm as he reaches for the receipt the teller hands him. He walks away from the counter with a rack of chips, but within a few seconds, he pulls his phone out of his pocket and appears to answer a call. He looks around and walks back to the counter of the cage—off to the side this time, where he won't be in anyone's way—and sets the chips down. He pulls a pen or pencil from his pocket and writes something on the back of his receipt. A minute later, he hangs up the phone and pockets it.

He stares at whatever he's written.

"He's memorizing it," Carlos says.

Thirty seconds later, Carpenter wads up the piece of paper and looks around for a trash can. There's one in a nearby corner, and he tosses the balled-up receipt toward it.

"He missed," Ava says, almost breathless.

"Back up the video," Carlos says. "Please."

The guard rewinds the recording. He tries to zoom in but the picture only gets blurrier. Still, it looks like Ava is right. The ball of paper overshoots the can and lands behind it on the floor, hidden in the corner behind the bin.

On the screen, we watch as Carpenter returns to the cage and cashes in the chips he just bought. He receives another receipt, which he pockets.

"That's the one we found," Carlos says. "Let's go see if we can find the one he threw away."

We rush back down the hallway and into the casino, leaving the manager and guard behind. It takes a moment for us to orient ourselves within the clanging labyrinth of slots, but soon we hurry past the machines on our way to the cage.

In my mind, I'm preparing myself for the fact that the receipt will be gone. Whoever comes around to empty the garbage bins will have noticed it and thrown it away. We'll have to confiscate all the garbage in the dumpster and ask Ryan to okay a team of techs to sift through it.

But when we arrive at the garbage can, the wadded-up receipt is still there, wedged into the corner with some napkins and a used coffee cup that also didn't make it into the trash bin. Carlos puts on a pair of gloves before reaching down to pick up the receipt. Slowly he unfolds it.

On the back, written in sloppy cursive handwriting, is an address and nothing more.

The address is on Old Pueblo Road.

"Isn't that the road we're on right now?" I ask.

Ava nods.

"I know where that is," she says, looking up at Carlos and me. "It's the old Tigua community center. It's been abandoned. They're building a new one and haven't made up their mind whether they should tear it down or use it for something else."

I remember seeing it when Carlos and I drove onto the Pueblo to meet Ava for the first time.

"What the hell would Carpenter want there?" Ava says.

"I don't know," I say, "but let's go find out."

CHAPTER 57

RYAN LOGAN STANDS in the garage bay where a half dozen CSI technicians go over the van they've impounded. Bright construction lights have been set up around it, giving everyone plenty of light to see by. They're dusting for prints, scouring for DNA—soon they'll dismantle the whole thing to look for any contraband or other kinds of evidence hidden deep inside.

Ryan is supposedly supervising what's going on, but his mind is elsewhere. He's thinking about Rory Yates.

He's mad at the Texas Ranger.

But he's also mad at himself.

He's upset that he let Rory get away with talking to him like that, angry with the Ranger for meddling with his investigation. But, if he's honest with himself, he knows his anger is mostly—if not entirely—born from jealousy. He hates

Rory for being his equal in the charity shoot—and for being more than a match for him in the field.

Rory's legend has only grown since he joined the task force. Ryan's afraid his own has diminished. He wants the kind of admiration Rory has earned.

Ryan has never fired his gun in the line of duty, and until that day comes, he'll never get the kind of respect and approbation he wants. It doesn't matter how many shooting competitions he wins. It doesn't matter even if he could beat Rory at next year's charity shoot.

He needs to be tested in a real gunfight.

Rory makes it look easy. He's a natural. The way he and Carlos rushed into the gunfight at the raid left Ryan awestruck.

He is jealous of Rory Yates and self-aware enough to know that he shouldn't be—that it isn't professional. He'd tried to set aside his jealousy. When Rory and his team had wanted to travel to Colorado and Arizona, Ryan thought this would be a good way to keep him out of sight. He wasn't banishing Yates to a wild goose chase. Yates was banishing himself.

He certainly hadn't expected Rory to almost single-handedly take down one of the brothels, rescuing four more women and—again—proving himself to be a genuine hero to the members of the task force. Ryan had snapped when he kicked Rory off the team. But the decision—more of an emotional response than any sort of conscious, thoughtful judgment—had backfired. Not only had it not gotten rid of Rory, but it had also weakened Ryan's esteem in the eyes of his team members.

They think even more highly of Rory now, he's sure. And they think Ryan was acting petty, jealous, small-minded.

Juvenile.

And the worst part is that Ryan agrees with them. He has to stop competing with Rory Yates. He has to find a way to work with him, not against him. He has to get Rory back over to his side. Even if there were no other reason, he needs to do it to win back his team.

"Sir?"

Ryan shakes himself from his thoughts. An agent standing next to him making a report asks, "Did you hear me?"

"Sorry," Ryan says. "Please start over."

"I just wanted to tell you about the car. We were able to track down a previous owner. He sold it on Craigslist about a month ago."

Ryan nods. It had been the same with the previous vehicles they'd recovered. The plates were stolen. But not the cars.

"I'm not sure it makes much difference," Ryan says, "but at least we know."

The agent nods and starts to back away, but then one of the techs shouts for Ryan to come over to the van.

Ryan walks to the back of the van, where the doors are hanging open.

"You'll want to see this, sir."

The techs have applied fingerprint powder to the inside of the doors and now dozens of prints are easily visible. Whoever left them—Marta Rivera, they assume—arranged her fingerprints into words.

On the door to Ryan's left, a message reads:

TAKING ME

TO MR Z

But that isn't all. On the inside of the other door, she's written the message:

RANGER

TRAP

Ryan stares at the words.

"Should we call Yates?" the agent next to him says. "Or Castillo?"

Ryan grabs his phone from his pocket and scrolls through the contacts. He holds the phone to his ear, looking nervously at the other agent. Carlos's number goes straight to voicemail. He tries Rory's.

"Come on, Rory," he mutters. "Pick up the damn phone."

CHAPTER 58

AS WE COME out of the casino, we spot a woman walking ahead of us through the parking lot, wearing a white blouse and a puffy black skirt over dark hose—the work uniform of a casino employee, I assume. The woman has a slight limp and it dawns on me who she is. Apparently Ava is one step ahead of me.

"Isabella?" Ava says loud enough for the woman to hear.

Isabella Luna, the woman we believe might have been the first eagle feather victim, turns around and greets us with a puzzled expression. I'd forgotten she worked at the restaurant inside the casino.

Recognition fills her face after a brief moment of confusion.

"Hi, Ava," she says, stopping so we can approach. "What are y'all doing here?"

"Working on a case."

"The missing girls who disappeared on the solstice, like me?"

"No," Ava says. "Another one."

"I guess y'all are busy, aren't you?"

"Busier than a one-legged man in an ass-kicking contest," Carlos says, and this makes Isabella smile.

"Guys," Ava says, "can I talk to Isabella alone for a minute?"

Carlos and I let her. We're in a hurry, but we also know this conversation could be important.

"We'll bring the truck around," I say.

A minute later, Carlos and I drive up to where the two women are talking. They're chatting like old friends. I'm antsy to get going, but I know Ava must be feeling the same way. She wouldn't linger like this if she didn't have a good reason.

"How are you holding up?" I ask Carlos, remembering that he spent the whole day driving from Houston to El Paso, and he's been busy with me ever since. "You didn't have dinner, did you?"

"I'm okay," he says. "Who needs food when you've got adrenaline?"

My eyes drift to the clock on the dash. It's just after 3:00 a.m. Carlos checks his phone and comments that the battery is dead.

"Shit," I say aloud, remembering that I never called Megan to tell her I wouldn't be back tonight.

I pull out my phone and debate whether to call or text. Even if she was trying to stay up for me, I'm sure she's drifted off to sleep by now.

I'm a terrible boyfriend, I text, hoping the sound of the phone doesn't wake her and she gets it in the morning. Carlos and I got busy working on a case. I don't know when I'll be finished.

I send the text and pause for a moment considering whether I should write a follow-up message. I type, By the way, I'm staying a Texas Ranger. Probably until I die. I hope you're okay with that.

But before I can press Send, my phone starts ringing.

It's Megan.

"Did I wake you?" I ask.

"I'm a night owl," she says. "I'm usually just getting home from work about now."

I tell her I can't talk long and apologize again for not contacting her earlier.

"That's okay," she says, "I'm just grinning from ear to ear that you called yourself my *boyfriend*."

I hadn't even realized I'd done it. I'm glad she can't see me now because I can feel the blood rushing to my head.

"I'm going to change my Facebook profile right now," she quips.

Outside the windshield, Ava gives Isabella a hug and then heads toward the truck. My phone beeps in my ear, and I see that it's Ryan Logan calling me.

"I better go," I say to Megan. "I'll call you tomorrow."

"I take it you're not hanging up your hat?" Megan says.

"Is that okay?" I ask, wondering if she was hoping I would quit for good. Willow would have been happy if I'd quit, I'm sure.

"It's fine with me," Megan says. "You look damn fine when you're all gussied up in your hat and badge."

Carlos scoots over and Ava slides in next to him. I tell Megan again that I need to go.

"Be careful," Megan says, and then adds with exaggerated emphasis, *"boyfriend."*

I try to switch over to the call from Ryan Logan, but I've missed him. I consider calling him back, but before I can mention that he called, Ava says, "You know we don't really need to drive. It's just right over there."

She points through the windshield. In the gloom of the streetlights, the dark building with boarded-up windows is visible from where we are.

"Well, we're already in the truck," I say, shifting into gear. "Might as well drive over."

"What did you and Isabella talk about?" Carlos asks Ava as I drive.

"She's agreed to let me interview her again," Ava says. "Just me. I think I might be able to get her to open up if it's just the two of us."

"Excellent work," Carlos says. "It was probably a mistake for Rory and me to be there the first time. Maybe what she needs is to talk to a fellow Tigua. And a woman."

"And a friend," I add, regretting that I shot down Ava's original idea of talking to her one-on-one.

We don't have time to talk anymore. I'm pulling up to the old community center already.

And I've forgotten all about calling Ryan Logan back.

CHAPTER 59

I DRIVE INTO a parking lot with weeds growing up through its many cracks. The building is a large, two-story adobe structure. The outside walls are as cracked as the parking lot and have been sporadically tagged with graffiti. Plywood sheets are nailed over the windows.

A temporary chain-link fence has been erected around the building, with tumbleweeds and garbage trapped in the links. The gate to the fence had been chained closed, but it looks like the chain has been broken by bolt cutters or a hacksaw.

I circle around the building once and note another panel van parked at the far end of the lot. We stop by it first, finding it unlocked but empty. But the presence of the van—Carpenter's vehicle of choice—makes us think Carpenter might still be inside the building.

As we approach, we notice the entry doors had also been

chained, and those chains have also been cut and left lying on the sidewalk.

The front door squeaks as I swing it outward. Inside is pure blackness. The tile on the floor under my flashlight reminds me of my high school, the pattern outdated, the colors scuffed from wear. There is a front desk area and a bank of chairs bolted to the floor. The vinyl of the chairs is cracked and spilling stuffing. As I sweep my flashlight across the spiderwebs underneath the chairs, a black widow scurries into the shadows.

Carlos flicks a light switch, but nothing happens. No doubt the electricity was turned off long ago.

"Hello," Ava calls out. "This is the Tigua Tribal Police and the Texas Rangers."

Her voice echoes and is followed by silence.

"Come out with your hands up," Carlos shouts.

No response.

I have a terrible feeling that, somewhere in the darkness, we're going to find the body of Marta Rivera. We know Carpenter was at the casino then dumped the van ten miles away at Ascarate Park. The only reason I can think that he would have been here was to discard her corpse before switching vehicles. My mind imagines the worst—the young woman raped, tortured, even dismembered, left as a warning to us to back off.

"There are three floors," Ava says, now keeping her voice to barely more than a whisper. "Should we split up?"

"Three?" I say, remembering only two from the outside.

"The ground floor. The upstairs. And the basement."

The lobby splits into two corridors, which, Ava explains, creates a rectangular hallway going around the building. If we split into two groups, each taking a hallway, we'd meet somewhere in the middle. And whichever way we go, somewhere around the halfway mark, we'll come to a stairwell leading up and down.

"Wait," Carlos says, ducking down and shining his light closely at the floor. "Look at this."

Ava and I kneel, as Carlos points out a faint footprint visible on the floor. A thin film of dust covers the ground and, if you look closely, you can tell that someone has walked through here. Now that we know what to look for, we shine our lights forward and see more of the boot treads recorded in the dust from when their owner walked deeper into the facility.

We shine the lights at our own footprints, which look similar, suggesting that the other prints might not be much older.

"I think these tracks are new," Carlos says, his voice barely more than a whisper.

"Let's follow them," I say, keeping my voice down. "Together."

Ava points out that there are tracks going in, but none coming out. Unless he found another way out, Carpenter or whoever else broke into the community center is still inside.

The three of us proceed as quietly as we can into the darkness.

Carlos and Ava lead, side by side, with me in the rear, checking behind us. Our boots make noise on the floor, but we are as quiet as we can be.

Chunks of plaster have fallen off the walls, and a few of the rectangular panels in the ceiling have dropped to the floor, exposing wiring above us. The boot tracks lead in and out of doors, as if the intruder was looking for something. One room contains old tribal decorations stacked against one wall: banners and costumes and drums. Another is used for the storage of old archery equipment: large hole-strewn circular targets along with bows and quivers of arrows leaning in the corner. Another room holds sports equipment, including a rack of deflated basketballs and a wrapped-up volleyball net. A trampoline is folded in half and shoved up against the wall, the canvas fraying and many of the rusty springs hanging loose.

It occurs to me that perhaps the intruder was merely an ordinary burglar looking to steal something of value. If Llewellyn Carpenter was going to discard Marta's body here, wouldn't there be two sets of prints? Or at least marks in the dust where she was being dragged?

We come to a place in the hallway where stairs lead up and down. Here, the tracks become more complicated. Boot marks show the person walking upstairs and downstairs, then more tracks continuing down the hallway on this floor, then more coming back. The tread points in both directions on the upper and lower stairwells.

We don't need to discuss it to understand what we're seeing. We can tell where the intruder went, but — if he's still in the building — we don't know where he is now.

It seems safer if we stick together, but we don't want him — whether it's Carpenter or someone else — to slip out behind us. We're going to have to go different ways.

I indicate that I'll go down in the basement.

Carlos says he'll go up the stairs.

Ava will stay on the ground floor.

"Be careful," I whisper. "And call out if you need help."

With that, I descend alone into the blackness of the basement.

CHAPTER 60

CARLOS JOGS QUICKLY up the stairs, keeping his light beam steady in front of him, his Colt leveled and ready to fire.

At the top landing, the boot tracks travel down a dark corridor and veer left into a doorway. Carlos hurries to the door and tries the handle. It's unlocked, so he yanks the door open and swings his gun and light inside. The room is packed with exercise equipment, large mats folded up and shoved against a wall, with upright punching bags filling the rest of the space. Some of the bags are cylinders with tufts of padding coming out of holes, but others are meant to look human, with muscular foam torsos and heads with scowling faces. Carlos darts his flashlight around, making sure none of the human forms are actually people.

As far as Carlos can tell, the tracks go into the maze of boxing bags, but no tracks come out.

He sweeps his light across the room, spotting a window on the other side. Through broken glass, he can see the lights of El Paso. If there had been plywood covering the window, it's been knocked down.

He wonders if there's a fire escape over there or perhaps some kind of scaffolding. The window might be low enough that the intruder could jump to the ground without too much risk of serious injury.

Carlos steps into the collection of punching bags, easing past them while keeping his gun and flashlight pointed in front of him.

"If you're in here," he says, "identify yourself and come out with your hands—"

He senses movement in his peripheral vision and spins around. A man lunges from the shadows. Before Carlos can get his light or his gun on the person, a heavy metal object smashes into the side of his skull. His knees forget what their function is, and the hardwood floor rushes up toward him. When he crashes down, he rolls over and tries to orient himself. Although he kept his grip on his Colt, the flashlight slipped from his grasp and is spinning on the floor, causing a strobe effect. Carlos can see the lower half of a human: boots, jeans, a hand holding an enormous pair of bolt cutters, at least two feet long.

Black-red liquid drips from the bolt cutters, and Carlos has the numb realization that it's his blood.

He tries to raise his gun, but his attacker's free arm reaches down and grabs the weapon. The flashlight—spinning slower now—completes a turn and illuminates the arm connected to the hand taking his gun away.

A tattoo of a snake coils around the forearm.

Carlos knows he needs to move. Shout. Alert Rory and Ava. Do something!

But his body just doesn't seem to be listening to his mind's instruction. Carlos's head collapses back onto the floor, and his eyes close.

The last thing he is aware of before passing out is the sound of Llewellyn Carpenter's boots walking back across the floorboards.

CHAPTER 61

AT THE BOTTOM of the stairs, I come to large double doors, which had been chained shut, but the cables—just like upstairs—now lie in a heap on the floor. The doors contain small rectangular windows, reinforced with diamond-shaped wire in the glass. I can see nothing but blackness on the other side.

There's a rotten-egg stench in the air. I'm afraid the smell is from some kind of rotting body. Maybe an animal that somehow got stuck down here. Or a human that was dumped.

I swing open the door, aiming my gun and flashlight inside.

The smell intensifies exponentially. A cold chill sluices through my veins when I realize what it is.

Natural gas.

I freeze in my tracks, uncertain whether I should proceed. Apparently they turned off the electricity but not the gas, and somewhere down in this basement is a leak. I know I should alert Carlos and Ava—tell them to get out of the building—but it occurs to me that it's probably just an open valve, which I could easily close.

I holster my gun—if I fired a shot, I'd blow up the whole damn basement—and I take out a handkerchief from my pocket to cover my mouth. I move forward, cautious but quick, into a spacious room with a dozen or more circular tables and stacks of chairs along one wall. Across the room is a counter for serving food, with a rolling divider—like a miniature garage door—separating the dining area from what I assume is the kitchen. I search the dusty floor for tracks and see them leading toward the kitchen. I head that way.

The basement is warm and stuffy, and I can feel my shirt clinging to my skin. I use the handkerchief to wipe a rivulet of sweat running from my hat band down the side of my face. I shine the light under every table I pass.

The smell is overpowering now, and my head is starting to hurt.

I shoulder the door to the kitchen open and shine my flashlight inside. The air is so thick with gas that I gag. My eyes water. I take a step forward and almost fall over when a wave of vertigo hits me. This doesn't seem like such a smart idea now, but I've come this far and I don't want to turn back until I see where the gas is coming from.

An industrial-sized grill, like the kind you'd see in a restaurant, sits across the room, and I hobble toward it, careful of my steps.

I hear gas hissing.

I get to the other side of the stove, and panic grips my heart when I see what's happening.

The pipe coming out of the wall has been cut in two—probably by the same tool that cut the chains—and a thin line of white vapor sprays into the room.

I hear a loud clattering noise in the direction I just came from.

Chains.

I burst out of the kitchen and run across the dining area. Through the small windows on the doors, I spot the light of a flashlight out by the stairwell. The doors themselves rattle as whoever is out there feeds the chains back through the handles.

I draw my gun and give one of the doors a solid kick. The metal door only opens a crack before closing again. I shine my light through the door window to see a man outside the door, his face covered in a gas mask—not your typical paper-thin painter's mask but an air-purifying respirator. Through the Plexiglas face shield, I can tell the man has a scar going through his left eye, just like the image of Llewellyn Carpenter in his mug shot.

I point my SIG Sauer at him through the window.

"Go ahead," he says, his voice muffled but audible through the mask and doors. "You'll blow the whole goddamn building to kingdom come."

CHAPTER 62

AS I AIM my pistol at Llewellyn Carpenter's face, I'm tempted to do as he says. I'd willingly sacrifice my own life to keep the evil son of a bitch from kidnapping any more women. But if I pull the trigger, the explosion will not only kill us; it might also kill Ava and Carlos.

Assuming they're still alive.

Carpenter has a look of demented glee on his face as he steps back from the window.

"Carlos!" I shout. *"Ava! Get out of the building!"*

My throat is thick with mucus, making it hard to breathe. My eyes stream tears, blurring my vision. My head pounds with the worst headache I've ever experienced.

I keep my light on Carpenter, who wears a small knapsack and has a large set of bolt cutters tucked into his belt. Next to the tool is a sight that stops me cold.

Carlos's Colt sticks out of his waistband.

"Ava!" I scream so hard my vocal cords feel like they're going to shred. *"There's a gas leak. Carpenter is going to blow the building up!"*

Working with a bemused grin on his face, Carpenter sloughs off his knapsack and reaches inside, pulling out a small rectangular canister of what looks like lighter fluid. He pops the top off the canister and squirts a stream toward the door. Then he pulls out Carlos's gun and begins ascending the stairs, leaving a trail of flammable liquid behind him.

"Ava!" I roar. *"It's a trap. Get out!"*

I shake the door with all my strength, but the chains won't budge. I might be able to punch out the window—even with the reinforcement wire—but that wouldn't do me any good. It's too small for me to crawl through, and I couldn't simply reach through and unlock the doors. I would need something to break the chains. If not for the gas, I'd shoot through the door until I hit the chains. But the moment the first spark ignites inside the gun, flames would fill the basement and burn me alive. The concussive force might blow the whole building off its foundation.

I pull out my phone to warn Ava, but—it must be because I'm in the basement—I don't have any service.

I spin around and shine my light throughout the room. If my flashlight wasn't already on, I'd worry that it might be enough to ignite the fumes. But it's waterproof, and I assume no gas can get inside where there might be sparks between the contacts.

I'd been so preoccupied lately with all my close calls in gunfights, I figured a bullet was waiting for me in my future.

I never dreamed that the way I'd go would be natural gas poisoning—or being incinerated in a fiery explosion.

It's hard to see because my eyes are streaming water, but I search for windows high on the walls. I don't remember seeing any low windows along the base of the building, and I don't find any here, either.

There's no way a building like this would pass fire code without two exits from the basement. So there must be another way out. The question is can I find it before I pass out?

As I try to take my first step, I collapse onto my hands and knees. I retch thick soapy bile.

If it wasn't for the fact that Ava and Carlos are out there—I refuse to believe that Carlos is dead—I would just take a deep breath and fall asleep. But as long as my partners are still at risk, I can't give up.

I crawl forward through the tables. When I get closer to the kitchen, I notice another door. It's one of those kitchen doors that swings either way, and I put a weak hand against it. On the other side is a long hallway and at the end, a short staircase runs up to what I assume is an outside door. Although I can only see the bottom foot or so of the exit, it looks like another set of double doors.

I rise to my feet and stagger down the hallway, falling on the steps and crawling upward.

The gas is so thick that every breath hurts my lungs. My brain feels like it's on fire inside my skull. I reach the doors and rise to my knees to find the push bar.

But the doors are chained together.

If the doors budged an inch, I might be able to wedge them open and at least put my face to the crack to inhale fresh oxygen.

But the doors won't open at all.

It's over.

I'm going to die.

CHAPTER 63

AVA HAS MADE it all the way around to the lobby again when she hears shouting. She can't quite make out what's being said, but she can tell by the tone that something is wrong.

She draws her gun and runs, aiming her flashlight ahead of her. A figure appears in the beam, backing up the stairway with a gun in one hand and some kind of canister spraying liquid in the other.

She doesn't know who it is, but she can at least tell it's not Carlos or Rory.

"Freeze!" she shouts.

The man turns to her, wearing a gas mask of some kind. Something in his body language and the cut of his hair makes her suspect it's Llewellyn Carpenter. The snake tattoo on his forearm verifies her suspicion.

He doesn't look particularly alarmed by her presence.

"Can you smell it?" he asks, his voice distorted from the mask.

For a moment, Ava doesn't know what he's talking about, but then she smells a sulfurous rotten-egg odor emanating from the stairwell.

Now that she notices it, the air is thick with the stench.

"If you squeeze that trigger," Carpenter says, "the whole basement of this building is going to be one hell of an inferno. Your Texas Ranger buddy is at ground zero. He'll be dead in an instant. But you," he says, nodding into the flashlight beam blasting him in the face, "it won't be quick. You'll run out of the building engulfed in flame, with your eyes melting in their sockets like butter."

"You'll die, too," Ava says.

Carpenter shrugs. "You've got a few options here. Run out now and save yourself. Or try to save one of your friends. The white guy's downstairs breathing gas. Your Indian buddy is upstairs with a cracked skull." Carpenter takes the bottle and starts spraying the liquid again. "Or," he adds, "you can pull that trigger and we all get a taste of what hell feels like before we go there."

The smell of gas is thicker now, nauseating Ava.

"I'm not going to hell," Ava says, and she lowers her gun and runs back down the hall the way she came.

Instead of running outside, she turns into one of the rooms she and Carlos and Rory explored when they first came into the building. She holsters her gun and sprints past the archery targets they saw earlier. In the corner, she finds the bows and quivers of arrows. She snatches one bow, but the string is broken. She tosses it aside and grabs another, taking a second to run the flashlight up and down it to make sure it's functional. Then she yanks an arrow out of a quiver and slides the nock over the string.

It's not a particularly good bow, and the aluminum arrow isn't the quality she normally uses—and it certainly isn't *her* bow, which she's used for years and shot thousands of times.

But it will have to do.

CHAPTER 64

WHEN SHE RUNS back out into the hallway, Carpenter has passed her. She holds her flashlight in her teeth, her hands filled with the bow and arrow, and runs down the hallway. At the doorway, she looks out to find Carpenter by the chain-link fence, circling. The pale blue light of approaching dawn fills the sky behind him.

Ava spits the flashlight out. There's enough light for her to see by.

When Carpenter hears the clatter of the flashlight hitting the ground, he turns to look at her. She's standing just inside the doorway—covered in darkness—and it's likely he can't really see her. Only her shape. He points the gun at her to keep her where she is. He's still grinning, knowing she won't shoot her pistol, won't risk the natural gas reacting with the spark of the firing pin.

He doesn't know she's traded her gun for a bow.

The last spurt of lighter fluid comes out of the bottle, and he discards it. He leans over, placing the gun barrel only inches from the liquid, close enough that the discharge from the Colt will ignite the fluid and carry the flame through the doorway and down the hallway. When it reaches the point where the air is thick with gas, the hallway will burst into flame — probably blasting her out the door like a cork shooting off a champagne bottle.

Ava draws back the bow. She aims it at Carpenter's chest, center mass, but then reconsiders. He's the only one who knows where Marta Rivera is.

She needs him alive.

Carpenter moves his finger inside the trigger guard.

Ava doesn't have time to think. She lets her body remember the hours and hours of training, the years of competition, the way the bow became a part of her.

She lets the arrow fly.

Carpenter must hear the *twang* of the string, because he hesitates, looking toward Ava's shape in the doorway.

The arrow sinks into his forearm, sliding through the radius and ulna bones and stopping two-thirds of the way through. Carpenter roars, dropping the gun with a clatter and staring at the three-foot-long arrow poking through his arm.

"What the fuck?" he screams.

Ava tosses the bow aside and sprints toward Carpenter, who falls to one knee, clutching his forearm. The tip and shaft of the arrow are coated in blood. He hears her pounding footsteps and reaches for the gun with his left hand. Just as he puts his hand on the grip, Ava's boot comes down on his fingers.

Carpenter gasps, looking up at her looming over him.

Ava lifts her other leg and drives the sole of her boot directly into Carpenter's face.

He falls backward, the mask askew, his nose spilling blood. Ava grabs the arrow, holding both sides of the shaft, and drags Carpenter the remaining few feet to the fence. He howls in pain and reaches for Carlos's Colt, but it's too far away now.

When she makes it to the chain-link fence, she pulls out her handcuffs and latches the wrist without the arrow to the metal bar at the bottom of a panel of fencing.

"You're under arrest, you motherfucker," she growls.

She reaches down and rips the mask off his head. The transparent plastic of the face shield is cracked from where she kicked him. She tosses the useless mask aside then yanks the bolt cutters from Carpenter's belt. She scoops up Carlos's Colt and shoves it into her belt, then sprints toward the building, where she picks up her flashlight and keeps running. She debates for a moment who to help first, Rory or Carlos, but Rory is closer to the leak and might be in more imminent danger. She leaps down the steps, taking two at a time, and finds the chained doorway.

She places the bolt cutters around a link and hesitates, fearing the metal-to-metal contact might make a spark.

But she doesn't have a choice.

The gas is so thick here, she can't imagine what it must be like on the other side where Rory is. She presses the two sides of the cutter together and grunts at the effort. The chain snaps and falls to the floor. She rips the door open and shines her light inside.

"Rory!" she shouts.

But there's no answer.

CHAPTER 65

WHEN LLEWELLYN CARPENTER sees the woman run into the building, he takes his cuffed hand and rattles the metal circling the fence pipe. He takes a deep breath and steels himself for what he's about to do.

Then he presses the end of the arrow against the concrete and slides the shaft through the hole in his wrist. He grits his teeth and growls in pain, the veins bulging on his neck. When most of it is through, all but the fletching, he takes the bloody shaft between his teeth and uses his mouth to yank the arrow the final few inches.

Fresh blood spills from the wound as he spits the arrow onto the ground. He sits on his hands and knees, snarling from the pain. He tries to move his fingers and finds that his thumb and forefinger seem to be okay, but the others won't move at all.

In a minute, he's going to knock the temporary fence down so he's shackled to one panel. Then he's going to drag it over to the Texas Ranger's truck and see if the door is unlocked. He's hoping for handcuff keys, but a shotgun might do to blast the fence beam to bits.

All of that is on his to-do list, but there's something else he has to take care of first.

He shoves his fingers into the pocket of his jeans, wincing in pain, and comes out with a Zippo lighter pinched between his thumb and forefinger.

He flicks it open and examines the flame.

It's about a seven- or eight-foot toss to get the lighter to the wet trail of fluid leading into the doorway. In the air, the flame might blow out. Or he might miss.

But he's going to try.

Llewellyn Carpenter isn't the kind of man who quits. Another man would have surrendered when the Texas Rangers and FBI raided the warehouse. Another man would have given up when the Ranger showed up at the brothel.

Llewellyn had gotten away both times.

He might not get away this time, but he'll at least make sure none of those three piece-of-shit cops live to testify against him in court.

He holds the lit Zippo sideways, like a flat rock he's about to skip across water. He moves his arm slowly in a throwing motion, getting a sense for the movement. Finally, he cocks his arm back and lets it fly.

The orange flame soars through the air, hits the pavement, and skids toward the wet spot. The Zippo stops a centimeter outside the wetness, like a shuffleboard disc skidding to a halt just short of the scoring line.

"Shit," Carpenter says, disappointed.

Then he watches as the dancing flame stretches toward the liquid. The wet spot flares up. A six-inch flame darts along the trail of fluid and disappears through the door of the community center. Orange light fills the hallway. He hears a *whoosh*, like a furnace kicking on — only a hundred times louder. Hot air exhales from the doorway, blowing against Carpenter's face. The rectangular entrance fills with a bright fiery light, illuminating a malevolent grin on Carpenter's face.

He laughs like the devil at the pit of hell, ecstatic that he's just claimed three more souls.

CHAPTER 66

AVA TRIES TO run across the basement, but stumbles into a table. Her throat burns. Her lungs ache. She gags, and tentacles of white phlegm dangle from her mouth.

She pushes on, her head spinning.

She looks toward the kitchen and spots a corridor. At the end is the dull glow from another light. She shines her light and locates more stairs—and a person lying motionless on the steps. She staggers forward, finding Rory unconscious, his flashlight discarded on a step beside him.

She doesn't bother to shake him. Instead, she goes straight for the door, positioning the blades of the bolt cutters around the link of the chain. She presses the handles together, but she doesn't seem to have the strength to cut through the metal.

She feels unconsciousness threatening and thinks what a cruel joke it would be if she passed out now.

She heaves with all the strength she has left. The handles snap together and the chain falls away.

She pushes the double doors open to the blue morning light, getting a whiff of the most beautiful clean air she's ever smelled.

"Wake up, Rory," she chokes, trying to rouse him.

She hears a noise—like a jet engine starting up behind her. When she turns to look, warm wind blows against her face. The corridor blazes with a reddish-orange light.

Ava grabs Rory under the armpits and, with a strength she didn't know she had, drags him up the stairs and out into the morning air. She jumps on top of him just as a cyclone of fire explodes out of the doorway like the breath of a dragon. A thunderous *BOOM* fills the air. The boards over the windows on the first floor explode outward, followed by glass shards and spouts of flame.

Ava, keeping her body pinned atop Rory, has never felt such heat. Tendrils of fire thrash above her, and then the dragon's breath retreats into the basement door.

Black smoke billows out.

Ava quickly checks to make sure neither of them is on fire, then she grabs Rory and drags him to the chain-link fence. It's a safe enough distance—for now. Behind them, fire crawls from the windows up the side of the building, like reverse waterfalls of red and yellow flame.

Ava shakes Rory. Tears stream down her soot-covered cheeks as she yells, "Wake up! Rory! Wake up!"

His eyes flicker.

"Don't you die on me, Ranger!" she screams.

He lets out a soft cough, and that seems to open the flood-gates of his lungs. He hacks violently, rolling onto his side, each cough seeming to rip him apart.

"It's okay," she says, patting his back. "Get that shit out of your lungs."

He sits up, taking big wheezing breaths. He blinks and looks around, seeming to understand most of what happened while he was out.

"Where's Carlos?" he croaks, barely able to speak.

"Still inside," Ava says, and they both turn to look at the community center and the columns of flame swelling from its windows and growing by the second.

CHAPTER 67

I CAN'T STOP coughing.

My lungs feel like they're being scraped by a cheese grater.

"Can you walk?" Ava asks.

I nod but don't waste my breath on speaking. She helps me up. While I was in the basement, dawn arrived, and now the air is filled with a soft muted light. Flakes of ash drift down on us, and the air stinks of smoke.

We jog around the building inside the perimeter of the fence—me still hacking terribly—until we find Llewellyn Carpenter trying to push the fence he's been handcuffed to away from the building. He's managed to disengage one panel from the rest of the temporary fencing and is dragging it toward my truck.

I reach into my pocket and grab the key fob. The truck beeps as I lock the doors.

Carpenter spins around, and the look on his face, seeing us alive, is priceless.

Ava runs up and gives him a shove, and he and the fence panel topple over.

"I should kill you," she growls.

"Wait," I say, catching up to her and putting a hand on her shoulder. "We need him."

We're far enough from the building that we're not in immediate danger, but we can feel the heat, like standing next to an open oven. We uncuff Carpenter from the fence and then recuff his hands behind his back. He winces when I click the handcuff ring over his injured wrist.

"You keep an eye on him," I say to Ava. "I'll go look for Carlos."

"You can't go in there," Ava says.

The second floor of the building doesn't seem to be fully engulfed yet, but I'm not sure how to get up there. Through the smoke pouring out of the front entrance, we can see flames consuming the interior walls.

"I have to try," I say.

I circle around the building, looking up and down for another entrance that might not be on fire yet. I find a side door, but the metal handle is hot to the touch, and I can hear the engine of the fire just on the other side.

I keep going, and when I round a corner to the back of the building, I spot a sight that fills me with joy.

It's Carlos.

Hanging out a second-floor window by his fingertips.

I run toward him, just as he jumps down, hitting the blacktop and rolling dexterously with his momentum. I grab him by the shoulders and help him up.

"Are you okay?" I ask, my voice still shredded from all the coughing.

He takes one look at my smoke-stained face and says, "Are you?"

"I'll live," I say, as we move away from the building.

"Me, too," he says, reaching to touch a place on his scalp where his hair is matted with blood. "I'm just embarrassed," he adds. "I can't believe I let that son of a bitch get the drop on me."

"He got the drop on me, too," I say. "Ava took him down."

Carlos stops before we round the corner of the building, grabbing my arm to keep me from walking.

"Is he alive?" Carlos asks.

I nod. "He's got a goddamn arrow hole through his arm, but I don't think he's going to die from it."

"Good," Carlos says. Then, with the building blazing next to us, he adds, "I've got an idea."

CHAPTER 68

I LEAVE CARLOS at the back of the building and run to the front, where Ava has moved Llewellyn Carpenter from the fence to near my truck, his hands cuffed together behind his back.

"There's no way in there," I say. "Carlos is gone."

"Goddamn it," Ava says, her voice cracking and her eyes threatening to spill fresh tears—and not from the smoke in the air.

I hate keeping her in the dark, but Carpenter has to believe Carlos is dead. Ava's reaction is going to make it believable.

Carpenter, blood still dripping from his nose, chuckles at the idea that he got at least one of us.

"I should never have shot you in the arm," Ava growls at him, her emotion showing through uncharacteristically. "I should have put the arrow through that psychopathic brain of yours."

I hold her by the arm, afraid she might take a swing at him.

A fire truck arrives along with a whole host of police vehicles. While Ava keeps guard over Carpenter, I run up to talk to them. Keeping my voice low, so neither Carpenter nor Ava can hear, I tell the responders that the building is vacant as far as we know.

When the first ambulance arrives, we ask a paramedic to wrap Carpenter's arm up. The wound is swelling, and we have to undo his cuffs.

"This man needs to go to a hospital," she says.

"Not yet," I say, and my tone keeps her from arguing.

We put Carpenter in the back of a Tigua cruiser. The rear doors won't unlock and a thick Plexiglas barrier separates the front from the back. Even then, we station one of the Tigua officers by the car.

"If he tries to break out in any way," I say, "shoot him with every bullet you've got in your gun."

The officer nods, unsure if I'm serious.

Ava adds, "Then reload your gun and shoot him again."

With Carpenter safely locked away, I walk Ava away from his car as we watch the firefighters dousing the building with their hoses.

"You told them there's someone inside, didn't you?" Ava asks.

"I need to let you in on a secret," I say, "but you have to show no physical reaction that Carpenter can see."

She nods.

"Carlos is alive."

Her eyes dart toward me and then settle back over the

firefighters. I've got to hand it to her — she can hide her emotions well.

"You're lucky I can't show a reaction," she says, "or I'd smack you."

"I'm sorry for lying," I say, "but the deception was Carlos's idea."

I explain to her what Carlos's plan is, and once she's on board, we ask the Tigua officer if we can take his car, with Carpenter in the back. Five minutes later, Carpenter is sitting in the Tigua Tribal Police station's interview room. With the bandages, we can't cuff his hands together, but we latch his good hand to the eyebolt in the table. He sets the other arm onto the surface of the table. Red spots are starting to leak through the bandages.

"I don't know what the hell you think you're doing," Carpenter sneers. "You need to take me to a hospital."

"We will," I say. "Soon."

"I want a lawyer," he barks. "This ain't justice."

"Justice," I say, "would be injecting you with heroin and letting men pay to rape you. I'd say talking to you for five minutes before taking you to see a doctor is mild by comparison. Especially," I add, waving dismissively toward his arm in an effort to bait his anger, "for such a minor injury."

"Minor injury?" he cries, holding up his bandaged arm. "Does this look fucking minor to you?"

I'm glad he's angry. This might be the only way to save Marta Rivera. Ryan Logan had said that none of the people they'd arrested from any of the raids were willing to say a word about the criminal organization they worked for.

I have to get Llewellyn Carpenter to talk.

Ava and I sit across from him as if this is a normal interview. There's nothing normal about it. We're still wearing our guns, still covered in soot and stinking of smoke, interrogating a suspect who should be in an ambulance right now.

"Don't waste your time, Ranger," Carpenter says. "I ain't saying shit."

"We've got you for kidnapping and attempted murder," I say. "You'll do a good bit of time. A decade at least. Maybe less, if you're lucky."

He stares at me, trying to see where I'm going with this. I made sure to give a low estimate of his future incarceration. I want him to think about the possibility of freedom in ten years.

"But," I add, "killing a police officer is capital murder. A death sentence."

He smirks, but I can tell my words are having an effect.

"If this was any other state, you'd grow old on death row," I say. "You'd have a nice cell all to yourself away from other prisoners while your lawyer filed appeal after appeal. That wouldn't be a bad life, actually. But this is Texas, where the average time spent on death row is less than ten years. That means, a decade from now, you won't be walking out on parole, smelling the fresh air. You'll be lying on a slab while a doctor shoots you up with potassium chloride. If you're lucky, you won't be conscious when your sphincter lets go and you shit your pants."

He glowers at me with his one good eye, burning like a green flame. It gives me satisfaction that I've managed to wipe the smirk off his face.

"That's what's going to happen," I say, "unless you cooperate. If you help us out, on my honor, I will testify in every court hearing you ever have that you shouldn't be given the death penalty for the murder of a Texas Ranger."

I don't mention that I know for a fact he didn't kill a Texas Ranger—that Carlos is alive and well, and on his way to the station now, if not here already.

"We're not waiting for a lawyer," I say to Carpenter. "We're not waiting for the FBI. This is a deal between you and me. It's a onetime offer, and it expires in two minutes."

CHAPTER 69

HIS SMIRK IS back.

"That's not how this works, Ranger," he says. "Cutting a deal takes lawyers and judges and lots of signatures on dotted lines."

"It also takes time," I say, "and that's one thing Marta Rivera doesn't have. My primary goal here is to save her life."

The interview room seems stuffy to me, but it might be that I'm feverish from being so close to the fire—or so close to dying. Either way, I can feel the sweat running down my chest. I hope it doesn't run down my forehead and give Carpenter a clue to how nervous I am. I'm acting tough, but it's a bluff. I need information only he has, and I don't know any other way to get it.

"If we wait to get the FBI and a bunch of lawyers involved," I say, trying to come across as sincere, "then your boss, Mr. Z, is going to know you've been arrested. He's going to move the women he's still got prisoner. He might kill them. And he'll do whatever he can to cover his tracks."

Carpenter shifts in his seat, pleased that he might have some kind of leverage here. His eyes dart to the one-way mirror on the wall.

"Anyone out there watching us?" he asks.

"I don't know," I say truthfully, since I'm not sure if Carlos has shown up yet. I don't mention that we positioned a video camera to record the conversation.

"No one we've arrested associated with these missing women has been willing to roll over," I say. "Maybe they know that if they talk, something will happen to someone important to them. Maybe an accident. Like a gas leak."

Now Carpenter's expression changes to a look something akin to satisfaction. I realize it could very well be that Carpenter is who these other men are afraid of. But he also should know he's replaceable. If he is Mr. Z's enforcer, who the other minions are afraid of, Mr. Z might now be in the market for a new guy to do the kind of dirty work Carpenter does. Maybe he already has such a person, an equal to Carpenter or a subordinate who's been waiting in the wings for this kind of chance. Carpenter's life could be in danger, or the life of someone he cares about, if there is such a person or thing.

"Once he knows you're in our custody, you and everyone or everything you care about could be in danger. You might be an evil son of a bitch, Carpenter, but I'm guessing there's something in this world you care about."

Carpenter seems contemplative for a moment.

"I've got cats," he admits, his tone different now.

"Cats?"

"Yeah, ten of them. At my house in Roswell. The neighbor feeds them when I'm not home."

"I'm guessing Mr. Z won't have a problem threatening your cats to buy your silence. Maybe he'll kill two or three to send a message."

"And how are you going to protect them?"

"I'm going to put Mr. Z in a Texas penitentiary," I say, as if the answer is obvious. "And if you want to shorten your sentence, you can testify against him. But that's a different deal for a different day. I need to catch him first, and that's what this deal is for. All I'm promising is that I'll sit in every courtroom and hearing for the rest of your incarcerated life, and testify that I don't think you deserve the death penalty. I can't keep you out of prison, but I can probably keep you from dying in prison."

He shakes his head. "You'll betray me."

"Carpenter, you're absolute scum," I say. "If anyone deserves to be on death row, it's you. But I keep my promises, and I promise that if you answer two questions for me, I'll shout from the goddamn rooftops that you deserve to live."

Of course, I don't mention how easy my promise will be to keep.

"First," I say, "where is Marta Rivera? Second, who is Mr. Z?"

We sit quietly, staring at each other for almost a full minute. Ava has sat unobtrusively beside me the whole time, letting me do the talking. Which is what I should have done for her during the Isabella Luna interview.

Carpenter takes a deep breath, resigning himself to becoming a rat.

"I dropped Marta off at Mr. Z's house," he says. "That's the last I saw of her."

"His personal residence?"

"There's a building at the back of his property with dorms. Or cells. Whatever you want to call them. He keeps a few girls there. He has clients come over every now and then. But they're mostly for his own use. He likes Indian girls the best."

I feel Ava grow tenser beside me.

"And who is Mr. Z?" I say.

Now he gets a grin on his face, as if he can't help himself. Like a comedian who can't help but smile before delivering a punchline.

"Garrison Zebo," he says, in a tone that suggests I should know who that is.

Ava, always so stoic, recoils an inch or two in surprise recognition.

"Who the hell is Garrison Zebo?" I say.

CHAPTER 70

CARPENTER MAKES A face like he can't believe I don't know.

Ava pulls out her phone, types into the web browser, then holds the phone toward me.

On the screen is an image of someone I recognize but can't immediately say from where. He's a fiftysomething man who is very blond, very tan, and standing with a politician's grin on his face in front of a sign that says ZEBO AUTOMOTIVE.

Then it hits me.

Mr. Z is the car salesman I saw on Megan's TV yesterday.

"Zebo Automotive asked the tribe to hold a Memorial Day car auction at the community center parking lot a few weeks ago," Ava says. "Some of the proceeds were supposed to go to tribal charities." She squints her eyes at Carpenter, who sits before us with a smug expression. "That's how you knew the gas was still on."

Carpenter nods. "They opened the door so Garrison wouldn't have to use a porta-potty. He poked around in the dark while he was in there." He taps his forehead with his bandaged hand. "Mr. Z remembers things, you see, and when he thought about where we should set a trap for you, he figured doing it on tribal property would keep everyone looking in the wrong place."

"Did you abduct any women at the event?"

He shakes his head. "That would draw attention," he says. "I did scope out a few pretty little things for later." He grins and says, "But that was three questions, and I only promised to answer two."

I think for a moment about the case and say, "No wonder you had an endless supply of automobiles at your disposal. That's why none of them were ever reported stolen or missing."

"Automobiles are one thing Mr. Z doesn't have a shortage of." Carpenter chuckles—as if now that we've come to an arrangement, we can share a good laugh together.

But he won't be laughing in a second.

Behind me, the door to the interview room opens. Carlos walks in, holding a white gauze pad to his bloody scalp. Carpenter sees him and he scowls at me, the rage clearly simmering under his skin. With his scarred white eye and his burning green one, he looks truly sinister.

"I thought you were a man of your word," he spits at me.

"I am," I say, rising from my seat. "I promise to tell anyone who wants to know that you did not kill Texas Ranger Carlos Castillo." I gesture with my arms to Carlos. "Which, as you can see, you clearly didn't."

Cops lie in interrogations all the time, but when I give my word, even to criminals, I don't break it. My words might have been deceptive, but I haven't made a promise I can't keep. Any guilt I feel for tricking him disappears easily and is replaced by satisfaction once I remind myself of everything he has done—that this man kidnapped and trafficked women.

We got you, you son of a bitch, I think.

"Ava," I say, "let's move Mr. Carpenter to one of your holding cells until the FBI gets here. Then they can do with him what they want."

Ava nods and moves to unlock the handcuff from the eyebolt on the table.

"Is it time to call Ryan?" Carlos asks me. "Let the feds know what we know?"

I turn my head slightly toward him, a momentary lapse of focus at the worst possible time. The instant I tilt my head away—the fraction of a second where both Carlos and I are distracted—is the same moment when Ava unlatches Carpenter's handcuffs from the table. Carpenter, as quick as a snake, throws his bandaged arm around her neck. With his other hand, he draws her pistol from its holster.

He positions himself behind her, using her as a shield, and wedges her gun under her chin, finger on the trigger—ready to blow her brains onto the ceiling.

CHAPTER 71

CARPENTER'S ONE GOOD eye peeks from around Ava's skull.

"Get your hands up!" he barks. "And move away from the door."

Neither Carlos nor I move — not our hands, not our feet.

"I said get your goddamn hands in the air."

I ignore him and make eye contact with Ava. She looks nervous, but not as scared as she should be. One of the FBI agents said recently that I have nerves of steel, but I feel like my nerves are nothing compared to hers.

She looks a hell of a lot less worried than I feel.

Carpenter has me in a familiar position — with a hostage blocking me from getting a good shot. I can't let him get away again.

"Listen here, Carpenter," Carlos says. "You don't want to do this."

"You listen to me, you stupid fucking Texas Rangers," Carpenter says, "either you put your hands up right now or I'm going to—"

"No!"

It's Ava speaking, not me.

"You listen to me," she says, doing her best to talk with the gun pressed to her chin. "You're going to let go of me and put *your* hands in the air."

Carpenter harrumphs.

"If you don't," she says, "Rory's going to shoot."

"My ass," he says. "He'll hit you instead of me."

"You wouldn't sound so cocky," she says, "if you'd ever seen him shoot. I have."

Carpenter lets out a chuckle, and then he starts barking orders at Carlos and me again. I'm only halfway paying attention to him. My eyes are focused on Ava's intense stare.

"Do it, Rory," she says quietly. "Take the shot."

"It's too dangerous," I say.

All I can see of Carpenter is about an inch of his face, just enough to glimpse his one eye peeking from behind Ava's head. It's a shot I might try with paper targets on a range. But with someone's life at stake, it's too risky.

"I believe in you," she says, and something about the conviction in her voice gives me confidence.

I take a deep breath and focus.

This is what I do, I tell myself, *and there's no one who does it better.*

Carpenter barks, "You go for that gun, Ranger, and I'll blow this bitch's brains out."

"You won't even see my hand move," I tell him. "Drop that gun now or die."

"Go fuck yourself," Carpenter snaps. "There is no way you're that—"

Before he can complete his sentence, my bullet plunges into his one good eye and explodes out the side of his skull. His head jerks back, and his grip on Ava loosens. Ava doesn't move, just lets him slough off her back like molting a snakeskin.

My ears ring from the sound of the shot in such a tight space.

Ava reaches up and touches the side of her face, making sure the bullet didn't nick her.

"I felt it graze my hair," she says. "I felt the heat of the discharge on my face."

"Are you okay?" I ask, holstering my gun and taking a step toward her.

She throws her arms around me and holds me in a tight hug. She was so strong through the ordeal. Now she lets her emotions loose. Feeling her tremble in my arms makes it sink in what just happened—and what could have happened if I'd missed. My limbs start to quake and a wave of sickness washes through me.

"I'm sorry he got the drop on me," she says. "I never should have worn my gun into the interrogation room."

"No need to apologize," Carlos says, putting a comforting arm on her shoulder. "He got us all."

"And I shouldn't have worn my gun into the interview, either," I say, looking down at Carpenter's corpse on the floor.

A sea of crimson is spreading from his skull. "If one of us was going to make the mistake, I'm glad both of us did."

The door bursts open and one of the Tigua officers asks if everyone is okay. We all leave the room — it's a crime scene now — and as we do, we hear some kind of hubbub coming from the lobby.

"I just heard a gunshot," a familiar voice shouts to someone out of sight. "I want to know what the hell is going on."

It's Ryan Logan.

And he sounds pissed.

CHAPTER 72

ON SHAKY LEGS, I follow Carlos and Ava through the building to the lobby. When he sees us, Ryan gapes back and forth between us with a look of astonishment. We're dirty and soot-covered and disheveled, our clothes torn and wrinkled and bloody.

I open my mouth to try to explain what's happened, but before I can get a word out, Ryan rushes forward. I recoil, almost expecting him to hit me, and instead he throws his arms around me. The second time in the last two minutes that I've been fiercely hugged. I'm too stunned to hug him back. My eyes drift over his shoulder to Ava and Carlos. Carlos frowns and holds his hands up in a "beats me" expression.

"I'm glad to see you all alive," Ryan says, letting go of me and shaking Carlos's hand and then, to my surprise, Ava's. "Marta Rivera left another message in the van that said you were walking into a trap. But I couldn't get a hold of you."

I smack my forehead and say, "Shit. I forgot to call you back."

"When I heard on the scanner that there was an explosion and fire on the Pueblo," he says, "I thought for sure you all were dead."

He says he arrived at the scene and got word that we'd been there and left with a suspect. He headed to the station to check to see if we were here, and he heard a gunshot as soon as he opened the door.

"What the hell did I miss?" he asks.

"Let's get you caught up," Carlos says, waving for him to follow us.

Thirty seconds later, we're all standing outside the interview room, looking in at Llewellyn Carpenter's dead body through the one-way glass. Carlos stops the video recording.

I tell Ryan what happened at the community center, then about our interview with Carpenter.

"Sorry we didn't wait to involve you," I say. "Time was of the essence."

Ryan, who doesn't seem the least bit angry at us for doing what we did without his authorization, says that he'll call in a crime scene team to look at the interview room. And he'll have someone check out the van in the parking lot next to the burning building. Maybe there's something useful in there.

"How long before you can get a raid together?" Carlos asks him. "We need to go after Zebo."

"It's not something you can just throw together," Ryan says. "A few days at least. I'm not sure the word of a dead man is going to be enough to get a warrant."

Carlos points to the camera and says the interview is recorded, but Ryan still looks skeptical.

"That's not going to work, Ryan," I say, preparing for an argument. "Zebo is probably looking at the TV right now, waiting for reports of Texas Rangers killed. Or if anyone's been arrested. If he doesn't hear from Carpenter—and if he doesn't hear about any dead Rangers—he's going to know he's compromised."

"We don't even have twenty-four hours," Carlos says. "This time tomorrow, he'll be in the wind."

"And," Ava adds, "we'll never find Marta Rivera."

I'm afraid Ryan is going to feel ganged up on, but as he looks back and forth between us, he genuinely seems interested in our arguments.

"What do you think we should do?" he asks.

"Let's go after him," I say. "Right now. We do it ourselves."

Ryan has an expression on his face like he can't believe what we're asking him to do. But then he looks in at the dead body of Llewellyn Carpenter. It feels like we could end this thing once and for all—today—but if we don't, if the so-called Mr. Z slips through the cracks, we might never bring this case to a close.

Ryan takes a deep breath.

"Rory, our approaches to law enforcement have been at odds since you joined the task force," he says to me. "Maybe it's time I give up the fight and try it your way."

CHAPTER 73

GARRISON ZEBO WATCHES the news coverage of the fire on the seventy-seven-inch television in his spacious living room.

Zebo is wearing a Neiman Marcus cashmere robe, with a pair of Dolce and Gabbana house slippers. His exposed legs are shaved clean and are orange from the tanning bed he has in his bedroom. He sips from a lemon-carrot-ginger drink as he flips through the local channels, trying to find one that has any new information.

So far, the news coverage hasn't revealed much. He settles on one station simply because it has the best imagery: a helicopter view of firefighters hosing down the building while a huge column of black smoke rises into the sky, the haze blotting out the view of Mexico in the distance.

The reporter narrating the coverage doesn't know anything: how the fire started, if anyone was inside, what the building even was used for. All he has to work with are colorful descriptions of the scene, which the camera captures better than he can.

Impatient, Zebo picks up his cell phone and calls Llewellyn Carpenter.

No answer.

He sends a text and asks for an update. He's starting to feel antsy. He's been looking for Carpenter's van in the aerial footage but can't find it. The existence of the fire suggests he was successful, but it's always possible he blew himself up in addition to that Texas Ranger he was after. Zebo doesn't care if Carpenter is dead or alive—as long as he hasn't been arrested.

The anchor explains that the FBI plans to make a statement, and then there are a few moments of discussion between the anchors about why the FBI would be involved at all. Why isn't the fire department making the statement?

A minute later, an agent named Logan appears on camera, standing before a bank of reporters in front of the Tigua Tribal Police Station. This is the same guy who was on the news after the raid, Zebo remembers. At that time, he looked smug and full of himself. Now, with his wrinkled suit and haggard expression, he looks like someone who would like to be anywhere but on TV.

Zebo turns up the volume.

The agent states that there is no word yet on what caused the fire—that will only be known after a full investigation—but he wanted to let the public know that three law enforcement personnel were believed to have been in the building.

The reporters at the press conference bombard the agent with questions, almost none of which he answers.

Why were the law enforcement personnel at the location?

"I can't comment at this time."

Do they suspect the fire was caused by arson or an accident?

"We won't know that until we conduct a thorough investigation in conjunction with the fire department."

But there is one question he answers: Are the law enforcement officers members of the FBI?

"No," the agent says. *"The officers in question are two Texas Rangers and a member of the Tigua Tribal Police."*

The agent cuts off the interview, and Zebo mutes the sound. He pumps his fist in the air like he's been watching a sporting event and his team just scored.

"Two Texas Rangers!" he exclaims.

He reaches for a silver bell sitting on the coffee table. He gives it a hearty ring, and within seconds, his butler arrives. Zebo calls him Alfred, after the stuffy butler in the Batman movies. But the name is meant ironically. His Alfred is more of a bodyguard/head of security than a butler. Zebo's Alfred is six foot six, built like a heavyweight boxer, and clad in tactical gear, with a sheath knife on one hip, a radio on the other, and a Beretta in a holster at the small of his back.

He calls the prison at the rear of his property a dormitory.

He calls the women held there his lovers.

He calls the heroin he injects into them medicine.

And when he has johns over to the house—only his highest-paying clients—he tells them how much his lovers are looking forward to pleasuring them.

"Alfred," he says to the mercenary he calls his butler. "I want to celebrate. Bring me the new girl. The one Carpenter delivered the other day."

"Marta?"

"Yes," Zebo says, turning the volume of the TV back on and focusing his attention on the news coverage. "It's time for her to start earning the medicine we've been giving her."

CHAPTER 74

RYAN LOGAN RETURNS to the station after his press conference to find me in the investigation room with a laptop opened to Google Earth. Ava and Carlos just stepped out to make a phone call that might help us, and Ryan and I have a moment alone.

"One of the agents showed me the recording of your interview with Llewellyn Carpenter," he says, looking contemplative.

For a moment, I expect him to find some fault with my approach. The way I questioned Carpenter without getting him medical attention could certainly be seen as unethical. But the interview with Carpenter isn't what Ryan wants to talk about—it's what came after.

"That shot you made," he says. "I've never seen anything like it. That's a shot you can be proud of for the rest of your life."

I open my mouth to show some modesty, but he waves me off.

"On a range," he says, "shooting at paper targets, I could probably try that ten times and get it right once or twice. But this isn't a range. Those weren't paper targets."

I nod, not knowing what to say. There's a big difference between shooting at targets with wax bullets and drawing your gun in life-or-death situations. There aren't any do-overs when it comes to real people and real bullets. That's what I felt Ryan didn't understand during the raid, when I stopped him from taking a bad shot.

I can see he understands it now.

"When you hear about shooters like Jelly Bryce and gun-fighters from the Wild West," Ryan says, "you never know if you should really believe the stories, or if maybe the legends have taken on a life of their own. Seeing you in that video, I can believe some of those legends." He nods at me. "You're a special breed, Rory. They don't make them like you anymore. You might be the last of your kind."

This last sentence he says with both admiration and res-ervation. In his tone is the wish that he could be like me and the realization that he isn't. However good he might be with a gun, there's a gulf between us that he doesn't feel he'll ever be able to bridge.

"Being able to shoot a gun isn't the most important part of being in law enforcement," I say. "I've seen that time and again working with Carlos and Ava. I'm not half the cop they are. Or you," I add, earnest in my compliment. "I know we've had our disagreements, Ryan, but I respect all that you've done with this task force. There are a lot of women being reunited with their families because of you."

He nods his appreciation, but I can see my words don't cheer him.

I want to warn him that the situation we're heading into is likely to get bloody. I want to ask if he's ready, but I know he might see that as disrespectful. And, given the respect he's just shown to me, I don't want to insult him.

Before I can figure out what to say, Carlos and Ava return.

"Just got off the phone," Carlos says. "Our plan should work."

"Someone want to tell me what's going on?" Ryan says.

Carlos points to the Google Earth image of Garrison Zebo's property.

Zebo's acreage abuts the foothills of the Franklin Mountains in an upscale area of El Paso. The property includes a large mansion and several other buildings on a campus thick with trees and other vegetation. A large blue pool sits behind the house, so close it looks like you could dive from the deck into the water. One of the large outbuildings looks like a garage, and considering Zebo owns a car lot, we suspect that he probably has some nice automobiles stored there. Another building, near the back of the property, looks like it could be storage, or perhaps even a guest house for visitors.

We assume the women are held there.

A thick wall—probably concrete or flat rocks concreted together, a popular style here in El Paso—runs around the perimeter of the property, topped with razor wire.

There is also a gate out front, with a small guardhouse.

"If he's got women there," Ryan says, "then he's going to have armed men guarding them."

I'm afraid Ryan is going to call off the operation, but then Carlos speaks.

"There," Carlos says, pointing to the screen. "That's our way in."

Behind the property, an aqueduct runs through the foothills, carrying steel-gray water along a path that people probably use for running or horseback riding. These kinds of acequia trails are common in this part of the Southwest, where every ounce of water is precious.

On Zebo's property, we can see a small drainage creek running down a hill, passing right behind the building where we think the women are housed and toward the back wall. The streambed is dry in the picture, but when there's a rainstorm, it probably fills up. It's hard to tell exactly how, but the streambed leads under the wall, where it intersects the main waterway. Without some kind of outlet, the back of his property would flood.

"Just got off the phone with the water company," Carlos says. "The pipes they use in that area should be big enough for us to crawl through—although it might be a tight fit."

"Should we wait for nightfall?" Ava asks.

"No," Ryan says, surprising all of us that he's the one to endorse this seat-of-the-pants mission. "Let's get this show on the road."

"Not just yet," Carlos says, and all eyes turn to him. "Ava, you're not going to like what I have to say."

"What?" she asks.

"I don't think you should go with us," Carlos says to her. "It should just be the three of us." He points to himself, then to Ryan and me.

I'm shocked. I don't know why he'd want to leave her behind.

Ava visibly bristles.

From her face, I can tell she feels betrayed.

CHAPTER 75

RYAN, OF ALL people, comes to her defense.

"She saved your asses back there at that fire," he says to Carlos. "We shouldn't leave her out." He turns to Ava. "I was wrong to exclude you before, and he's wrong now."

Carlos says that his recommendation for her to stay behind is not meant to be a slight about her abilities in the field.

"It's not that at all," he says to her. "You need to stay behind to interview Isabella Luna."

He explains that no matter what happens at Garrison Zebo's place, those of us who go will be preoccupied afterward for the rest of the day, probably the rest of the week. There will be reports to file, statements to give, interviews to handle—and all of that is only if it goes well and we arrest Garrison Zebo and save Marta and any other women who might be there.

If anything goes wrong—if it turns out Carpenter was

lying and that Garrison Zebo isn't Mr. Z, or if Zebo gets away, or we don't find the girls—then our asses will be in serious trouble for rushing into this thing without warrants and approval from our supervisors. We could come out of this with the blackest of black marks on our records.

Whether we end the day law enforcement heroes or pariahs, we'll be indisposed for a good twenty-four or forty-eight hours. Maybe longer.

"Fiona Martinez might not have that long," Carlos says, referring to the latest eagle feather victim.

Isabella Luna was found ten days after her disappearance. If the same thing has happened to Fiona as happened to Isabella four years ago, there might still be time to save her.

"Last night at the casino, Isabella agreed to talk to you," Carlos says. "If she'll open up to you in a way she wouldn't when Rory and I were there, we need to know what she knows."

At this point, Ryan gets a phone call and steps away for a moment.

Carlos goes on to explain what he's been wanting to talk to us about but hasn't had the chance—that he spent his evenings on his Houston trip scouring the phone records and social media accounts of the four missing eagle feather victims. In three of the four cases, he found people reaching out to them on social media right before they disappeared.

"The names were different," Carlos says, "but in all the instances, a person contacted them, acting like an old friend, or at least an acquaintance, and said, 'Do you remember me?' And in all three cases, the person said they'd met at a powwow."

He explains that he figured out that the accounts were bogus, used as a way to find out where the women were living.

"So what does all this mean?" Ava asks.

Carlos says that he thinks the women were all targeted at powwows. The abductor saw them, maybe met them in some capacity, and then tracked them down later through social media.

"But why not abduct them when he first met them?" I ask.

"Powwows are crowded places," Carlos says. "It would be hard to just take someone. Plus," he adds, "we know whoever it is waits for the solstice. We don't know why, but we've got four feathers left behind after four solstices. That's no coincidence."

"It's not," Ryan agrees, coming back into the conversation while putting his phone away. "The crime lab just called. Last night, I told them to move your eagle feathers to the top of the queue. High priority."

We all stare at him, stunned.

"I just got word," he says, "all four feathers were a genetic match. They came from the same bird."

I feel a cold chill.

Ryan says, "If there was any doubt of the link between the cases — and I guess I was the only one with any doubts — it's gone."

None of us can believe the about-face Ryan has demonstrated.

"Look," he says, "I owe you all an apology. I didn't take your theories on the feathers that seriously. But when I saw the message from Marta Rivera that you were all heading into a trap, I thought you might all be killed. I realized we're all on the same side, and after you survived the morning—no thanks to me—I feel like I've been given a second chance to work *with* you all, not against you."

He turns his attention to Ava, who he's had the longest-running feud with.

"Carlos is right," he tells her. "You go talk to Isabella. Try to get her to remember something—anything—about the day she went missing. We," he adds, gesturing to Carlos and me, "are going to do everything we can to save Marta Rivera. You go save Fiona Martinez."

Ava stares at him, her expression unreadable. Ryan extends his hand.

"Okay," Ava says finally, and, in a sight that I wouldn't have imagined possible a week ago, she shakes with Ryan Logan.

CHAPTER 76

RYAN DRIVES AN unmarked FBI sedan along the dirt road-way paralleling the canal. To the left of us is the muddy waterway and, beyond it, the desert foothills rising into the rocky Franklin Mountains. To the right are the mortared stone walls of the properties that abut the open space. The houses—multiple stories with manicured lawns and clear-blue swimming pools—are among the most upscale I've seen in El Paso.

"This looks like the one," I say, pointing ahead.

While most of the houses' walls are only waist-high, allow-ing us to see some of what's on the other side, Zebo's rock wall is ten feet tall and lined at the top with razor wire—a measure of security that might seem excessive if we didn't know what he was hiding in there.

Ryan parks the car and the three of us clamber out, all

wearing our Kevlar vests. Carlos carries his shotgun. Ryan and I are relying on our pistols.

It's a hot day, and the unforgiving West Texas sunlight beats down on us. My shirt is already wet with sweat.

Not wanting to be seen, we hurry toward the canal, where a corrugated pipe sticks out over the brown water. I hop down into the canal, getting wet from my waist down, and shine a light into the tunnel. It looks to be about ten feet long, the bottom coated with branches and mud. A frightened frog hops away to the other side.

"I'm going in," I say, and try to wedge myself inside.

I make it about two feet, my body squeezed like a sardine in a can, before wiggling back out.

"I'm not going to make it with this on," I say, and unstrap my Kevlar vest and toss it on the slope.

I climb back inside the tunnel. It's still a tight fit, but I can move easier now. I make my way forward, feeling the grip of claustrophobia. The pipe doesn't get any narrower, but the muck along the bottom grows thicker, making progress difficult. The air is stagnant and smells like river water.

"You okay, Rory?" Carlos calls from behind me, his voice a tinny echo in the narrow tunnel.

"Almost there," I say, and wriggle onward.

I slide out of the other side, my clothes coated in mud. I'm in the bottom of a wash and don't have much of a view of Zebo's property—just trees and brush—but I do have a glimpse of the building where we think the women are imprisoned.

"It's clear," I call into the pipe, keeping my voice close to a whisper and letting the echo carry my words.

As I wait, I pour the water out of my boots while keeping an eye out. The slope is crowded with native trees—border piñon, subalpine fir, and Chihuahuan pine—which no doubt help keep people from seeing what happens on the property from higher up in the Franklin Mountains.

But the dense foliage will also give us cover as we sneak up the dry wash.

I hear a shuffling sound as Carlos makes his way through the pipe. Something metal clunks inside the cylinder, and I wince, worrying that someone will hear. A minute later, I find out what the sound was as the barrel of Carlos's shotgun protrudes from the pipe. I take it and use my free hand to help Carlos out. More svelte than me, he managed to keep his Kevlar vest on.

A few minutes later, Ryan squeezes through. A few inches shorter than me, he was able to keep his vest on, too.

"Are we ready?" Ryan asks, breathing heavy, more from the adrenaline than the effort to get through the pipe.

"Wait a minute," Carlos whispers, beginning to unstrap his vest. "Take this, Rory."

"No," I say, stopping him. "You keep it."

There's no way I'm going into this protected while Carlos isn't. I'm not having another Ranger die before my eyes.

"Damn it," Ryan says. "We should have folded up your vest and shoved it through."

He's right. Carlos managed to get his shotgun through. Any one of us could have wadded up the vest and shoved it ahead of us in the cylinder. I hadn't thought of it at the time. I'd been too anxious about getting through.

"I'll go back and get it," Carlos says, extending the shotgun for me to take.

"No," I say, showing Carlos my empty hands that won't hold his gun. "The longer we dick around here, the more likely we're going to be discovered. Let's go."

Without waiting for an answer, I start creeping up the wash. Carlos and Ryan have no choice but to follow.

CHAPTER 77

I MAKE MY way up the arroyo to the backside of the building. I try to keep quiet, but it's not easy wearing cowboy boots and walking through a rocky, debris-strewn ditch. I stop and listen. Birds chirp. In the distance, I hear the rumble of cars on the main thoroughfare.

The cackle of radio static comes from the building, and I hear someone talking.

When Carlos and Ryan catch up to me, I whisper, "There's at least one guard."

Ryan suggests one of us circle around the building so we can get the jump on him from two sides, but I'm worried that we'll make too much noise. The ground is littered with tree branches and rocks, and none of us has the shoes for stealth. And if we have to use our guns, we might be caught in each other's cross fire.

"Let's just rush him," Carlos whispers. "Scare the ever-loving shit out of him."

We creep forward as quietly as possible, slowly making it around the side of the building, which looks almost like a motel. The guard—dressed in black with a pistol at his hip—has his phone out, checking Twitter or looking at porn.

The three of us burst from cover.

"Put your hands up," Carlos hisses, the shotgun leveled on his chest, "or I'll blow a hole in you so big we'll be able to see what you had for breakfast."

The guard, in a state of disbelief, looks back and forth between them and me. His hand drops toward his pistol.

"Don't you fucking do it!" Ryan growls.

The man's hand hesitates, inches from his pistol's grip. Then he realizes he's outgunned and raises his arms into the air.

"Smart move," Carlos says. "Now turn around and put your hands against the wall."

The man does as he's told, positioning himself between two of the cell doors. Carlos moves his shotgun to his left arm and reaches to disarm the guy. But the guy—moving fast enough that he could hold his own in a quick-draw competition—snatches his pistol out while spinning around.

My gun is in my hand, but Carlos is between him and me. I might be able to shoot around him, the way I did with Carpenter when he had Ava in a headlock, but in that case, they were both still—and I'd been readying myself for several seconds.

I don't have that kind of time.

Things are moving too fast.

Carlos tries to swing the shotgun, but it's big and bulky and his opponent is already bringing up the pistol, pointing it above Carlos's Kevlar vest to his face.

I can see it all happening. The man is going to pull the trigger. The bullet will go through Carlos's skull. I'm helpless to stop it.

I open my mouth to scream, but when I hear the gunshot, my breath freezes in my throat.

The guard's head jerks to the side as a bullet passes through his brain. He collapses onto the ground, and both Carlos and I turn to see Ryan Logan holding his gun in both hands, looking as shocked as the rest of us.

"Thanks," Carlos says to him. "I owe you one."

"That," I say to Ryan, nodding my respect, "is a shot you can be proud of for the rest of your life."

He looks at me and swallows, then, giving me a sheepish smile, says, "So much for keeping things quiet."

"Yeah," Carlos says. "Let's get moving."

Carlos digs through the dead man's pocket and finds a set of keys. We open the door of the first room, guns ready. A woman lies on a mattress on the floor, dressed in skimpy lingerie. She is asleep or dead, her long dark hair covering her face.

"Marta?" I say, speaking loud to try to rouse her even though, apparently, the gunshot outside her door didn't.

She rolls over, brushing her hair back from her face.

It's a young Latina woman.

Not Marta.

CHAPTER 78

MARTA STANDS IN the basement, trembling with fear.

The room is spacious, but holds almost nothing. There is a king-sized bed covered in black rubbery-looking sheets, a door to a small bathroom, and another door to a closet full of lingerie: brightly colored corsets, lace bustiers, see-through body stockings, crotchless teddies.

A big man in a black shirt with a gun escorted her here and told her to wait for Mr. Z.

Her legs feel weak. She wants to sit on the bed, but she feels like that would be giving up—a gesture of supplication she's not ready to concede to.

The door to the outside opens and an overly tanned white man walks in wearing a robe. Marta takes a step back. The man approaches, grinning at her like the Cheshire Cat from *Alice in Wonderland*.

Marta recognizes him. She's seen him on TV—Garrison

Zebo, the blowhard car lot owner always boasting about sur-
pluses of inventory and how everything must go. She almost
opens her mouth to tell him she recognizes him, but she bites
back the words. If he knows she can identify him, that means
he'll never let her leave.

Then it hits her—he is never going to let her leave.

"I know what you're thinking," he says, pointing to the
closet. "There are so many choices, it's hard to pick."

She starts to sob, and she's afraid her legs are going to collapse beneath her.

"Don't cry," he says, his tone darkening. "If you're going to
cry, then Uncle Z will give you something to cry about. Keep
it together, and this will be more pleasant for both of us."

Marta bites her lip and fights back tears.

"That's better," he says, then he looks her up and down like
he's appraising a car's value. "You look fine. Why don't you go
ahead and sit on the bed?"

Her legs feel numb beneath her as she approaches the bed
and sits down.

Is this really happening?

"You look tense," Zebo says. "How about I give you something to loosen you up?"

He withdraws a small key from his robe and inserts it into
the drawer of the nightstand. He reaches inside and pulls out
a syringe, then a small baggie of brown powder, roughly the
size of a strawberry.

"This is what you want, isn't it?" Mr. Z says to her, raising
a knowing eyebrow.

She's never wanted something so badly. Not just for the

high and the release from the sickness she's been feeling, but also because she knows the high will anesthetize her from what is about to happen. If she's flying through the clouds, she won't be bothered by what is happening to her body back on earth.

Mr. Z prepares the injection. He pours the powder into the spoon and holds the lighter to its underside. The heroin bubbles as it melts, the air filling with an acidic vinegary smell.

From outside, they hear the sound of a gunshot.

The noise is muffled down here, underground, but it's still noticeable. Mr. Z stops what he's doing, setting the spoon and lighter down, and grabs a cell phone from his pocket.

"What the hell was that?" he barks into the phone.

Marta stares at the heroin. It's almost ready. She can't wait. She moves toward the nightstand and picks up the spoon and lighter. With shaky hands, she holds the flame underneath the metal and watches the powder liquefy. Mr. Z eyes her but doesn't do anything about it. He seems amused that she's preparing her own injection. He turns away from her, paying attention only to the conversation.

With shaking hands, she slurps up the brown liquid into the needle.

"Don't bother me if it turns out to be nothing," he says into the phone, then he pockets it into his robe.

As he turns around, Marta lunges at him and jams the needle into his shoulder. He winces in pain, but before he can pull away, Marta squeezes the plunger and releases the heroin into him.

He whirls around and belts her across the face.

Marta collapses, and he looms over her, smirking as he looks back and forth between her and the syringe protruding from his arm.

"You know," he says, "when you inject heroin into a vein, it takes effect in seconds. But when you put it into muscle," he adds, tugging the syringe out of his shoulder with a wince, "it takes a good five or ten minutes to kick in."

He pulls out his phone while Marta stares at him from the floor, her whole body trembling.

"Come get me in five minutes," he says into the phone. "This bitch just shot me up with her heroin." There's a pause and he adds, "Just the muscle. I'll be high as a damn kite, but not for a while. Five minutes will give me enough time."

He pockets the phone and holds the syringe like a knife, glowering at her like a panther ready to pounce.

"Plenty of time for me to kill you."

CHAPTER 79

"GET ME OUT of here," the Latina woman hisses from the mattress on the floor.

"No one will hurt you anymore," I say. "Where is Mr. Z?"

"With the new girl."

"Where?" I ask.

"Where he always takes us," she says. "The basement."

Outside, the dead guard's radio buzzes.

"What's going on?" a voice says. *"Was that a gunshot?"*

Carlos grabs the radio and says, "I shot a rattlesnake. That's all."

There's a long pause.

"I'm sending Jenkins and Ramirez," the voice says.

"Roger that," Carlos says, acting like nothing is unusual.

"What the hell do we do now?" Ryan asks.

I tell him that we need to open the other doors—fast—and get all the women out.

"You take them out the way we came," I say. "Call for backup. Carlos and I will look for Marta."

He opens his mouth to argue, but Carlos says, "You've got to get these girls out of here. If everything goes to shit, you've got to at least save them."

He nods in agreement, and we work together to throw open the other rooms and help the women out. There are three, and they all look terrible—emaciated, bruised, unclean.

There's no telling how long they've been here.

No telling what's been done to them.

We direct them to clamber down the embankment with Ryan. The prospect of escape has given them new strength.

"We've got company," Carlos says.

Two men jog our way through the trees, both wearing black like the guard Ryan shot. Only these guys are carrying TEC-9s.

"Go!" Carlos shouts to Ryan. "We'll cover you."

With that, he starts blasting his shotgun in the direction of the men. They dive for cover behind trees. The range isn't in Carlos's favor—not with a shotgun and plenty of bushes and tree branches in the way—but with each shot spraying nine balls of double-aught buck, the men have to keep hidden. It gives Ryan and the women time to run down the hill. Within seconds, they're out of sight.

Which is a good thing, because Carlos's gun is out of shells.

The men step out from hiding and open fire with the TEC-9s. Carlos dives on me, and the two of us fall inside one of the doorways. Bullets tear through the walls, showering us in adobe dust and chunks of cinder block. Beams of sunlight poke through every bullet hole.

Carlos is lying on top of me, pinning me down. It's only when I feel warm liquid wetting my shirt that I realize he's been shot.

CHAPTER 80

MARTA TRIES TO scamper backward, but Zebo moves with a frightening quickness and grabs a fistful of her hair as he kneels. She scratches his face with one hand and reaches to block the syringe with the other. He slams her head down against the floor. The carpeting does very little to soften the concrete underneath, and for a moment, Marta's vision threatens to go black.

Zebo brings the syringe down in a stabbing motion. She moves her head to the side and manages to throw her arm in its way, and the needle slices the skin of her forearm before jamming into the floor.

He holds the syringe up and examines the needle, which is bent like an elbow.

Marta's ears ring from the blow, but her faculties are returning to full alert. She tries again to wriggle away from Zebo, but he tosses the syringe aside and throws himself down on her with practiced dexterity. He has a lot of experience holding women down.

"No!" Marta screams, and she digs her fingernails into his face, scraping up trenches of skin.

Zebo roars in pain and throws wild punches that glance off her forearms. He wraps his hands around her throat.

She tries to breathe, but her airway is cut off.

Outside the door, more gunfire erupts. Several loud blasts, one after another, followed by automatic fire. At the noise, Zebo flinches, loosening his grasp. Marta flails, reaching for his eyes. He recoils, and she manages to shove him off of her.

She scrambles away toward the door. Zebo lunges and grabs her ankle. She kicks at him, but he manages to get hold of both legs. He yanks her to him and throws himself on top of her again. She digs her nails into his arms, but he doesn't stop. He grabs her by the neck with both hands and squeezes.

Blackness threatens to overtake her.

Her muscles weaken. Her fingers loosen their grip on his arms.

She wants to hang on—the heroin should take effect any second—but she has no fight left in her. Atop her, Zebo growls like an animal, a long string of saliva dangling from his mouth.

His face is the last thing she sees before the darkness takes her.

CHAPTER 81

THE SHOOTING STOPS, and I heft Carlos off of me onto the debris-covered floor. He grunts quietly as I look for the wound.

Blood trickles out of a hole in his side, just below one of the Kevlar panels. The bullet hole is low enough to miss his lung and heart, but in a spot to do plenty of damage to other organs. I can't find an exit hole, which means the bullet is lodged somewhere inside him.

His stomach?

His liver?

"Hang in there," I whisper.

I assume the two armed men are approaching the building, coming cautiously enough that I've got at least thirty seconds—maybe a minute—before they get here. I tear off my T-shirt, wad it up, and press it firmly against the wound.

"I'm going to get help," I say.

Carlos gives a slight shake of his head. "Don't worry about

347

me," he utters, having trouble speaking from the pain. He covers the balled shirt with his own hand, signaling to me that I can remove my own. Then he fixes me with an intense stare. "Go get Marta."

As I gape at him, rage fills me. It wasn't long ago that I watched Kyle Hendricks die in the act of saving my life. I saw the life leave his eyes, and I had to stand in the Medal of Valor ceremony accepting my award while his mother accepted his.

Now Carlos is going to die.

No!

Goddamn it. No!

With adrenaline flooding my veins, I rise to my feet. The smart thing to do would be to wait in the room, my gun at the ready, and as soon as either gunman popped around the corner, I could shoot him. But I'm not waiting, not while my partner is bleeding to death.

I run out the door.

One gunman appears off to my left. I shoot him in the face before he can pull the trigger. Instinct tells me that the other man is going around the building, flanking us, and I spin around in time to see him coming around the corner, swinging the TEC-9 at my running body.

I dive to the ground, sliding through dirt on my left shoulder while aiming my pistol with my right. He lets loose a burst of gunfire, all of the shots sailing above me, and I shoot him through his gritted teeth. The gunfire ceases, and he collapses to the ground.

I don't waste a moment. I jump to my feet and sprint toward the mansion.

CHAPTER 82

RUNNING, I PASS a huge outbuilding with five vehicle bays. Two of the garage doors are open, revealing a sixties-era Shelby Cobra and a brand-new Tesla Roadster. From here, I can see the house, with the pool behind it and a peninsular deck extending from the second story like a massive diving board.

As I arrive at the swimming pool, I slow for an instant, considering my next move. Before I can decide, an armed man runs out onto the deck. Muscled like a professional wrestler, he wields a TEC-9 with two hands. I dive into the water just as he lets the gun rip. Bullets pierce the surface and dart through the water, followed by comet trails of bubbles. I swim along the bottom, doing an underwater breaststroke like a frog, careful to keep my SIG Sauer in my hand. Bullets continue to rain into the water, so many that his magazine must be almost empty.

When the firing stops, I press my boots against the bottom and push myself to the surface, almost directly underneath the shooter. I can't be sure my gun will still fire after being submerged, but I don't have time to think about it. The man pops a new magazine into his TEC-9 and leans over the balcony railing.

I shoot him in the throat before he can fire.

He teeters, clutching his neck as blood dribbles down into the pool. Then his body tumbles over. I lunge out of the way, and he hits the pool in an explosion of water. A plume of crimson spreads from the body as it bobs to the surface.

I grab the edge of the pool and haul myself out.

I move toward the stairs, my boots sloshing water. I almost run up the steps to the balcony toward the house, but I spot a door, tucked away under the stairs, and I remember that the woman said Mr. Z took Marta to the basement.

I kick the door open and race down a set of stairs, taking three at a time. There's another doorway at the bottom. I hesitate, readying my gun, listening. I make out some kind of *thud*.

I raise my foot to kick the door open.

Garrison Zebo—recognizable from his bleached hair and leather-tanned skin—is slumped on the floor atop Marta Rivera.

Neither appears to be conscious.

I throw Zebo off of her. His eyes are open—he's awake—but he's as flaccid as a noodle.

"Marta!" I shout, checking her pulse and listening for breath.

I find a faint beat in the artery in her neck. Her eyes flitter open. Then she bolts upright, taking a gasping breath, looking around in terror.

"It's okay," I say. "I'm a Texas Ranger."

She throws her arms around me, and I hold her trembling body. Through the open door, I hear sirens, close and getting closer.

"You're safe."

CHAPTER 83

AVA PULLS HER SUV up in front of Isabella Luna's small brick house. She has showered, scrubbed off the soot and the smell of smoke, and changed into a fresh uniform. Her hair has been washed and stretches down her back in a damp braid. She takes a deep breath, knowing the importance of this interview.

Ava approaches the front door of Isabella's house as her phone beeps with an incoming text. She stops, midway up the walk, and checks the message.

It's from Rory.

Marta is safe.

Ava closes her eyes and breathes a big sigh of relief. Then another text comes in.

Zebo arrested.

She feels a jolt of satisfaction. Then a third text comes and robs her of her good feelings.

Carlos is injured. On his way to hospital.

If you pray, say one for him.

Ava looks up from the phone, blinking back tears. Thunderclouds are overtaking the sky as the sun sets, creating a feeling as ominous as this news. She starts to text Rory back, but Isabella opens the front door.

"Ava?" she says. "I saw you pull up."

"Hi," Ava says. "Is now a good time?"

"It's as good a time as any, I guess."

Just then, another text pops in from Rory.

Let me know what happens with your interview. Call me. No matter how late.

She puts her phone away and hurries the rest of the way up the walk, where Isabella gives her a hug.

"Thanks for agreeing to talk to me," Ava says, trying to put thoughts of Carlos—and how bad his injury might be—out of her mind.

"I'm not sure how much help I'll be," Isabella says, leading her into a nice living room with hardwood floors, a kiva fireplace, and a worn leather couch with an accompanying love seat. The coffee table is messy with newspaper clippings, printouts from online articles, and copies of police reports. A cardboard box sits on the floor, its lid ajar. Inside, Ava spots similar documents.

"I got out this old box of stuff from my disappearance," Isabella says. "I thought it might jog my memory."

"And?" Ava says, sitting on the love seat to give Isabella the couch.

"Nothing."

Ava glances over the articles, with headlines like:

Tigua Girl Missing After Powwow
Police Seek Information in Missing Girl Case

And finally:

Missing Girl Found Alive

Ava can see why the articles haven't jogged Isabella's memory. They're all about everyone else's experience. Not her own.

"What do you remember about the powwow where you were last seen?" Ava asks.

"Not much," she says, shrugging. "It was just like any other powwow. I guess the cool thing was that this one was in our backyard. It felt kind of special because of that."

Ava asks what the last thing she remembers is, and Isabella says she's not sure. She has memories of the event—dancing, competing, laughing with friends—but she isn't sure what order they happened in. Ava presses for more information, but every question she asks is met with a quick dismissal. As much as Isabella says she is willing, she doesn't seem to *want* to help.

Ava gets the feeling that it isn't that Isabella can't access those memories.

It's that she doesn't want to.

Ava feels frustrated that while Rory and Carlos were putting themselves in danger to save Marta Rivera, she is just spinning her wheels with Isabella Luna. But what did she expect? She's just rehashing the same questions they already asked.

She has to find a new approach if she wants to get the answers she needs.

CHAPTER 84

"ISABELLA," AVA SAYS, "four other people have gone missing under similar circumstances. Three of them have been gone so long that it's unlikely they're still alive. But one might be alive. You can help her."

Isabella lowers her head. If she remembers, the only way to get her to talk might be making her realize she can help someone else.

"Are you *sure* that you don't remember anything that happened to you?" Ava asks, staring at Isabella's lowered head.

She's going to tell me, Ava thinks.

Instead, Isabella raises her head and says defensively, "How do you know the cases are linked?" Isabella doesn't give Ava time to think. "They all went missing from their homes, didn't they? They all had an eagle feather left behind. What happened to me is not the same at all."

356

"What *did* happen to you?" Ava says. "I want to know. I want to help you."

Isabella makes a *pfft* sound with her lips. "You want to help me? It's a little late for that. Where were you four years ago?"

Ava feels the opportunity slipping away.

"I'm here now," Ava says.

Isabella opens her mouth to speak, but then stands abruptly.

"Excuse me a minute," she says, visibly quaking.

Isabella disappears into the hallway. Ava lets her go. Maybe a moment alone is what she needs.

A minute goes by. Then two. As she waits, Ava flips through the old articles about Isabella's disappearance. The coverage was extensive, probably because she went missing from such a public place. It occurs to Ava that the news coverage of Fiona Martinez, the latest victim, has been minimal by comparison.

Ava's heartbeat accelerates as she thinks of something Isabella said.

They all went missing from their homes, didn't they? They all had an eagle feather left behind. What happened to me is not the same at all.

She and Rory and Carlos never told her the women had gone missing from their homes. And while they had asked her about eagle feathers, she doesn't think they mentioned why. Because the press doesn't know there was any connection between these years-apart cases, those details have never been in the newspaper or on TV.

She knows something, Ava thinks. *And it's time she comes clean.*

She steps into the hallway, where she finds three door-ways, two of which are open. One of the open doors leads to a bathroom. Another to an office. The third, the closed door, must be her bedroom.

Ava raises her hand to knock, but something in the office catches her eye.

On the desk sits a photograph. As Ava approaches, she sees it's a picture of five girls. All Native. All wearing traditional regalia. All smiling and happy.

All holding small dreamcatchers, with five eagle feathers on each and the words ORDER OF THE GOLDEN EAGLE stenciled in the centerpieces.

They are all younger than their more recent photos, but Ava easily recognizes each of the girls.

Fiona Martinez.

Rebecca Trujillo.

Chipeta Tavaci.

Tina White Wolf.

And there with the other eagle feather victims, smiling like she's among friends, is Isabella Luna.

Ava spins around to look for Isabella, but something else catches her attention. In the corner, to the left of the door in a place that was out of her sight when she first walked into the room, a feathered dreamcatcher hangs from the ceiling, the same as the ones in the photograph, except this dream-catcher has only one feather.

The other four—identical to the feathers left at the victims' homes—are missing.

CHAPTER 85

ISABELLA APPEARS IN the doorway like a ghost, holding forth some kind of object in her hands. Ava is paralyzed with confusion, and before it registers that the item is a Taser gun, the young woman pulls the trigger.

Electrodes fly through the air, trailed by electrical wires. Ava reaches for her pistol, but the probes land on her uniform and fill her body with the worst pain she's ever experienced. She tries to lift her gun, but every muscle in her body is locked up.

Heat burns through her bloodstream.

She drops to her knees. Then onto her chest. Abruptly, the electricity stops coursing through her veins, but still she can't move. Her muscles were iron a second ago, but now they're jelly. Isabella walks over to her and pries her pistol out of her fingers. She tucks it into her waistband and then leans back down to disconnect the electrodes.

Ava's handcuffs are fastened to her belt, and Isabella pulls them off. Ava tries to resist, but her limbs won't cooperate. In seconds, her hands are cuffed behind her back as she lies face down on the hardwood floor, still gasping from the pain.

"Please...Isabella," Ava says, having trouble forming the words. "Don't...do this."

Isabella takes the gun and presses the barrel against Ava's temple.

"If you try to yell for help," she says, "I'll kill you with your own gun."

CHAPTER 86

I'M SITTING IN the back of an ambulance parked on the street outside Garrison Zebo's house. I'm holding an oxygen mask over my face with one hand and have an IV needle in the other. Someone gave me a fresh T-shirt, but my jeans and boots are still damp. The EMT helping me strongly encouraged me to take a ride to the hospital to get checked out, but I insisted I wouldn't leave the crime scene yet.

The oxygen is helping me feel better, clearing my lungs of the lingering effects of the gas I inhaled this morning. The IV is giving me a small boost of energy. I can't remember the last time I ate. And it's easily been thirty hours since I slept. Tomorrow my body will be full of aches and pains, but for now I'm still running on the fumes of my adrenaline.

The sun has dropped below the horizon, and, in the distance, the sky is filled with clouds pulsing with heat lightning.

The whole street has been closed with police tape, and

there are numerous police officers, FBI agents, and crime scene technicians running around. From where I am, I can see Ryan Logan standing on Zebo's lawn, coordinating everything. I have a newfound respect for him. Managing the craziness of all this can't be easy. He is constantly being updated, relaying information, making decisions. In the time I've been sitting here sucking oxygen, he's probably already talked to the director of the FBI and the governor of Texas.

As I wait for the IV to drain into my body, I check my phone, which—thank God it's water resistant—survived my dive into Garrison Zebo's pool. I've got two dozen missed calls and texts, all from family and friends asking if I'm okay after seeing reports of what happened at Zebo's on the news. Both Willow and Megan were among the callers. But the message I'm really waiting on hasn't come yet.

I haven't heard from Ava.

Ryan breaks off a conversation with another agent, then heads over toward the ambulance.

"You ought to let them take you to the hospital," he says.

I shake my head no, then turn off the oxygen canister and hang up the clear plastic face mask. The IV bladder is almost empty.

Ryan updates me on the investigation. Agents quickly scavenged some of Zebo's files and found the locations of two more brothels we didn't know about, one in a mining camp in Carlsbad, the other outside a truck stop in Amarillo.

"We've got people headed to both now," he says. "We're bringing down the whole organization tonight."

The women held captive at Zebo's house, including Marta,

have been taken to the hospital, and agents are contacting their families as we speak. As for Garrison Zebo, Ryan informs me, he's in stable condition.

"Let's hope he gets pretty much the same treatment in prison that the girls he abducted got from him," Ryan says.

"Any word about Carlos?" I ask.

Ryan has a forlorn expression. He nods.

"Tell me," I say.

"He's in surgery," he says. "They've got to get that bullet out."

I nod. That doesn't sound so bad.

"He flatlined on the operating table," Ryan adds. "His heart stopped beating, and they had to zap him with the paddles to bring him back."

"Shit," I say, a lump filling my throat.

"There's nothing we need you for that can't wait until tomorrow," Ryan says. "I'll get one of the agents to give you a ride to wherever you want to go."

I stand up and tug the IV needle out.

Ryan extends his hand.

"You did good today, Ranger," he says.

I nod, giving his hand a shake. All our animosity is finally behind us.

"You, too," I say.

A minute later, Agent Kara Prince, who I met at the hospital, pulls up to give me a lift.

"Good news," she says. "Marvin came out of his coma."

It's a relief, of course, but now I'm worrying about Carlos.

"Where to?" she asks.

"The hospital," I say. "I'll pay Marvin a visit while I'm waiting for my buddy to get out of surgery."

As she pulls away from the curb, I lean my head back and try to rest. But I can't stop wondering why Ava hasn't called. I try her number. The phone just rings and rings. I tell myself to worry about this in the morning. Still, I can't shake the feeling that something might be wrong. Ava is a consummate professional.

She would have called.

"On second thought," I say to Kara, "can you take me somewhere else?"

CHAPTER 87

TEN MINUTES LATER, Kara pulls up next to the Tigua community center, or what's left of it anyway. The second story has collapsed onto the first, leaving a pile of blackened debris. Tendrils of smoke drift into the sky. The cracked and weed-filled parking lot is damp with water. One fire truck is still there, with the firefighters keeping an eye on the rubble to make sure the fire doesn't spark to life again.

My truck is sitting where I left it.

I thank Kara and promise to stop by to see Marvin later, then I nod to the firefighters and climb into my truck and start the engine.

Before Ava and I took our trip to Colorado and Arizona, we stopped at her house so she could pick up a few things. I don't recall the address, just the vicinity, and after a few minutes of driving around, I pull up out front.

There's no sign of Ava's SUV, but the garage door is open,

full of weight-lifting equipment. The radio is playing pop music—Kelly Clarkson, I think—and Marcos is lying on a bench, pressing up a bar loaded with four 45-pound plates. He slams the bar onto the rack and sits up, smiling at me as he wipes his brow with a towel.

It seems too late to be weight lifting, but Ava had said Marcos, as a trucker, keeps irregular hours.

"Hey, Rory, what's up?" He looks me up and down. "Man, you look like shit."

I tell him I'm trying to find Ava.

"She went over to Isabella Luna's house," he says. "That was a while ago. I guess they really got to talking."

I ask him if he knows where Isabella lives. He doesn't know the address but knows the street and what the house looks like. After he gives me some basic directions, he looks at me with serious concern.

"Something wrong?"

"Probably nothing," I say. "Try not to worry."

Three minutes later, I pull up in front of the residence. Ava's police SUV isn't here, either. But I figure I'll check anyway. The Pueblo is small enough that Ava could have walked here.

As I approach the house, Isabella swings the door open, smiling.

"Oh, hi, Rory," she says. "Ava and I are just finishing up. Want to come in?"

She has a flushed, happy look on her face, like she's been laughing—or maybe just had a glass of wine. Whatever I was worried about goes away. Her demeanor sets me at ease.

"Just for a minute," I say.

She opens the door for me and I step in.

"She's in the living room," Isabella says, pointing down the hall.

I take one step forward as Isabella shuts the door behind me.

Suddenly, I feel two side-by-side stings on the back of my shirt, like I've been shot simultaneously by twin rubber bands. I try to turn, but electricity vibrates through my chest and limbs. I drop to the floor, unable to control my cramping muscles. My body writhes on the hardwood, my muscles consumed with painful spasms. The pulsating waves of electricity cease, but I'm still momentarily paralyzed. I try to reach for my gun, but my hand just won't do what it's told.

"I'll take that," Isabella says coolly, plucking my pistol from its holster.

CHAPTER 88

ISABELLA TOWERS OVER me, retracting the cords of the Taser. Her expression—so animated before, so happy—has been replaced by cold indifference. She reaches into my pocket and pulls out my cell phone.

"Where's...Ava?" I manage to grunt.

She pats my belt and says, "Where are your handcuffs?"

"In my truck," I croak, my voice hoarse.

She lets out an annoyed huff, then takes a few steps away.

Now would be a good time to jump to my feet, to try to disarm her, but my body won't listen to my mind's commands. Feeling is coming back into my muscles, but not fast enough. Isabella returns and, at her direction—and with great effort—I roll over and cross my wrists at my lower back.

Isabella ties them together with twine, cinching the rope

tight. She kneels and tears off a length of duct tape and presses it over my mouth. She tells me to get to my feet and points which way I should walk. I do as she asks, even though standing takes considerable effort, especially with my arms bound behind me. She walks me into the kitchen and directs me to a doorway. I shoulder my way through to a garage.

Ava's SUV is parked inside.

With Ava locked in the back.

Isabella opens the vehicle's door and gestures for me to get inside. I slide in next to Ava, who apologizes with her eyes. Her mouth is duct-taped, too.

Isabella opens the garage door and slides behind the wheel. She sets my gun on the passenger seat, next to Ava's pistol and her handcuff keys. A Plexiglas barrier separates her from us, and the back doors of the SUV, like all police vehicles, won't open from the inside.

As she pulls out onto the street, she says, "You two don't try to get the attention of other drivers. If I hear any sirens, I'll shoot you both and then myself."

She drives in silence, heading southeast out of the city on I-10.

I'm furious with myself for getting into this situation. When Isabella answered the door, I had thought she looked flushed but happy, as if she and Ava had been having a laugh. Instead, she was excited, scared, nervous—but she put a smile on her face and disguised those emotions with cheerfulness. I was so ready to have my worries alleviated that I wasn't paying attention as closely as I should have been.

Her smile disarmed me.

Behind my back, I strain against the twine around my wrists. Ava's hands are cuffed—there's no way she can get them free—but there might be a chance I can loosen my restraints.

As I pull against the rope, I can hear the twine whine, and I know I have to make some noise in order to cover the sound. I move my lips, try to stretch my jaw, and eventually get my mouth open. The flap of duct tape hangs off my chin.

"Isabella is the eagle feather killer?" I ask Ava, loud enough for Isabella to hear.

Ava nods. She moves her mouth and tongue, straining to break free of the duct tape over her lips. One corner of the tape is curling up.

"Forgive my intimacy," I murmur, and I lean toward her, like I'm going to kiss her, and put my teeth over the tape. Biting hard, I tear it from her face.

She takes a deep breath and tells me that she found a picture of all five women, back when they were teenagers, and a dreamcatcher with a feather identical to the ones we'd found—missing four of its five feathers.

Isabella watches us from the rearview mirror, apparently unconcerned that we can now talk. The moment has passed when screaming for help might do us any good. Isabella pulls the SUV off the highway and heads into the desert to the north. The headlights illuminate nothing but a two-lane road with sagebrush crowding both sides.

"You killed all of them?" I say to Isabella. "Fiona? Chipeta? Rebecca? Tina?"

She eyes me in the rearview mirror.

"Why?" I say, keeping my voice calm. "I want to understand."

She meets my gaze in the mirror.

"I didn't do anything to them that they didn't do to me first," she says.

CHAPTER 89

IT WAS TINA'S idea.

She was the oldest and the most self-assured. They all looked up to her. Coming from different states and regions of Texas—the five of them had been brought together only by the luck that they'd each won in their respective categories at the powwow. The girls' winners' circle was dubbed the Order of the Golden Eagle. The boy winners were called the Order of the Bald Eagle.

After they'd gotten a passerby to take their picture together using Isabella's phone, Tina had said they should celebrate, skip out on the event—go somewhere else, just the five of them.

Isabella was excited to have a new group of friends. She knew Rebecca, the other Tigua, but the others came from Colorado and Arizona and Houston, which was just as far away and just as exotic as the other states.

"No one will notice we're gone," Tina said. "Come on. We'll come back before they miss us."

Fiona was the youngest and seemed the most worried.

"What if we get caught?" said the Arizona girl, who had just turned sixteen.

"I'm on probation," Tina said, saying it like this was something to be proud of. "I could end up in juvenile detention. I've got the most to lose. I'm not afraid."

This claim made the others feel ashamed for their cowardice. Although, later, Isabella would conclude that this statement should have raised alarm bells with her. Tina hadn't yet proposed they do anything illegal.

"You two are both from around here," Tina said to Rebecca and Isabella. "Where can we go to have a little party?"

Rebecca knew of a place outside the city, a cliff overlooking a dry riverbed.

"It's very secluded," she said. "No one ever goes there."

Isabella asked her parents to hold her dreamcatcher so she wouldn't lose it, and then she snuck away with her new friends. They laughed as they navigated around the crowds, avoiding friends and family. It felt like they were on a secret mischievous mission that no one else could find out about. Around them, people danced and sang and played drums, the smell from the food filled the air, and no one noticed the five teenage girls sneaking into the parking area and piling into Chipeta's Jeep.

They sped out of the city, giggling and waving their arms in the air.

The farther they went into the desert, the more Isabella became worried, but Tina and the others didn't seem to mind. Even Fiona had gotten on board with the adventure. Tina passed around a flask, and this helped Isabella loosen up. By the time they arrived at the overlook, Isabella felt aglow in the warmth of the alcohol.

The view was spectacular.

They were parked atop a cliff overlooking a creek bed with a trickle of water running through it. The sandstone rocks were reddish, and various desert plants grew out from the cracks. Beyond the creek, low rolling hills stretched for as far as they could see, blanketed in sagebrush and cacti. White clouds sailed across the horizon.

It was a hot day, but a light breeze blew over the landscape, keeping them comfortable.

When the flask was empty, Tina said, "I've got something else."

She pulled out a glass bottle about two inches long, full of white powder. She unscrewed the lid, which was connected to a snuff spoon big enough to hold a single snort.

"Who wants to go first?" Tina said.

None of the other girls had ever done cocaine, but Tina was a persuasive leader. She did the first bump and had such a look of ecstasy on her face that Rebecca and Chipeta decided to try.

"You don't have to do it if you don't want," Isabella said to Fiona, who looked scared.

"I'll do it," Fiona said, "but only if you do. Only if everyone does."

Isabella thought it couldn't hurt to try. She snorted a spoonful and blinked her watering eyes. Instantly her face felt numb. The numbness moved through her like a warm fire, and soon her skin tingled all over her body.

She smiled what felt like the biggest smile she'd ever had, and that was enough to dispel Fiona's fear. The youngest girl took a snort.

They built a fire and Chipeta cranked her radio, and the five girls danced around at the top of the cliff, careful, despite how stoned they were, not to go near the edge.

Time slipped forward, and the sun began to set. The longest day of the year was coming to an end. The clouds to the west were bathed in brilliant shades of red and pink and purple—so much more vibrant and beautiful because of the drugs in their bloodstreams.

Some of the girls said they should head back.

Isabella didn't want to.

She didn't want the party to end. She urged Tina to pass around the vial of coke one more time. She kept dancing even though the others stopped. Time slipped forward again, and they were in darkness.

Arguing.

The moon broke from the horizon and rose into the sky, casting a ghostly blue glow over the land.

"Come on, Isabella," Tina said, grabbing her arm. "It's time to go."

"Let go of me!" Isabella snapped.

She yanked her arm free, and in doing so, lost her balance. She stumbled near the cliff edge. It wasn't a sharp drop-off, but a sloping, gradual one. Her feet slipped, and she fell to her knees, sliding away. She flung her arms out to stop her slide, but she couldn't. Tina stepped forward to grab her, but Isabella was already past the point of no return.

She tumbled off the cliff wall, screaming as she fell into the darkness.

CHAPTER 90

ISABELLA WOKE UP to daylight, her leg broken to pieces, a large gash in her head. She screamed for her friends.

They were gone.

They'd left her to die.

Ten days later, after she had crawled—dehydrated, starving, sunburned, snake-bitten—down the creek bed to the highway, she claimed that she couldn't remember what happened.

None of the girls ever came forward.

But Isabella did remember. She remembered all of it, and as she lay in the hospital, as she went through hour after excruciating hour of rehab, she planned her revenge.

Every year, on the solstice, she brought one of the girls out to the cliff where they'd last been together. She used the year in between to track down the next girl, figure out where she was living, and come up with a plan to abduct her.

Isabella had won her Order of the Golden Eagle dreamcatcher for archery, and the girls all knew how good she was. So when she aimed her bow at them and told them to back up toward the cliff edge, all four had done as they were told. The slope is gradual at first, and as the girls inched backward, they probably thought they could keep their footing. But, as Isabella knew too well, eventually the ground became too sandy, the angle too steep. Their feet slipped out from under them and they slid off the edge, screaming just as Isabella had.

Each of the girls cried and apologized and offered an excuse for why they'd left her behind. The versions changed slightly from year to year, but the stories were similar enough that she understood.

Like before, it was Tina's idea.

After Isabella had fallen, the girls yelled her name, but only silence echoed back to them. They wanted to get help, but Tina questioned whether that was wise. At first, the other three couldn't believe what Tina was proposing. Just drive away? Leave her?

But Tina explained that no one knew that Isabella had been with them. They could return to the powwow, act like they'd been there the whole time, and pretend this never happened. The alternative, she said, was that they all get in serious trouble. They'd run off; they'd drunk alcohol; they'd used cocaine. Their parents would be the least of their worries. They weren't on tribal land—who knew what the white authorities would do to them? Maybe they'd try to call it manslaughter.

Maybe murder.

The girls fought and cried and screamed, but one by one Tina wore them down. Fiona, the youngest, was the last to hold out. When Tina argued that Isabella was obviously dead and they couldn't help her—they could only hurt themselves—Fiona finally relented.

The four girls made a pact, sealed by tossing their dreamcatchers into the fire, to pretend they'd never come out here—to forget they'd ever known each other.

The four of them drove back in silence, the desert air chilling them. They made it back to the powwow, and besides a few inquiries from family and friends, no one thought anything of their absence—not even when news of Isabella's disappearance surfaced the next day. Besides the brief ceremony where they were handed their dreamcatchers, the girls, as far as anyone else knew, had never had any meaningful interaction.

The powwow organizers had planned to make a big deal out of the competition winners—send out news releases and publish their names in the Tigua tribal newsletter—but when Isabella went missing, the tribe didn't want to draw any kind of attention to the powwow. They wanted everyone to forget it ever happened, so the names of the five girls were never connected in writing.

Never linked in anyone else's memory.

CHAPTER 91

AS ISABELLA NAVIGATES the SUV on a winding gravel road, a coyote darts in front of the vehicle, its eyes glowing in the headlight beams.

"I left behind the feathers thinking that maybe the other girls would hear about what was happening and figure it out," she says. "If they were afraid enough, maybe they'd finally come forward and admit what they did. But I don't think a single one of them knew that the others had gone missing. They hadn't kept in touch. And no one connected them together. When an Indian girl goes missing, it's not like it makes national news."

I've managed to loosen the twine behind my back as Isabella talked. My wrists are raw and my fingers are tingling from a lack of circulation, but a few more minutes and I might be able to squeeze my hands free.

Isabella pulls the vehicle to a stop and shuts off the

headlights. She takes Ava's gun, leaving mine in the cab, and climbs out. She opens our door for us and gestures for us to exit. She takes several steps back, ensuring that neither of us can rush her without giving her plenty of time to pull the trigger.

We're on a high plateau, near the edge of a cliff overlooking rolling high-desert hills. I can hear the faint trickle of a streambed below. El Paso is a distant glow on the horizon, its light pollution far enough away that above us the sky is filled with stars and a bright half moon. The storm forming earlier has dissipated to a few lingering clouds, and the moonlight illuminates enough of the valley below that I can make out brush and trees and distant plateaus—in other words, a whole lot of nothing for as far as the eye can see.

"So you brought them out here?" I say, working against the rope restraints behind my back. "You aimed your bow at them and told them it was either the cliff or an arrow?"

"And that's what you plan to do to us?" Ava asks.

"Since I have this," Isabella says, holding up Ava's gun, "I left my bow at home this time."

She points with the gun toward the place where the ground begins to slant.

Ava and I walk toward the edge. I keep my hands hidden. I need time, so I try to keep Isabella talking.

"Did they express remorse?" I ask.

"Of course," Isabella says. "They begged and pleaded, said they were sorry." Her expression changes, and for a moment I see what might be regret. "Fiona was the hardest for me. She was a sweet girl. I saved her till last, thinking maybe I wouldn't go through with it. Let her off the hook. But..." She shrugs. "She made her choice."

"Isabella," Ava says, taking a tone like a friend. "I can see how you think you've created some sort of justice. They wronged you. I get it. But what about us? Rory and I never hurt you. All we ever do is try to help people."

"Then you should have been here four years ago," Isabella says. "Maybe things would have turned out different."

Isabella moves the gun back and forth between us as we inch toward the edge. "Keep going."

Facing death has been on my mind for the last several days. Kyle Hendricks sacrificed himself to save me. Carlos sacrificed himself to save me.

Now it's my turn.

I grit my teeth and try one last time to squeeze my hand through the rope. Skin burning, my right hand finally slips free. I keep my hands behind my back, clenching and unclenching my fists to give them circulation, the twine hanging loose around my left wrist.

From somewhere behind us, down in the canyon, we hear a faint, strange sound coming from far away. It could be the mew of a bobcat or the yap of a wild dog.

Or it could be a human groaning in pain.

My eyes go wide, as do Isabella's. She hears it, too.

"That could be Fiona," Ava says. "She might still be—"

"I said, keep moving!" Isabella snaps, lowering the gun and firing a round at our feet. A bullet strikes the rock between us, ricocheting loudly out over the canyon.

She could have easily hit one of us, and it wouldn't have bothered her a bit if she did.

It's now or never.

Time to die.

"*Run, Ava!*" I shout as I hurtle my body forward, swinging my arms around to tackle Isabella.

Isabella raises the gun and shoots.

CHAPTER 92

THE BULLET STRIKES me in the upper chest, on the right side, just under my collarbone and close to my shoulder. I feel the *thump* when it hits. The shot staggers me, but it doesn't stop me. I fly at her like an out-of-control train jumping off the tracks. My left hand reaches for the gun but misses, and so I lower my left shoulder and slam into her.

She and I go down in a pile of limbs and grunts. The gun goes flying, skidding over the loose rock and coming to a stop near the cliff's edge.

Ava—acting quick—jumps on Isabella and tries to pin her. Her arms are still cuffed behind her back, but she uses her weight and her legs to keep the woman down.

I sit up and a wave of dizziness crashes into me. The front and back of my shirt are wet with blood from where the bullet went in and where it punched its way out.

Isabella thrashes beneath Ava. She grabs Ava's braid and

yanks her off. Then she scrambles toward the gun. Ava jumps after her, throwing her weight on her again, but she's severely disadvantaged without her arms.

I rise to my feet—moving in slow motion. I take one step toward the fighting women but stop myself. I turn and head to the vehicle. I use my left hand to open the door. I reach across the seat to retrieve my gun. When I grab it and rise back out of the car, a lightning bolt of pain explodes from the wound.

I raise my gun with my left arm, but I can't hold it steady. I've always been useless shooting with my left hand, and even with the bullet hole near my right shoulder, I switch the gun to my dominant right hand. I place my left hand underneath my right, helping to lift the arm.

Ava and Isabella are in the danger zone now, where the ground begins to slope. Isabella strains to reach the gun with Ava on top of her. Isabella's fingers are inches away.

I try to keep the sight steady on Isabella's head, but it veers wildly.

Ava tries to pin Isabella's arms with her knees, but Isabella heaves beneath her, giving herself just enough space to move.

She grabs the gun and swings it upward. She aims it at Ava's face.

I squeeze the trigger.

Blood sprays from Isabella's face, and her arm goes limp.

I let out a breath of relief, but then realize that both women, tangled together, have begun to slide over the edge. I force myself to my feet and stumble forward. Ava scrambles to get off of Isabella's body, but she's sliding across the sandy grade.

I lunge forward and throw my left hand out. I get a grip on the collar of Ava's shirt just as Isabella's body slides out from under her and disappears over the edge.

I hear her body crash into the brush below.

CHAPTER 93

FLAT ON MY chest, my body spread out, I tell myself not to let go. Ava scrambles with her feet, using me for leverage. I slip downhill, and it feels like both of us are going to pitch forward off the cliff. Then Ava gets a good foothold and throws her body up to the flatter surface.

We crawl away from the edge, grunting and gasping. I slump to the ground, and Ava jumps to her feet and runs to the SUV, where the handcuff keys are lying on the passenger seat. I put my hand over the entrance wound, trying to slow the bleeding. Ava runs back to me with her arms freed and a first aid kit in hand.

She tears off my shirt and dumps a packet of quick-clotting powder on the entrance and exit wounds, then begins to wrap me up in hemostatic gauze.

"You're lucky," she says. "Looks like the bullet missed your artery, missed your shoulder blade. I don't hear any sucking sounds, so it missed the top of the lung."

"Thanks," I say when she's got me good and wrapped up, with bandages running around my chest and shoulder. The kit doesn't have a sling, so she fashions one with tape and secures my arm to my body.

She gives me a nod and thanks me in return. We share a brief moment, looking at each other, two partners—two friends—who just survived a terrible ordeal. Then the moment is over and she's back to business.

"Move as little as possible," she says, leaving me sitting in the dirt as she runs to the car to call for help.

I ignore her and rise to my feet. The worst of the shock is gone, so I'm no longer nauseated and dizzy. I walk over toward the edge—not too close—and look out at the canyon below.

"*Fiona!*" I shout.

There's no answer.

A minute later, Ava comes back, looking flustered.

"No cell service," she says. "All I can get is static on the radio. We're going to have to drive back to civilization."

"I'm not going with you," I say.

"What the hell are you talking about?"

I gesture with my good arm toward the canyon.

"Fiona might still be alive," I say. "I'm going to look for her."

Ava argues with me. She says we can look for her together, but I tell her that this would waste precious time. We need help out here — and we need the most capable of us to go get it. That's her.

She says that I'm going to kill myself trying to get down into the canyon, but we can both see a place where the cliff flattens into a gentler slope.

"Give me that first aid kit," I say. "And if there's any food in your car, I'll take that, too."

Ava digs out a stash of Gatorade and PowerBars she keeps under her seat. She hands the Gatorade to me and stuffs the PowerBars in the first aid kit. I chug half the bottle and wedge the kit into my pants pocket.

I pick my gun out of the dirt and try to put it on my belt, but I'm using my left hand and the holster is on my right. Ava finally helps me get it into place, giving me a look of disapproval that I'm stupid to be doing this.

"Drive safe," I say.

"Don't pass out," she says.

As her taillights recede into the darkness, I walk parallel to the cliff edge. The slope flattens out somewhat, and a seam of rock cuts down the hillside at an angle. Ordinarily, Ava would have a flashlight to give me, but in the aftermath of the explosion this morning, she wasn't sure what happened to it.

I can see well enough in the moonlight that I don't really need it.

I make my way down on wobbly legs.

"Fiona!" I call. "Can you hear me?"

Traveling is slow, but I finally make it to the bottom, where the sandstone streambed is filled with shallow puddles and trickling tributaries connecting them. I make my way back downstream, heading toward where the cliff looms over the canyon.

"Fiona!" I call again. "Are you out there?"

Up ahead, I hear a noise. It could be an animal moving in the brush. A coyote or a javelina.

But something about it sounds more human—a large form slinking through the brush.

"Fiona?" I say.

The canyon is deathly quiet, filled only with the sound of water filtering through the rocks.

I get a cold chill.

Could it be?

I saw blood spray from her face before she fell over the edge. But she survived the fall once before. Maybe she survived again.

"Isabella?" I call.

Somewhere in the darkness, I can hear raspy, labored breathing, like an injured animal waiting for its final pounce.

CHAPTER 94

ISABELLA REMEMBERS THE snake.

The way it bit her even after it was dead.

I am the snake, she thinks. *I am dead. But I have one bite left.*

She landed atop the bones of the other girls. Last time, the fall had knocked her out and she didn't experience the full pain of the impact. But this time, she remained conscious, and as her bones shattered, the instant agony had been unlike anything she'd ever felt.

She wanted to die right then and thought about putting the gun, which she'd somehow held on to, against her temple and pulling the trigger.

But she's a fighter. She proved that once before, and she will prove it again.

She crawled down into the creek bed to a small overhang she remembered. A nice place to hide from the elements.

Or a Texas Ranger.

Her face is gushing blood, but the bullet only took off part of her nose. It hurts, but it's not the most painful part of her existence right now. Only adrenaline and hate are keeping her going.

She hears him coming, calling out Fiona's name.

Isabella crouches inside the small rocky cave, holding the gun close to her chest.

I have one bite left.

CHAPTER 95

I FIND THE skeletons of the women, their clothes in tatters, their bones gleaming white in the moonlight. I count three skulls. Around the vertebrae of one of the necks is a silver necklace, which I recognize from the photo of Chipeta Tavaci.

I'm sure the other two are Rebecca Trujillo and Tina White Wolf.

I suspected all along that they were dead, but to be confronted with their remains is still hard. I feel overwhelming sadness that these women were killed. That we weren't able to save them.

But there's no sign of Fiona.

If she were here, her remains would be more fresh. Which means—dead or alive—she's out there somewhere in the darkness.

And there's no sign of Isabella, either.

A trail of blood leads through the brush toward the creek. It's hard to follow in the moonlight, the splotches of red getting lost in patches of dark dirt. Now is when I wish I had a flashlight.

I draw my pistol—with difficulty—and walk forward with the gun in my left hand, where it feels uncomfortable and awkward. I curse myself for never practicing with my left.

I don't call out anymore. Now I try to be as silent as possible. There's a small drop-off into the creek bed, which I hobble down. My boots sink into two inches of water. Any trace of blood has been washed away.

I kneel and squint and look around, trying to figure out where she could have gone.

A shot rings out behind me as a bullet zips by my ear. I drop onto the ground and roll over in the water, my injury exploding with pain. I attempt to get my gun up, but between the pain and the sling and my clumsy left hand, I can't seem to get oriented.

Isabella Luna leans forward out of the darkness of an overhanging rock, her gun leveled at me.

Before I can act, I hear a wild screeching noise. The sound startles Isabella as well as me, and she hesitates.

A ghostly female form lunges out of the brush, balancing on only one leg while holding a rock the size of a bowling ball above her head and screaming like a banshee. With long dark hair hanging over her face and skeleton-thin arms straining to hoist the stone above her, she looks more like a phantom from a horror movie than a human.

Isabella swings the gun toward the apparition, but the phantom is too fast. She slams the rock onto the top of Isabella's skull with a sickening *crack*.

Isabella goes limp, and her gun hand falls into the water.

The apparition—Fiona Martinez, emaciated and haggard but very much alive—drops onto the ground, sobbing.

"I'm sorry, Isabella," she cries. "I'm so sorry."

I'm not sure if she's apologizing for leaving Isabella here all those years ago or striking her with a rock just now.

Or both.

Fiona puts her face in her hands and weeps. I see that the back of one hand is swollen like a water balloon, punctuated by an enflamed red welt.

My eyes drift to Isabella, whose face lies in a puddle, the clear liquid turning a dark crimson in the moonlight.

No breath ripples the water.

EPILOGUE

CHAPTER 96

I'M ON THE road driving to headquarters in Austin. It's a typical Central Texas day—humid and hot as hell but otherwise beautiful.

I've been suffering through rehab for my injury, and I've finally gotten to the point where I don't have to wear a sling. I've got two matching scars—one where the bullet went in and one where it came out—not to mention a lot of lingering pain. But the doctors seem to think I'll make a complete recovery in time.

I remain skeptical.

To say I used to be good with a gun is an understatement, but who knows if I'll ever be as good again.

Maybe I won't be as accurate.

Maybe I won't be as fast.

And if I'm not, I'm going to have to live with that. I've always said how good you are with a gun isn't what makes you a good cop. I might have to find out what kind of Texas Ranger I am without a gun.

As the tall buildings of the city appear in the distance, I get a phone call from Ava Cruz, and I answer it via Bluetooth.

"What's up?" I say, happy to hear from her.

She says she just got off the phone with Fiona Martinez's mother, and she wanted her to deliver a message to me.

"She told me to tell you thank you for keeping your promise," Ava says.

I remember talking to the woman in the back room of the Flagstaff gift shop. She looked like an older version of her daughter and had been adamant that Fiona was still alive. I was just trying to give her the reassurance that we wouldn't give up hope.

I'm glad we didn't.

"How's Fiona doing?" I ask.

"She's in therapy," Ava says, "and she has the support of her family. She feels terrible about abandoning Isabella, but she was young and made a stupid mistake. I hope she learns to live without too much guilt."

Once she was in the hospital and we were able to talk to her, Fiona told us that she'd considered trying to crawl downstream but a scorpion had stung her hand, and that was the final straw for her—she'd decided to give up and die. Which, lucky for me, was the only reason she was still in that spot when I came down looking for her. She was near death's door, but she'd heard our voices and the gunshots—and used her last ounce of strength to smash the rock over Isabella's head.

"The next time you talk to her," I say, "remind her that I came to save her, and she ended up saving me."

"Speaking of saving lives," Ava says, "what about Marta? Have you heard from her?"

"She wrote me a really nice letter," I say, "talking about how thankful she was. She's going to have to testify against Zebo when all this finally goes to trial, and that will be hard. But she's a fighter. She's going to be okay."

Ava updates me on the latest with Ryan Logan's task force. She's a member now. I haven't been involved since we closed the cases on Garrison Zebo's trafficking ring and the eagle feather murders. Unfortunately, there are plenty of other missing women to find, so Ryan and Ava are still busy. As for me, the powers that be in the Rangers have pulled me back to my usual duties in Waco.

For now.

I have a good idea what they have planned for me next—and it's not what I have planned for myself.

I tell Ava I miss her and to stay in touch. I want to tell her how thankful I am—for her partnership and her friendship. But I know she feels the same way, and it's okay that the words go unsaid on both sides.

When I park at headquarters, I check my phone before walking inside.

I have a text from Megan.

Are we still on for tomorrow night?

Megan got the job at Baylor. Even though things started hot and heavy between us, we've slowed down, having only hung out a few times since I got out of the hospital. I managed to make it to her graduation, where Neil—aka Dr. Stephenson—hooded her with tears in his eyes. I thought he had the hots for her, but I see now he saw her more as a surrogate daughter.

Megan is staying at her folks' ranch, busy looking for a place to live and preparing her teaching materials for the upcoming semester. Now that it seems like our lives are returning to some semblance of normalcy, we've scheduled our long-awaited date. But now that we *can* move forward, both of us seem a little trepidatious. It's as if neither of us ever really thought this could happen, so now that it can, there's some fear about moving forward.

I'm game to give it a shot, if she is.

You bet, I text, then walk into headquarters for my scheduled appointment with Captain David Kane.

I sit in the same seat I did back in June when he told me he wanted me to take the lieutenant's exam.

"Rory," he says, leaning over his spotless oak desk, "we're about to have a lieutenant opening in Company C. How do you feel about relocating to Lubbock?"

"Let me stop you right there, sir," I say, as politely—but firmly—as I can. "Maybe I'll take the lieutenant's exam one day, but I don't think I'm the best Ranger for the job, right now."

We talk for a few more minutes, but when he realizes there's no convincing me, we don't have much more to say. He's not too happy with me, but this isn't the first time I've pissed off one of my superiors.

It won't be the last.

On my way out, I stop by a certain office door and give it a knock.

Carlos beckons me in with a broad smile on his face. The last time I was here, we hardly knew each other. This time, I give him a great big hug, holding on tight.

"Careful," he says. "I don't want you to rupture anything."

I laugh and let him go. After the bullet punched a hole through loops and loops of his intestines, he still hasn't been cleared for field work, but the doctors say it's just a matter of time before he'll be 100 percent. At least now he's back to eating solid foods—and pizza.

"You want to go get a cup of coffee?" he asks.

"Let's get a beer," I say. "It's five o'clock somewhere."

He gives me a skeptical look, trying to figure out if I'm serious.

"Gotcha," I say, grinning from ear to ear.

CHAPTER 97

THE NEXT DAY is Saturday, and I find myself alone on the gun range Dad built on the property. In front of the earthen backstop, I set up a sawhorse and line up some empty beer and soda cans on it.

I leave the windows down on my truck with the radio playing, tuned to our local country station, 99.9 WACO-FM. Willow texted me early this morning and told me to listen. I'm guessing they'll be debuting her new single.

I stand back, my gun on my hip and my hand at the ready.

I draw and shoot the first can, which bounces away with a *tinging* sound. Drawing my pistol took only about half a second, but it felt glacially slow compared to what I used to be able to do.

As I shoot the rest of the cans, I never miss. And each draw gets a little faster than the one before. But my speed is nowhere near what it used to be.

I holster the pistol, disgusted with myself, and on the radio, the DJ says that Willow Dawes will be up next, on the hour.

I rotate my arm like I used to do before football practice. There's some stiffness in my shoulder—a little bit of pain— but I push the discomfort away. I take a can and prepare to toss it in the air, to try to shoot it before it falls, but then I get another idea. I dig into my pocket and pull out a quarter. I remember what was going to be the tiebreaker between Ryan and me. Dropping a coin from shoulder height and trying to shoot it as it passed by, just like his hero Jelly Bryce used to do.

Ryan missed.

I forfeited.

And so the tie remained. But no one else is here now—no child who might run into the line of fire.

I hold the coin at shoulder height. I take a deep breath. Focus.

Just then I hear the DJ say, *"I'm here in the studio with Waco's beloved daughter, Willow Dawes."*

I lower the coin. I must have heard that wrong. She can't be in the studio. She must be calling in from Nashville.

"Willow has been nice enough to give us a sneak peek of some of the songs on her upcoming album," the DJ says. *"Willow, tell us about the first song we're going to play."*

"It's called 'Texas Forever,'" she says, *"and my friend Rory Yates helped me write it."*

I stare at my truck, listening in absolute shock.

"You're talking about the Texas Ranger who inspired a certain song from your debut album?" the DJ asks.

"Yep," she says, laughing. *"We're still good friends, and the last time I was in town, he and I jammed on this song. He helped me come up with the lyrics."*

When the song starts to play, I'm even more surprised. With a professional band accompanying her lyrics, playing everything from a steel guitar to a fiddle to a piano, the song is a boot-stomping country anthem as catchy as anything on the radio. I won't be surprised if it's sung by college kids at field parties and beach campfires for the next decade.

After the song is over and the DJ cuts to a commercial, my phone rings.

"How does it feel to be a country music songwriter?" Willow says, laughing. "I gave you co-writing credit."

"I'm speechless," I say. "The song is amazing."

"You want to celebrate?" she asks.

"Whenever you're in town," I say.

"I *am* in town," she says. "I'm in the studio at WACO-FM right now. I could make you dinner at your place. I'll bring my guitar. We can sit on the porch and play like we used to."

"I'd like that," I find myself saying. "I haven't played in forever."

What I don't tell her is that I've been too afraid to try, worried that my injury might affect my ability to play.

"I could meet you in Waco if you want me to," I say. "Where are you staying?"

"I don't have a place yet," she says, and her tone shifts, making her sound uncharacteristically shy. "Maybe I could stay with you."

I'm so surprised I don't know what to say.

"Think about it," she says quickly, probably sensing my hesitation.

She says she has to go—they're going to interview her for a few more minutes and play more of the album—but she'll call me later.

As I hang up, I don't know what to think. Does Willow want to get back together? She certainly seemed to be suggesting it.

"Ah, crap," I say aloud, remembering I already have plans with Megan tonight.

I'm going to have to cancel with one of them.

The problem is, which one?

I'm not the kind of guy who dates more than one woman at a time. Part of me thinks that if Willow is interested in trying again, I should go for it. There was always something special about our relationship. But another part of me thinks that it's time for me to move on from Willow, once and for all. Megan *seems* perfect for me, but I really don't know her that well. We might find out quickly that we're not a good match. I *know* Willow and I are—it's only our careers that got in the way.

I sit on the tailgate and listen to the rest of the interview and two more of Willow's new songs, a fun romp called "Crushin' on a Cowboy" and a heartbreaking ballad called "Tell the Angels" about the fear of losing a loved one. Maybe it's hubris, but I can't help but think both songs are about me.

When the interview is finally over, I find myself in a foul mood. Part of me is thrilled that Willow might want to get back together—another part is irritated with her for not letting me move on.

What am I going to do?

I clean up the cans and the shell casings, preparing to head home and brood about the tough spot I'm in. Then I remember what I was about to do before the interview came on.

I take the quarter back out of my pocket and hold it at shoulder height. I pour the pain of my dilemma into a fuming single-minded focus.

I release the coin, snatch my pistol, and shoot.

The quarter lands in the grass at my feet. I lean down to fish for it among the blades of green. When I find it, I hold it up between my thumb and forefinger and examine the hole through the face of George Washington.

"So much for that tie," I say, unable to stop myself from grinning.

The truth is I don't really care about the draw with Ryan Logan. What I care about is the fact that my shooting ability is coming back. The shot was pretty easy, actually.

Now I have to figure out what to do about tonight.

If only love came as easy for me as shooting a gun.

ACKNOWLEDGMENTS

Special thanks to Captain Kip Westmoreland of the Texas Rangers.

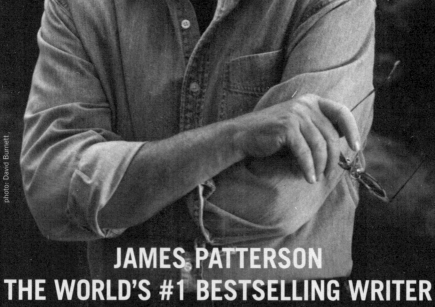

photo: David Burnett.

JAMES PATTERSON
THE WORLD'S #1 BESTSELLING WRITER

ABOUT THE AUTHORS

James Patterson is the most popular storyteller of our time. He is the creator of unforgettable characters and series, including Alex Cross, the Women's Murder Club, Jane Smith, and Maximum Ride, and of breathtaking true stories about the Kennedys, John Lennon, and Tiger Woods, as well as our military heroes, police officers, and ER nurses. Patterson has coauthored #1 bestselling novels with Bill Clinton and Dolly Parton, and collaborated most recently with Michael Crichton on the blockbuster *Eruption*. He has told the story of his own life in *James Patterson by James Patterson* and received an Edgar Award, ten Emmy Awards, the Literarian Award from the National Book Foundation, and the National Humanities Medal.

Andrew Bourelle is the author of the novel *Heavy Metal* and coauthor with James Patterson of *Texas Ranger* and *Texas Outlaw*. His short stories have been published widely in literary magazines and fiction anthologies, including *The Best American Mystery Stories*.

JAMES PATTERSON
RECOMMENDS

JAMES PATTERSON

TEXAS
★
RANGER

Officer Rory Yates comes home—to a murder charge

& ANDREW BOURELLE

TEXAS RANGER

So many of my detectives are dark and gritty and deal with crimes in some of our grimmest cities. That's why I'm thrilled to bring you Detective Rory Yates, my most honorable detective yet.

As a Texas Ranger, he has a code that he lives and works by. But when he comes home for a much-needed break, he walks into a crime scene where the victim is none other than his ex-wife—and he's the prime suspect. Yates has to risk everything in order to clear his name, and he dives into the inferno of the most twisted mind I've ever created. Can his code bring him back out alive?

JAMES PATTERSON
AND BRIAN SITTS
CRIME HAS A NEW ENEMY.
THE NEW YORK TIMES BESTSELLER
THE SHADOW
A THRILLER

THE SHADOW

Only two people know that 1930s society man Lamont Cranston has a secret identity as the Shadow, a crusader for justice—well, make that three if you include me, and it is my great honor to reimagine his story. But the other two are his greatest love, Margo Lane, and his fiercest enemy, Shiwan Khan. When Khan ambushes the couple, they must risk everything for the slimmest chance of survival...in the future.

A century and a half later, Lamont awakens in a world both unknown and disturbingly familiar. Most unsettling, Khan's power continues to be felt over the city and its people. No one in this new world understands the dangers of stopping him better than Lamont Cranston. And only the Shadow knows that he's the one person who might succeed before more innocent lives are lost.

JAMES PATTERSON

1ST TIME IN PRINT

THE MIDWIFE MURDERS

and RICHARD DiLALLO

THE MIDWIFE MURDERS

I can't imagine a worse crime than one done against a child. But when two kidnappings and a vicious stabbing happen on senior midwife Lucy's watch in a university hospital in Manhattan, her focus abruptly changes. Something has to be done, and Lucy is fearless enough to try.

Rumors begin to swirl, with blame falling on everyone from the Russian mafia to an underground adoption network. Fierce single mom Lucy teams up with a skeptical NYPD detective, but I've given her a case where the truth is far more twisted than Lucy could ever have imagined.

From the Creator of the #1 Bestselling Women's Murder Club

JAMES
PATTERSON

2 SISTERS

DETECTIVE
AGENCY

FIRST
TIME IN
PRINT

& CANDICE FOX

2 SISTERS DETECTIVE AGENCY

Discovering secrets about your own family has a way of changing your life...for better or for worse. Attorney Rhonda Bird learns that her estranged father had stopped being an accountant and opened up a private detective agency—and that she has a teenage half sister named Baby.

When Baby brings in a client to the detective agency, the two sisters become entangled in a dangerous case involving a group of young adults who break laws for fun, their psychopath ringleader, and an ex-assassin who decides to hunt them down for revenge.

For a complete list of books by

JAMES PATTERSON

VISIT
JamesPatterson.com

 Follow James Patterson on Facebook
@JamesPatterson

 Follow James Patterson on X
@JP_Books

 Follow James Patterson on Instagram
@jamespattersonbooks

Scan here to visit JamesPatterson.com
and learn about giveaways, sneak peeks,
new releases, and more.